Harvest of Mercy

Moses Oladapo Adio

WIPF *&* STOCK · Eugene, Oregon

Wipf and Stock Publishers
199 W 8th Ave, Suite 3
Eugene, OR 97401

Harvest of Mercy
By Adio, Moses Oladapo
Copyright©2019 Apostolos
ISBN 13: 978-1-5326-8098-4
Publication date 2/1/2019
Previously published by Apostolos, 2019

ACKNOWLEDGEMENTS

First and foremost, I like to thank God for His blessing on my life and for helping me as I wrote this novel.

I would like to appreciate Ms Laura Maisey for her amazing critique/editing service.

As every destiny needs a helper to evolve, I really bless God for granting me helpers of destiny in the following men of God:

Reverend Paul Jinadu, founder, New Covenant Church (Nigeria, UK and Worldwide). His ministry introduced me to Jesus Christ.

Bishop Joseph Akanmode, General Overseer, Grace Anchor Church, Ibadan, Nigeria. His ministry has provided succour to me during my wilderness experience.

Reverend Daniel Ofosu Bonnke, the General Overseer, Mercy Seat International Christian Centre (UK and Worldwide). He is a great influence in my writing ministry.

Finally, I want to appreciate my wonderful wife, Deaconess Susan Bamitale Adio, for being there for me at all times. I cannot measure the amount of spiritual and practical support she has given me.

Moses Oladapo Adio

ACKNOWLEDGEMENTS

PREFACE

It is quite amazing that, despite His power and dominion over everything that He created, the almighty God daily deals with each of us with immeasurable mercy. The rich men and women of this earth often misbehave due to their riches; kings and queens get intoxicated by royal splendour, while power goes into the head of the powerful. But the Giver of riches, positions and power sits upon the throne of mercy, handing out overwhelming degrees of mercy unto all and sundry. This is a mystery! It is, however, shocking and equally disheartening that, instead of appreciating God's love, people misconstrue it as frailty. And, because of His unfathomable depth of mercy, many 'fools' do not only say in their hearts that He does not exist, they say aloud and broadcast it to anyone who will listen.

Some of the characters in this book are very prosperous. But God's definition of prosperity is not the same as ours. Prosperity, in the divine dictionary, refers to exhibition of the three attributes of the Kingdom of God – righteousness, peace and joy in the Holy Ghost. Any earthly achievement is mere addendum, and God is always ready to bestow these. 'Seek ye the kingdom of God,' said Jesus, 'and all these things (your godly aspirations) shall be added unto you.'

Nobody can appreciate God unless they first come to Him. Those of us who, by His grace, are in His Kingdom know what we had missed outside His Kingdom. It's so heart-rending that we'd better forget it and focus on our glittering present and the even more glittering future we now have in Him!

This fiction portrays God's merciful forbearance with all people which daily draws many unto Him.

'Now unto Him that is able to do exceeding abundantly above all that we ask or think, according to the power that worketh in us' (Ephesians 3:20 KJV).

To Him and only Him be all GLORY!

Moses Oladapo Adio

CONTENTS

DEDICATION

This novel is dedicated to all missionary evangelists who work in the Far East, Middle East and North Africa, where the task of soul winning is at constant risk to their lives.

CHAPTER 1: LORD, HAVE MERCY

Show me a man
Who never reaps where he has not sown.
For, freely do we all pluck from God's orchard
That, without sowing or tending,
Daily do we reap a HARVEST OF MERCY!

The British Embassy, Monrovia, Liberia; July 1978

It was Samantha's first Monday at the Trade Department of the British Embassy in Monrovia. She stared unconsciously at every object as she sat morosely in her office that morning. The room was purposely carved out of a very large conference hall and was newly furnished. It had an air-conditioner in the wall close to the ceiling and a giant fan stood on the carpeted floor beside the file cabinet. On the well-polished wooden desk were two file trays, a telephone directory and a computer. On the wall behind Samantha's desk was a large notice board, on which was pinned a broad, multicoloured statistical chart.

Samantha suddenly rose and walked over to the standing fan, regarded it nonchalantly for some moments and then turned it on. She then walked sluggishly back to her seat and returned to her former posture – staring glumly at the objects on her desk. She suddenly remembered the folder which she had earlier on dropped carelessly under the desk. It contained her induction documents. As she opened the folder, there was a gentle knock at the door.

'Hi, I'm Amanda,' said the smiling visitor as she came in, without waiting for a response. She was a woman about Samantha's age and a staff member of the department, too. Samantha looked up from her desk, where she was trying to make her way through the folder.

'Oh, um, I'm Samantha.'

'Nice to meet you,' said Amanda. 'I wouldn't bother reading all that,' referring to the induction documents. 'Half of it is irrelevant. We'll tell you what you need to know. They're a good bunch of people here.'

Samantha gave a small smile but didn't answer. She hoped the woman would take the hint and leave her alone.

'Come to the bar with us tonight?' Amanda asked.

'Um, no thank you.' Samantha answered, keeping her eyes on the folder. She didn't want to make friends. They would only betray you in the end so what was the point?

'Alright, I see you again at break time,' said Amanda as she left the room.

But Amanda couldn't stop thinking about Samantha's coldness. She remembered her same attitude earlier that morning, when she was introduced to the rest of the staff members. She neither gave a hearty smile nor showed any interest, even when the head of the department had joked, 'Now, I have a rare privilege of personally leading Miss Collins to her office.' While everyone clapped or smiled, Samantha had responded with a half-hearted 'thank you, sir.'

Many weeks went by and Samantha still refused to fraternise with her colleagues. She didn't care much about her dressing; she neither dressed smartly like the rest of the ladies nor applied her makeup. But, despite her weirdness, she was very hard-working. She never left office at closing time until she treated all the files in her in-tray. And she had a perfect relationship with patrons and prospective patrons of British businesses who were referred to her office for one thing or another. 'Thank you for doing business with British firms. I can guarantee that British firms are among the best for this service or product,' she would say.

And because of these official qualities, she was liked by all and sundry. But there remained the big negative – her cold attitude to every staff member. Various reasons were adduced to this by her colleagues. While some said she was arrogant, some said she suffered from an inferiority complex. Someone once opined that the job wasn't her ideal choice; she might have been compelled to take it by her circumstances.

It was month of December. The annual end-of-year party of the Trade Department was fast approaching. The party, which was organised for top entrepreneurs and reputable bankers in the country, afforded all staff members an opportunity to mix with the invited members of the public. There would be a keynote address read by an invited banker after which all attendees would take to the floor. It was an occasion everyone always looked forward to; a time when they could come out of their shells and show off their true social colours. This year's party would be particularly interesting for the obvious reason of seeing Samantha socialise for the first time. No one could wait to see her dance and possibly participate in the characteristic small talks with the invited guests. About a week before the party Amanda had visited her office to chat about the party.

'Oh Samantha, are you aware that we will close very early on Friday and then come back in the evening for the party?'

Pretending she wasn't aware of any party, she had asked:

'What party?'

'The end-of-year party, of course,' replied Amanda.

'Attending a party is a matter of choice,' she snapped without looking at Amanda.

'No darling. We must all attend.'

Samantha turned around to the computer and stopped responding afterwards. And after one or two unanswered queries, Amanda left the office.

The large space within the embassy's sprawling compound was decorated to the fullest. The grass was trimmed down and the palm trees, which dotted the ground, were beautifully adorned with Christmas lights. White plastic chairs were arranged four per group, each group with a well-decorated table. Servers were contracted, and a popular radio DJ hired. Each embassy staff member returned for the party that evening wearing a different look. The ladies had their hair restyled and wore their most beautiful dresses, looking adorable in their specially applied make-up. The men wore black party suits with white shirts and black bow ties. The guests started trickling in a few minutes before the party started. And by the time the programmes commenced, all sorts of state-of-the-art automobiles had filled up the embassy's garage and other vacant spaces. Elation was written all over the faces of the top business people and the other distinguished professionals as they alighted from their expensive wonders-on-wheels. It could be deduced that the party had also served a purpose of reuniting these highly affluent people, considering their laughter and the way they embraced one another. Although Samantha came back for the party smartly dressed, she didn't mix with the partying people. Instead, she joined up with the contracted servers. This was, in fact, a ploy to ward off dance requests from the men, but even though she was the only white girl among them, and the only embassy worker to be serving, she felt more comfortable in their company than among the high-fliers.

'Now, I shall call on a distinguished banker, an epitome of banking and business, a young versatile gift to the banking industry, in the person of Dr Donaldson Jerome Weah, to come out and deliver a keynote address,' announced the MC. As was the practice, a bank was selected to present a keynote address. And the onus was on the management of the bank to select who, among their top managerial staff, was to deliver the address. The Director of Finance of the Wuteve Bank, who was Donaldson's immediate boss, was to deliver the address but he had an impromptu official commitment abroad. Donaldson was, therefore, picked as a substitute. His boss had offered to help him with ideas, but he politely rejected the offer. He preferred to do it alone; he never doubted his own ingenuity. What further proof of his brilliance did anybody need? He had a first-class bachelor's degree in Banking and Finance; an MBA; a PhD; two professional titles, and he was two-time winner of Central Bank of Liberia's Banker of the Year award! Why should a keynote address, titled, *African Banks and Consolidation – The Critical Parameter of Size to Become Regional Players,* pose any threat to him? Although it was his first time ever to represent his bank at such occasion, he put up a creditable performance, and his presence that evening had certainly turned a few heads.

Without exaggeration, Donaldson had a finely-built figure. Tall at six feet and ebony-skinned, the dimples on his cheeks would make any one ask for more when he smiled. He had a natural way of smiling that generously revealed his immaculate set of white teeth. And the meticulousness of his presentation that day, coupled with his mastery of the Queen's English, left all the embassy staff wondering if he had once lived in the Great Britain. But the truth was that Donaldson could adopt any accent or intonation. The popular accent of Liberians was American, but he loved BBC programmes, especially the news, which he regularly listened to on his radio. And, to impress his hosts, he had decided to display his mastery of their accent. But what really impressed his hosts, which included three British High Commissioners from Nigeria, Ghana and Sierra Leone, was not just the mastery of the English accent but the amazing facts and figures that were embedded in his awesome presentation. And when it was dance time, all the embassy ladies, with exception of Samantha, fancied a dance with him.

Donaldson had been eyeing Samantha ever since she had come up to serve him. He had been captivated by a ravishing beauty for the very first time. 'What a beautiful lady!' he said within himself. 'Is she actually a server here?' he wondered. Server or not, he must explore every available opportunity of getting closer to her. Meanwhile, as Samantha stood among the servers, she cleverly surveyed the guests as they arrived. The men seemed to have a common trait – arrogance. Their words and body language were full of it. She could see it from afar, but it became unbearable when she came near. Without saying 'thank you' as she served them, some of these men had proceeded straightaway to ask her name and phone number. How rude! Some of them were in company of friends or colleagues who chatted unnecessarily loudly about their various business exploits. But she noticed one young, handsome man who talked little and bowed as he exchanged greetings with everybody, including women. He was one of the few men who thanked her for serving him. He had said to her smilingly, 'Thanks for the royal treatment, madam!' And, later that evening, when the same man was called upon to give a keynote address, Samantha couldn't resist listening with rapt attention.

Donaldson knew that he would be approached for a dance by some ladies, but what he really wanted to do was approach Samantha. 'Oh gosh!' he had said within himself when two ladies simultaneously came forward. Not knowing which of them he should agree to dance with, he just looked into their eyes in turn and the they both smiled. Donaldson was saved from the situation by a man who tapped one of the ladies on the shoulder and said, 'Would you care to dance?' Donaldson still eyed Samantha who stood holding an empty tray. Suddenly, he saw a man in a white three-piece suit walk over to her. He missed a heartbeat! There was no doubt that the man had gone to make a dance request. If she obliged, Donaldson knew that his chances of getting closer to her would be considerably reduced. But some moments later, after a brief conversation, the man turned around and walked over to another lady and the two of them began to dance. Donaldson heaved a sigh of relief. But not long after that, another man, a well-known presidential adviser on banking and industry, rose from his seat and walked over to her. And within a few moments he was back on his seat alone. One of the embassy ladies then walked briskly to him and smilingly requested a dance. It was glaring that the lady had come to help him overcome his embarrassment. The man happily obliged. And the next moments the two of them were on the dance floor. At first Donaldson was very happy at the two men's 'misfortune.' But his joy was short-lived, and his hope turned to despair when he suddenly realised that he might suffer the same fate. Should he forget about the lady and concentrate on his dancing? But that was very difficult. He no longer seemed to have a control over his eyes as he kept looking at her. He would have to try, even if she refused to dance with him. He always believed that it was better to fail an examination than to be absent from it. According to him, today's failure would form part of preparation for tomorrow's success. Or, it might turn to be the main platform needed for tomorrow's success. He smiled at his positive thoughts. His dance partner smiled back, even though she didn't know why he smiled.

His mind was fully occupied with how to get to Samantha. It would be very rude of him to disengage himself from his partner too early and try to engage another. In fact, that wouldn't only be rudeness on his part; it would send the wrong message about his character in a public gathering! He heaved a quiet sigh. Unbelievably, his partner excused herself at that moment. 'I need to visit the ladies' room,' she said, smiling at him as she walked away. Donaldson barely noticed. The beautiful server was still standing there. This was his chance to talk to her.

He then walked over to her and said, 'The glory of an angel is better appreciated when she dances and not when she serves. You belong to the centre and not the corner, madam.' Bowing, he added, 'Would you please dance with me?' Donaldson was a vast reader of romantic novels. He had borrowed that approach from a novel he read while at university. And it worked! All the embassy ladies, who were anxious to see Samantha's reaction, cast furtive glances as he spoke to her. Without saying a word, she followed him to the dance floor where they danced to Heatwave's slow jam – *Always and Forever*. Donaldson loved the song, and he knew the lyrics as well as he knew his own name. As they danced, he gently sang the romantic lyrics. But he sang a bit louder when it got to where the singer said, *'And if you get lonely, phone me.'* That was the only time Samantha looked into his eyes. She had been dancing with head bowed right from the start. But Donaldson didn't expect her look of indignation. She had seen where he was heading and decided she needed to do something – and quickly, too.

'Sir, can you please excuse me now?' she asked.

'Em, em, you mean you want to go have a seat?'

'Yes.'

'Alright, can we go to my table? I've got an empty chair.'

'No.'

'Okay, can I have your card?'

'No.'

'May I know your name then?'

'Samantha.'

'My name is Donaldson – Donaldson Weah. And here's my card.'

'That won't be necessary sir.'

And as she turned around to leave, Donaldson added, 'Oh, can I have your office number?'

'No.'

'Can I come around and say hi to you one of these days?'

Samantha didn't respond to this last query. Instead, she turned around and walked away. Donaldson remained glued to the same point and stared at her as she walked briskly towards the service point. 'What kind of creature is this?' he wondered as he walked back to his seat, highly embarrassed.

It wasn't that Donaldson had a problem dating girls or having them hooked on him. How would a highly influential, handsome banking executive like him have dating problems? As a drop of honey attracts various kinds of insects he had always attracted various kinds of women anywhere he went. But he was such a strange young man who didn't have a penchant for ladies. To his friends, his disposition towards ladies was the only negative of his life. He drank alcohol, though modestly, and cracked lots of jokes. He related to all his friends and colleagues very well. He was so kind and generous. But when he was presented with a lady by friends, he found one excuse or the other to turn down the 'offer.' Sometimes, he would complain that the lady was too dark. And another time, she was too light complexioned. 'Oh, this one has an angelic smile but she's too short for my liking,' or, 'That one is too tall – taller than I. I can't cope with her.' Because of this, he was given all sorts of nicknames by his friends. Among his numerous nicknames were Pope and *Edingo*. Of all the nicknames, he hated being called *Edingo*. He didn't see anything funny in the nickname as it referred to a sexually impotent man. Even one of his university mates had shared a joke about a sexually impotent man, called *Edingo*.

CHAPTER 2: LOVES' HELPER

Samantha was the first lady ever to steal Donaldson's heart. As much as he tried, he couldn't get the memory of their meeting off his mind. At work everyone noticed the change in his demeanour. He was spotted resting his elbow on the office table with his chin on the palm and barely noticed when someone walked into his office. In his bid to suppress the thought of her he had once drunk himself to stupor. But that same night he saw himself holding her hand in a dream. When he woke up and realised that it was a dream, he became very sad and sat up helplessly in bed. With only underpants on and legs flung wide apart, he cut a picture of a drunkard who had come back to his senses only to realise that he had misspent all he had last night, including his transport fare back home! The alcohol had not helped at all. He felt very stupid to have thought it would! He then switched from blaming himself to his encounter with Samantha again. He tried to compare her to the lady he first danced with. No. In terms of beauty, he wouldn't be doing Samantha any justice by comparing her to that lady. Although he relished the honour of being approached for a dance by such a highly respectable woman, he really longed for Samantha. He still remembered how the opportunity of dancing with her came after her dance partner had excused herself. 'You'll never come back to me. Oh, Jesus Christ!' he had thought.

Donaldson neither believed in Jesus Christ nor attended church. He was used to using the name of Jesus as a swear word, nothing more. He didn't believe in existence of a God either. If there was a God, then he hated Him. 'How can a man in his right mind believe in a non-existent God?' was his position. How could anyone prove to him that God existed when he lost his both parents and had to undergo terrible situations as a child? Why did his parents' relatives take over his inheritance and refuse to take him in if truly there was a God? Donaldson got angry whenever anyone tried to convince him of existence of God.

That night, he had wished Samantha wasn't married. And when he had an opportunity of coming closer to her he surveyed all her fingers and discovered that she didn't have a ring on, which gave him hope. But his hope was short-lived. Samantha's attitude to him discouraged Donaldson from giving her a call. But after two weeks, while alone in his office, he finally plucked up the courage to call her on the Trade Department line. But as he reached for the receiver his hand became shaky; his nerve failed him. And he held on to the receiver without dialling the number, thinking of her possible reaction. He was in that position when his secretary burst in with a file in her hand.

'Sir, I tried to speak to you on the intercom without success. I thought you were using the phone. I just wanted to tell you that I have finished with the typing. May I sign for you and send them straightaway?'

'Oh, thank you, Samantha,' replied Donaldson. 'Let me just check them first.'

'Sir, what did you just call me? Samantha? Who's Samantha?' asked Agnes with a grimace.

'Oh Agnes, please pardon me. I didn't have enough sleep last night. You may drop the file and go. I will call you later.'

Twitching her lips, Agnes made for the door.

As soon as she left, Donaldson summoned up all his courage and dialled the number. The call was picked up by a male operator who transferred the call to the Trade Department. And another person – a lady – responded.

'Good afternoon. This is extension 124, the British Embassy Trade Department. How may I help you?'

'Good afternoon. My name is Donaldson Weah. I'm calling from Wuteve Bank ….'

'Oh Dr Weah!' the lady ecstatically exclaimed. 'How are you? I am Amanda. Do you remember? We danced together at our December party.'

'Oh Amanda!' exclaimed Donaldson. 'It's great speaking to you. How are you? The party was great, and you guys were amazing!'

'Thanks for the compliment, Dr Weah. We also thank you for honouring our invitation. How may I help you this afternoon?'

'Oh, thank you, Amanda. May I speak to Samantha?'

'Alright, one second ….' Smiling ecstatically, Amanda transferred the call to Samantha via the intercom.

'Hello, Samantha Collins on the line. How may I help you?'

'Hi Samantha!' responded Donaldson. 'How are you? It's me Donaldson.'

'Good afternoon. What can I do for you?'

'I would have called you earlier, but I thought you were away to Britain on holiday,' Donaldson lied. That was followed by a long silence which was eventually broken by Samantha.

'So, what can I do for you?' Samantha asked squeezing her eyebrows.

'I just wanted to say hello,' replied Donaldson.

'But I guess you realise that this is an official line which must be kept as such?'

'Of course, I do. I'm so sorry. Can I have your home phone then?'

'No. Good day sir!' she replied and hanged up. But Amanda had been eavesdropping through the intercom. And before Donaldson could hang up, she whispered, 'Hello. Don't hang up yet.'

'Who is it?' asked Donaldson.

'It's Amanda. I overheard your conversation with Samantha and I want to help you. We can't talk now but you may have my home number and give me a call later.' Although Donaldson took the number, he really didn't know what to say. He was completely shattered by Samantha's snub. He suddenly became dizzy and, despite the perfect air-conditioning in his office, he could feel cold sweat coming out of his forehead. He didn't even remember to thank Amanda before hanging up.

What sort of embarrassment did he subject himself to? Why did he call her in the first place? 'Oh my God!' he lamented. God? Was he going mad? What could a non-existing God do? As he spoke to himself he didn't realise that his voice was raised and Agnes, who was in the adjacent office, was listening. She left what she was doing and gently knocked his door. 'Yes, come in,' he responded as he adjusted himself on his chair.

'Sir, I overheard all you said. And I've just come to tell you that there is God who is the Creator of heaven and earth and all that is in them. He's the One who rules in the affairs of men. There is no problem that is too big for him to solve. He says, "Come to me, all who labour and are heavy laden, and I will give you …"'

'That's enough!' exclaimed Donaldson, banging a clenched fist on the table at the same time. 'I didn't invite you. Did I? Who told you that I'm heavy laden? And who complained about labour? Did you think you can fill my mind with your bigotry? But since when did the whole world become eavesdroppers? I tried to speak to a friend at the embassy and someone was eavesdropping there. And right now, in my office, another person is eavesdropping! Samantha – sorry, Agnes – don't you think this

17

world will be a better place if everyone minded their own business? I've already warned you not to talk to me about God, so let this be the last warning! Now will you please get out of my office?'

Agnes was a married woman in her early thirties. A devout Christian, she had a great evangelical zeal. She was one of those heaven-conscious people who believed that wherever a child of God found themselves they were there for God's purpose. And that purpose was to affect the lives of people around them and win them for Christ. That was the principle by which she lived. She never closed her eyes to any perceived vices but spoke out against immorality and godlessness anytime and anywhere. She was married to a lawyer, who was also a fervent servant of God, an assistant pastor. Agnes' husband was ready to help the poor who were cheated and oppressed. He argued their cases without taking a penny. And he never defended criminals with established criminal records. He wasn't as rich as his colleagues, but he had enough for his family, a wife and two children. Agnes was five years older than Donaldson and had been at the bank five years longer, too. She started as a confidential secretary at one of the branches. She was later transferred to the Monrovia Headquarters, on promotion, as a Personal Assistant to the Human Resources Director. That was a year before Donaldson joined the bank. She was, however, reposted to Donaldson's office as soon as he arrived at the headquarters. She had sought an audience with her new boss on their first meeting. That was after he was introduced to all senior management staff at an ad-hoc meeting. In his words of introduction, the Director of Banking Operations had said, 'Ladies and gentlemen, we have in our midst this morning a sagacious, young and dynamic epitome of banking and business. He's a tested and trusted professional who can pull a rabbit out of a hat. I'm pleased to introduce to you our new Senior Finance Manager in the person of Dr Donaldson Jerome Weah, Bachelor of Administration; Master of Business Administration; Doctor of Philosophy; Member, Chartered Institute of Bankers of Liberia; Member, Liberia Institute of Management and Member, the America's Association for Financial Professionals. There was a protracted round of applause.

Agnes introduced all the department staff to her new boss as soon as he settled down in his office. There were about ten of them, including messengers, clerks, copy typists and a confidential secretary. After the introductory formalities, she waited behind to have a closed-door meeting with him. But she got the shock of her life when she suggested starting their discussion with a prayer. Donaldson looked at her indignantly before replying that the only places for prayers were churches and personal homes. When Agnes replied that God was everywhere and that there was nowhere prayer couldn't be said, he quipped, 'Madam, I believe what you want to discuss with me is of importance. Can we go ahead and leave religion out of it?'

'Alright sir,' conceded Agnes. 'First, I want to congratulate you on two different things – your blossoming career and promotion. I'm sorry sir, but I've got to let you know that you are the youngest senior management staff of this bank, including all the branches. I don't believe that is by chance. I believe that God is at work in your life. It's quite amazing that a hapless orphan has risen to such a height at such an age. I'm convinced God's hand is on you. He loves you and sent Jesus to die to make you one of His children, you've got to appreciate all He has done for you by giving your life to ….'

'Enough, Agnes!' barked Donaldson. 'Now listen to me: I don't owe my achievements to any so-called God. My achievements are my own. They are the result of my determination to succeed, which was fired up by hard work and dedication to my stringent principles. And one of the principles is not to be deceived by a non-existing God or those who gullibly follow it. Listen to me, madam: I don't believe in anything supernatural. If you do, that's your business. But I should let you know that if you really want us to work together harmoniously in this department you mustn't try to discuss religion with me again. Have I made myself clear?'

'Perfectly sir,' Agnes replied as she turned to leave.

Agnes didn't speak about Jesus to her boss for months. But she never stopped praying for the salvation of his soul. Despite their different beliefs, however, they had a good official relationship. She perfectly understood her boss and smoothly coordinated the daily activities of the department. Most of Donaldson's administrative responsibilities were performed by her. She was very punctual and always arrived at work earlier than anyone. She always told her colleagues that Christians must set shining examples everywhere.

Two weeks after Donaldson had collected Amanda's number, he eventually made up his mind to call her. His unconquerable feelings for Samantha compelled him. The venue of their meeting was fixed for the ground floor restaurant of the posh Hotel Africa on the western coast of northern Monrovia. Hotel Africa was the largest and most beautiful hotel in Liberia in the 1970s. It was the meeting point for crème de la crème of the society. It was the only hotel in Monrovia that was patronised by government functionaries, wealthy businessmen, ambassadors of nations and their staff. Donaldson didn't frequent the hotel. Apart from that night, he had been there only once. And that was two years ago when it hosted an international banking conference. He didn't see any reason why he should patronise a hotel where a bottle of beer cost seven times more than it did elsewhere. He once told his friends that even if he won millions of dollars in jackpot he would still not patronise the hotel. He believed that the place was meant for three categories of people: thieving politicians, white bosses who were paid in foreign currencies, and government contractors who collaborated with corrupt politicians to embezzle public funds. Any officer of his company who frequented the hotel should be investigated for corruption. That was his opinion.

He had arrived a quarter of an hour ahead of schedule and took a seat where he could clearly see Amanda when she arrived. He then took a magazine from a small shelf beside his table and ordered a bottle of chilled beer. Amanda walked in few minutes later, accompanied by a white couple. She surveyed the large restaurant as she walked towards the counter, apparently to see if Donaldson had arrived. But he wondered why she had come with those people. Hiding behind his magazine, he decided to study their body movements and read their lips before showing up. About three minutes later, another couple came downstairs by the lift and hugged Amanda's friends. They shook Amanda's hand in turn before entering the lift with her friends, leaving her alone in the ground floor restaurant. Still surveying the crowded restaurant for Donaldson, she asked a waiter to get her an empty table. Just then Donaldson walked over to her.

'Hi Amanda,' he said smilingly.

'Oh, good evening Dr Weah,' replied Amanda ecstatically. 'I'm sorry I arrived behind schedule. I had to wait for my neighbours' guests from South Africa. My neighbours are also here, and they asked me to give them a lift.'

'I saw them,' replied Donaldson casually.

'Did you? I thought you had just come in.'

'No. I arrived before seven.'

'That means you had been watching me before you showed up?'

'Yes.'

'Why did you do that?'

'Because I had no idea why you brought those people to a meeting that was supposed to be confidential,' he replied smilingly.

Amanda sighed and smiled at the same time. After they had had a seat Donaldson ordered a dinner for both of them. And while they ate, he broke the silence by asking:

'Amanda, I can't wait to hear what you have to tell me about Samantha.'

'Okay, let's finish our meal first and I will relate a story.'

After their meal, Donaldson called for another bottle of beer for himself and a glass of Coca-Cola for Amanda who didn't take alcoholic drinks. And as they sipped their drinks Amanda began.

Several months after Samantha's arrival in Liberia, she was still refusing to fraternise with any of her colleagues. Amanda had taken it upon herself to investigate the reason for her attitude. She had always suspected that it wasn't her natural behaviour; something must have informed that. And, having stumbled on her previous job information, she was able to gather the required details from her brother's friend, who also knew Samantha very well.

Samantha was from Bermondsey, South East London. She lost her father when she was still a child and her mother passed away a few months before she came to Africa. She inherited the five-bedroom family property which she let out when she got a job with the British Embassy. She graduated from University of London with a bachelor's degree in Business Administration. Samantha had a broken relationship back home in England. There had only ever been one man in her life. His name was Dave and their relationship dated back to their high school days. Both of them were able to get a good job as soon as they finished their degrees. While Samantha worked as an Administrative Officer at the London headquarters of John Lewis Partnership, Dave was employed by the National Health Service (NHS) and posted to Saint Thomas' Hospital in London. The young lovers decided they would get married after working for two or three years. It had been an exciting courtship for them. They were very fond of each other and were always together whenever they were not at work. And, as expected of ecstatic young lovers, so many times they spent weekends together at Dave's flat. That was before trouble struck several months before their wedding.

Samantha had a younger female cousin called Bridget whom she accommodated in her flat at Bermondsey. Bridget was the youngest of four children of her parents and the only girl. For this reason, she always preferred Samantha's company. She initially spent weekends with her, but one day she asked Samantha if she could move in. And after Samantha had been convinced of her parents' consent she was allowed to move in.

Bridget's high school results were very bad. And after two consecutive unsuccessful attempts to gain admission into the university Samantha enrolled her at a private modelling school. It didn't take her long to prove that she had a very bright future in that career. Within her first year at the school she modelled at a few fashion exhibitions within and without England. Bridget couldn't stop thanking Samantha for helping her on the way to a promising future. And Samantha so loved Bridget that she never failed to buy her any fashion accessories she could find when there was a sale on: beautiful handbags, shoes, clothing and pieces of jewellery.

A few months before Samantha's wedding, however, a tempest of betrayals suddenly wrecked her relationship. Samantha had felt dreadfully ill during her morning team meeting. When it finally finished, she escaped to the ladies where her boss, Gwen, found her leaning over the sink, running cool water over her wrists.

'Are you ok? You should go home if you're not well. We can manage here, you know.' Gwen put a kind hand on Samantha's arm.

'Thank you, Gwen,' replied Samantha. 'I'll go to Dave's, I think. His place is closer than mine and I have a key.'

But as she pulled up in front of the flat she was surprised to discover that Dave was at home. His Ford was parked out front and she could hear music blaring from his heavy bass home stereo. She took out the keys from her handbag and opened the front door. As she walked down a short passage to the living room she was terribly shocked to find a lady's handbag and pair of shoes were lying on the living-room floor. On the coffee table were some takeaway leftovers and an empty bottle of wine. 'What is happening here?' Samantha asked herself as she bent down to have a closer look at the items. She picked up the handbag and immediately recognised it. It was the one she bought for Bridget on one of their shopping trips two weeks earlier. Was she dreaming? She headed for Dave's bedroom. That was the only thing she could remember as she woke up to find herself surrounded by a team of paramedics. She had collapsed on entering the room and finding Dave and her cousin making love on the bed. Unknown to Samantha, this was just one of many days off Dave had taken to carry on his affair with Bridget.

It was a terrible trauma for Samantha who nearly suffered a breakdown because of the incident. Her ordeal was worsened when about four months later, her mother lost her long battle with cancer. Samantha's bosses at work and friends stood by her. Her salary continued to be paid while she took three months off work, a gesture she appreciated. When she fully recovered, she summed up all her courage to pick up the pieces of her life again. But the straw that broke the camel's back came when she learned that Bridget was pregnant with Dave's child and they had concluded arrangements to get married. She made up her mind to leave England perhaps that would wipe off the unpalatable memory. And having resigned her appointment at the John Lewis, she applied for and got a job with the British Embassy in Liberia. The job advert was timely. Out of about fifty applicants interviewed she was among the three eventually taken. The double betrayal suffered by her, coupled with the demise of her mother, however, had a huge effect on her demeanour and general disposition towards others – especially men.

There was a long silence after the story. Donaldson took out a white handkerchief from his pocket and gently wiped his eyes. Amanda did the same.

'This is dreadful!' he said.

'Yes, it is, Dr Weah,' replied Amanda.

'And with this situation, what chances do you think I have of winning her over?' asked Donaldson.

'There are great chances, Dr Weah. But my question is: Do you like Samantha for a partner or just for fun of it?'

'Amanda, I don't have to hide my feelings from you. I like Samantha. If there is a way of helping her overcome her pain I believe she would make a very good partner.'

'Listen to me, Dr Weah. I strongly believe if we handle this matter very well you will surely win Samantha over.'

'How do you mean?'

'I studied her very closely at the party that night. I noticed that she didn't raise her head throughout the programme until you were introduced. And until you finished your presentation she didn't move her eyes away from you. I also noticed that you too were eyeing her, even when we were dancing. So, I pretended I was visiting the loo to create an opportunity for the two of you. And I was not disappointed – I came back to find you dancing with her! Dr Weah, you seem to have the magic, considering that she had turned down two dance requests before yours. You will get Samantha, but you will have to work for it if you truly want her. I want her to be happy again. And I'm convinced you're the man that can make her happy again. I will give you all the support that you need. Take her card. But don't call her until I ask you to. Her birthday is on March 27 – next month. Send her a surprise birthday gift on that day but keep her wondering how you knew about her birthday. Another secret: after Samantha left the John Lewis, one of the many poems written for her by her jilting fiancé was recovered from her office drawer. Have it. If you can't write a poem like that ask someone else to write it for you and have it sent together with the gift. Samantha loved romantic poems!'

Donaldson collected the paper and read through the poem which was titled, '*Blame Them Not.*'

BLAME THEM NOT!
Sack not that perfect waiter, who dropped saliva in customer's soup;
Rebuke not that dutiful cop, who mistakenly handcuffed a colleague
While the thief went singing Hallelujah; Make no jest of that brilliant doctor
Who took a sip from patient's sample urine, For they were all carried away
By none but Samantha's radiance and beauty.
BY DAVE 02/06/1974

'What a sugar-coated son-of-a-bitch!' he remarked.

CHAPTER 3: PEACE AND JOY

It was Saturday. As Samantha had no friends she neither went out on weekends nor received visitors. Although she had a cable TV installed in her three-bed room apartment, she never liked to watch British programmes. Any time she watched the BBC and saw some London locations, she was reminded of the reason she had left home. She had come to Africa to start her life anew, and she didn't like anything that could remind her of the bitter past. But the only thing she couldn't forget was the death of her loving mother and her parting words. And that Saturday morning, as she sat on a sofa watching a local programme absent-mindedly, she once again remembered. 'Samantha, you must be very strong to face the challenges of life. Never accept defeat. Tough times never last but tough people do. Don't pine over any man. One day you'll meet a caring man who will make you happy. He will shower you with unimaginable love and stick with you.'

'Now it's time for the broken-hearted to receive joy and sinners to receive salvation. Viewers, it's time to meet the woman of God, Pastor (Mrs) Elizabeth Smith, on our religious programme, *Peace in Abundance.*' The programme announcement caught Samantha's attention and grounded her flight of thought. Pastor Elizabeth Smith was a renowned television preacher and marriage counsellor. Her programme was aired on most television stations in Liberia. She was the President and General Overseer of "Peace in Abundance Ministries," which was very influential in Liberia. The mantle of leadership fell upon her after the demise of her husband, the founder of the ministry. Much like her late husband, she gave soul-piercing and marriage-mending messages. Many people testified to being helped by her ministry. After some introductory songs, the 'woman of God' appeared, 'Good morning, beloved! Hey, don't change the channel! Today's programme is meant for you–yes, you!' Samantha had never been so dazed. That instruction came just as she took the remote and was about to change the channel! 'That's a strange coincidence!' she thought. But the preacher dropped more bombshells, 'No – it wasn't a coincidence. God has specifically chosen today to speak to your situation. And if you shall be willing and obedient, what looks like a great mountain before you shall become flat. His Word says, 'For your shame you shall have double portion.' Shall we have an opening prayer?' For the first time in her life, Samantha was ready to listen to a Christian sermon. Although she neither closed her eyes nor said 'Amen' to the opening prayer, she listened with rapt attention. She returned the remote to the centre of the table and settled herself on the sofa.

Most of what the preacher said was a mystery to her. The woman had said, 'You think it's the end of the world because that man you loved and trusted has jilted you?' She also said, 'Do you realise that there is someone who loves you more than the mother or father you lost?' And she also added, 'Because one person has disappointed you doesn't mean everybody will. By one man death came to our world. But by another man life came to our world. What you need is Jesus Christ. He is the Giver of everlasting peace and joy. Give your life to Him now as you watch and listen to me. If you are ready, can you please say the following prayer along with me?'

Although Samantha liked the sermon and the preacher, she wasn't sure she was ready to give her life to Jesus. That preacher spoke so confidently and convincingly. But how could Jesus Christ give her peace and joy and mend her life? Even if Jesus made Dave divorce Bridget and come back to her begging, she would never take him back!

Should she give another man a chance? How would she know that the man was sent by Jesus and not by the same devil that sent Dave? But the preacher said Jesus would intervene only when one invited Him. How? By giving one's life to Him! The only thing that she didn't seem to agree with was the process of giving one's life to Jesus. It was too simple to have any effect. By merely saying some so-called words of confession and praying some simple prayer! She utterly disagreed with that process. How could mere words of your mouth give you joy and peace? The preacher didn't even ask her to come to her church to be prayed for. But did she even need another man?

Why was she bothering herself about the sermon, anyway? Even though she didn't need another man, perhaps it was true that she needed peace and joy. After all, the preacher didn't say Jesus would give her another man but peace and joy. It seemed Jesus knew precisely what she needed. Well then, if Jesus could first give her peace and joy she would consider giving her life to Him. 'That's a deal, God, okay?'

The following Monday was her birthday. It was four years since she last celebrated it. Dave had booked a posh restaurant where they treated friends and relatives. That was their last year together. Since then she didn't even remember when it was her birthday. Among her colleagues at work only Amanda knew when her birthday was – but pretended she didn't. At midday Samantha was called to reception to collect a parcel that was dropped for her by a local courier. 'Parcel?' she asked. There must have been a mix-up somewhere.

'Excuse me, I am not expecting any parcel,' she had argued.

'But it is addressed to Miss Samantha Collins of Trade Department of the British Embassy,' replied the receptionist via the intercom.

'Alright, I'm on my way.'

She stared at the parcel as she walked back to her office. What could this be and who was the sender? The sender didn't even write his or her name. All that was written at the back of the parcel was the sender's initials and post office address. She placed it gently on her office table. Resting her chin on her right palm with elbow on the table, she regarded the parcel for a while. She was lost in thought. At last she tore it open. 'What? Today is my birthday!' she exclaimed. The first thing she saw as she opened the parcel was a very beautiful birthday card. Next to the card was a gold wrist-watch packed in a beautifully ornamented glass case. But none of the items bore the sender's name. Who on earth could the sender be? Just then, she noticed that a medium size envelope had fallen off the parcel. She picked it up and tore it open. By Jove! It was a poem from Donaldson Weah.

HAPPY BIRTHDAY, ANGEL
I know I'm not worthy of your smile.
Neither am I worthy of your angelic embrace.
But allow me to make this birthday offering
At your beautiful and adorable altar
And let my offering be accepted by you,
Even if I'll still be loathed!
by Donaldson Jerome Weah

Samantha was dumbfounded. OK, it was a lovely poem, but how did he know it was her birthday? That was a great mystery. If she really wanted that question answered there was only one person she could ask. And that was Donaldson himself. Should she call to thank him? But would her action not be misconstrued by him? What if he thought that his gifts had ensured her change of heart? But it would be an act of ungratefulness not calling to thank him. She was confused. She took the wrist-watch and admired it once again. It was Swiss-made. It must be very expensive. 'It's beautiful,' she admitted. She read the poem and looked at the card again and again. Then she remembered her mum, the preacher and Jesus. Her mum told her that she would one day meet a caring man. The preacher said that if she believed, Jesus would give her peace and joy. Has Jesus begun the process of giving her peace and joy? Was Donaldson a caring man? But Dave had started off like that. Should she give

Donaldson a chance? No. Not so quickly. But maybe they could start off on a platonic basis. But the riddle of her birthday was still there.

Since Amanda was the administrative secretary, she was the one who sent out the party invites. There was a possibility that she still had Donaldson's number. But there lay the problem – Samantha had never had personal discussions with anyone at the embassy ever since her arrival three years ago. She had no friends among them. She had none anywhere! As she was still thinking, there was a gentle knock at the door. 'Yes, come in,' said Samantha. The door was slowly opened. It was Amanda! Samantha hurriedly packed the gift items.

'Hi there!' said Amanda smiling. 'Have you finished with that diskette? I need to print something from it urgently,' she added. But as she spotted the gold wrist-watch she exclaimed, 'Hey, what a beautiful wrist-watch! Have you just bought it? Can I have a look at it, please?' But Samantha didn't bother to reply any of her questions. Instead, she ejected the diskette from her computer and handed it over to her. Amanda took the wrist-watch from the table and admired it. 'How much did it cost, Samantha?' But there wasn't any response. 'Samantha, please tell me. I need to ask my fiancé to get me one like this.' Samantha quietly stared at her. She wasn't sure if she should discuss the matter or not. 'Oh, is that a birthday card? So, it's your birthday!' Samantha looked at the envelope and realised that the card wasn't properly hidden. Amanda had seen everything she thought she had hidden from her. Should she open up now? No … yes … no.

'I'd better leave since you don't want me to share in the joy of your birthday,' said Amanda as she turned around to leave.

But as she was about to close the door behind her, Samantha exclaimed, 'Hey, Amanda!'

Amanda couldn't believe her ears. Looking back, she asked:

'Did you call me?'

'Yes. Can you please get me the Wuteve Bank telephone number or, specifically, that of the guy who presented the keynote address at the last party?'

'You mean Dr Donaldson Weah?'

'Yes. I only have his official number – that of his department. I hope there's no problem?' asked Amanda.

'Amanda, please have a seat.' After Amanda had sat comfortably on one of the two visitor chairs directly opposite her table, Samantha asked, 'What do you know about that guy?'

'You mean Dr Weah? Well, I don't know much about him, but I will tell you the little I know. He's a very brilliant, award-winning young banking executive who has no appetite for ladies.'

'Are you sure of that?' interjected Samantha.

'Yes, I'm sure.'

'Then have a look at these.'

Samantha passed the poem and card to Amanda.

'Oh my God!' exclaimed Amanda. 'I can't believe Dr Weah wrote this! You must have hypnotised him! And who will ever loathe a writer of such a romantically captivating poem? This is awesome!'

'He gave me the wrist-watch too.'

'What?' Amanda exclaimed.

'Do you think I should call to thank him for the gifts? More importantly, I like to find out how he got to know my birthday?'

'You mean you didn't tell him about your birthday?'

'I didn't tell anybody. The last time I even remembered my birthday was four years ago until this guy reminded me today. Besides, I've only met him once – at the party. He tried to speak to me on an official line after that, but I snubbed him.'

'Do you like the guy?' There was a long silence which was eventually broken by Amanda. 'Listen, Samantha. You don't have to be shy. I'm a woman like you. I want you to believe that whatever happens between us today remains between us forever. I have been looking for an opportunity to come close to you ever since your arrival here. I always knew that you were such a pleasant person and that there must be reasons for your unwelcoming attitude.' Casting a quick look towards the door and lowering her voice as if suspicious of an eavesdropper, Amanda asked again, 'So, do you like him?'

'It's not that I don't like him,' began Samantha, 'but I have decided not to have anything to do with men for the rest of my life.'

'Why?'

'It's a long story …' she began to sob. Amanda moved closer and put her arm around her shoulders. She then took a tissue from a box and helped wipe her tears.

'I'm so sorry, Samantha,' said Amanda after Samantha had finished her story. 'As for Dave, all I can say is don't let him rob you twice. He robbed you of your happiness, don't let him rob you of God's plans for your life,' added Amanda.

What did she just hear Amanda say? Did she mention God? Does she believe in God?

'Excuse me, Amanda. Did you just mention God?'

'Yes. I said you shouldn't let a man deprive you of God's plans for your life,' repeated Amanda.

'Do you believe in God?'

'Of course, I do. Don't you?'

'And you believe in Jesus too?' Samantha asked further.

'Yes. Jesus is the Son of God. He gave Himself on the cross that we might be saved. He is the reason we exist. For the Bible says that nothing was made without Him.'

'This is strange!' exclaimed Samantha.

'What is strange?'

'Your being a Christian and quoting from the Bible, of course!' replied Samantha.

Amanda was the youngest of three children of Reverend Stuart Wilberforce who was the founder of the Divine Light Evangelical Church in Manchester, England. She and her siblings were brought up in the church, the eldest was now a pastor himself. Amanda, like any of her siblings, had a great zeal for soul-winning. Her modus operandi was spelt out in 1 Corinthians 9:23 *'I have become all things to all people so that by all possible means I might save some.'* As a result of that flexibility, many people believed she was too clubbable to be serious-minded. Some even thought she was a flirt. But whatever she did and wherever she did it had an evangelical motive. Through her, a quarter of the staff of the Trade Department had already become Christians. Many immoral men who thought she would easily grace their bed had found themselves listening to the gospel of Jesus Christ! One such man was Albert Shroud, a senior consular staff member at the US embassy. He had bombarded her with calls and texts, requesting a date. But the day she honoured his request, Albert wept like a baby and was led to Christ. Amanda was a specially anointed evangelist in the hand of the Lord. Her fiancé was also a firebrand Christian with an equal passion for evangelism. He attended her father's church in Manchester. She intended to apply to the Foreign Office in London for a transfer to England when her wedding approached. Top on her current evangelistic agenda were Samantha and her atheist boss. 'There is nothing God cannot do,' she always asserted. Amanda had exploited Donaldson's glaring desire for Samantha as bait to get at them both. She would work on Samantha first. And later she would go after Donaldson. That would be easier if Samantha became a Christian.

It was a golden opportunity for Amanda to preach to Samantha. It didn't matter if she missed lunch. She advised Samantha to call Donaldson and thank him for the gifts. But, she said, there was a relationship she had to seek first. It was that relationship that would smooth all other relationships. Relationship with God was the most important. Jesus had said, "But seek first his kingdom and his righteousness, and all these things will be given to you as well." So, to obtain God's peace and joy you must first give your life to Him.'

'Samantha are you ready to give your life to Jesus Christ?'

'There we go again,' Samantha said within herself. Was there any way of escaping all these 'you must give your life to Christ?' She blamed herself for seeking Amanda's advice. But she found her words comforting, even the Jesus bit. She realised that Amanda was a genuinely good person and would make a very good friend. So, despite the religious pestering, she had begun to like Amanda.

'Amanda, you are very nice. I'm sorry for the way I had treated you and everybody in this place for close to three years. It wasn't your fault, it was because of the trauma I went through. You know, for the first time in my life I listened to a Christian sermon on Saturday on LBC. The sermon spoke to my life circumstances. I've never heard anything like that before. The sermon was all about peace and joy, and I decided that if Jesus first gave me peace and joy I would consider giving my life to Him. That's my stand, Amanda.'

Amanda gave a half smile before replying, 'Samantha, you are funny. You act as if God owes you a favour! You are the one who loses without Him. It's only when you let Christ come into your heart that you can experience His joy and peace – not the other way around.'

Samantha was lost in thought. Should she give her life to Jesus and become a Christian? She would then have to attend church every Sunday. And midweek too! She would be reading the Bible and adhering to a long list of Christian do's and don'ts. Was that boring kind of life worth of living?

'So, Amanda was a born-again Christian?' she asked herself. 'I should have known by the way she's dressed and the fact she didn't take alcohol at the last end-of-year party. But how would someone know by the way she freely interacts with everyone – males and females? Honestly, I thought she was a flirt. But … wait a minute; my life is boring already! Why I am thinking that Christianity will make life boring? Can any life be more boring than mine? Amanda, who is a Christian, lives a very exciting life whereas I live most boring life.

'I still need to be given a little time to think before making my decision,' She said aloud.

It was 1 p.m. – the end of their break-time. Samantha apologised for preventing Amanda from having her lunch. But Amanda smilingly replied that the best lunch she had ever had was the privilege of chatting with her. Samantha, however, opened her sizeable office fridge and brought out a pack of biscuits and a bottle of juice which she offered Amanda as lunch.

CHAPTER 4: A PREACHING LUNATIC!

Precisely two weeks after receiving the birthday gifts, Samantha had not yet called to thank Donaldson or acknowledge their receipt. He had expected her call throughout the previous week, picking up every call with the alacrity of a desperate job applicant waiting for a call from the employment office. At least she ought to confirm their receipt, he thought. He had eagerly looked forward to hearing her voice. He then, somehow, remembered that she didn't have his number. He regretted not including his card in the birthday parcel. What an idiot he was! Should he call her? What if she didn't like the gifts? Calling her would then make him look even more stupid. But if she really wanted to call him she could obtain his official number from their telephone operator. Well, if she didn't call till Friday he didn't have to go on deceiving himself; he would forget about her. He decided to call Amanda, so he moved the telephone box nearer to himself.

'Amanda, it is precisely two weeks today and I don't know if Sam liked my gifts.'

'Are you sure she hasn't called you?'

'She doesn't have my number.'

'I gave it to her. She showed the gifts to me and asked if she should call to thank you.'

'I haven't received her call.'

'Relax, she will call you today.'

But she didn't call that day. It was a miserable evening for Donaldson as he left the office with still no word from Samantha. As he drove home that evening he decided to fill up his petrol tank. He branched off the road and stopped his car at a petrol station where there were about five cars already in the queue. As he joined the queue, he turned off the engine and rolled down the glass of his Mercedes. Not far from the petrol station was a man, dressed in rags, most likely homeless, begging for help from passers-by. When he saw Donaldson, he walked over to him. Regarding him silently for a few moments, he suddenly exclaimed, 'Because you have education, money, and a good job you think you have everything. But the greatest achievement of a man is salvation of his soul which is obtained free of charge through Christ Jesus. If you seek His kingdom the same way you seek after the love of that lady heaven will be happy with you. Don't bother to give me money. You need help more than I do!'

Donaldson was so embarrassed that he barely waited for his turn. And as he continued his journey he couldn't take his mind off the incident. It had even eclipsed the thought of Samantha. A madman preached Jesus to him! But the madman mentioned three things which were true: He had education, money, and a good job; he didn't seek God; and thirdly, he sought after the love of a woman. Could all those be coincidences? He became greatly disturbed. There was traffic holdup at that very moment. And from the car right in front of him he received yet another bombshell! There was a sticker on the back bumper of the car which read, 'WITHOUT JESUS THERE IS NO PEACE.' He regarded the car and its occupants from behind. It was a red, highly expensive Aston Martin V8 Vantage – one of the world's fastest and most expensive cars. Only five hundred and thirty-four Aston Martin's of that design were ever produced. The occupants were, without any doubt, the owners of the car. The man behind the wheel, dressed in African attire, laughed away as his wife chatted. Apart from being stupendously rich, the couple seemed to be truly peaceable and joyous. That was in sharp contrast to Donaldson's belief that only those who hadn't made headway in life ran after Jesus. He wondered how those rich and seemingly educated people could be bamboozled with religion. Yes. Jesus truly came here. But like Albert Einstein, Williams Shakespeare, Aristotle, and Gandhi, he died and was buried. He didn't need anyone to sell him a dummy about any resurrection. Jesus never rose, and he wasn't the son of God. And if he was, then he never existed since God himself never existed. Period! But what was all those 'Jesus, peace and Jesus' he had encountered throughout the day? Just when he thought he had got a break from Agnes; a poor lunatic and some rich-but-stupid individuals were waiting for him in the street. As for Agnes, anytime she preached to him again she would be suspended and recommended for transfer. That would teach the religious bigot a lesson.

He honked repeatedly as he approached the gate of his duplex. He normally honked twice when he approached the gate and the gateman, who vividly recognised the sound, immediately let him in. But that evening was different. As the car honked, he rolled down the glass and yelled, 'Alfred! Alfred! Alfred! Are you mad? Will you come here and open the gate for me!' The gateman, who was in his early fifties, ran like one being chased by a mad bull. 'Welcome sir,' he said, as he nervously looked into his master's eyes after opening the gate. Donaldson didn't bother to respond. He drove straight to the garage. He was met on the stair by his houseboy who bowed very low before him. He ignored him and went up to his bedroom. The houseboy then ran to the car, opened the back door and brought out a briefcase and some newspapers which he took upstairs to his master. And after he had set his dinner he returned to him, knocking gently at the bedroom door.

'Who is it? W...hat do you want?'

'Your dinner is ready sir.' But he didn't respond. And after the boy had waited for some moments without receiving any instructions he went to the laundry room to continue his work.

Donaldson made for the bathroom after changing into his pyjamas. The houseboy arrived few minutes later to deliver his laundered clothing and found the bedroom door ajar, while the bedside phone rang. Should he pick up the call? He was confused about what to do. On a good day, Donaldson was the most pleasant master in the world! He was very cheerful and not easily provoked. But the houseboy was aware that any trivial mistake that night could ignite a volcanic eruption. So what should he do – pick the call or leave the room? He made up his mind and picked it up.

'Hello,' he answered.

'Hello. Is that Dr Weah?' asked the caller – a lady.

'No, Madam. This is Rufus, his houseboy. He's having a shower.'

'Alright, please tell him to call me back. Take my number please. My name is Samantha.'

As he didn't know how urgent or important the call was, Rufus decided to deliver the message to his boss while in the bathroom. He then went to the bathroom and knocked gently.

'What is it? Don't you know I'm in the shower?' barked Donaldson.

'I am sorry sir, but a lady just called. Her name is Samantha.'

'What?' asked Donaldson ecstatically.

'Samantha sir,' replied Rufus. 'She said ...'

Donaldson didn't allow Rufus to finish his statement before rushing out of the bathroom. He shoved the boy out of his way as he ran half-nakedly with foams all over his body. Samantha had called his office that evening but the call was answered by the telephone operator who gave her the home number. Donaldson dialled her number and a conversation ensued. She apologised for her delayed call and then expressed her profound gratitude over the 'priceless gifts.' Donaldson, who was highly elated, had responded by saying that he was more grateful to her for accepting the 'token gifts.'

'But ... excuse me sir, how did you know it was my birthday?' Samantha asked, preferring to be formal.

'You see, Samantha, I feel uncomfortable with your being formal with me. We are friends. Aren't we?'

'Alright, I'm sorry. But you haven't answered my question,' she added smilingly.

'That's not for tonight, Samantha. I will tell you but that will not be over the phone. Do you drive?'

'No. I use an official car and chauffeur,' replied Samantha.

'Okay, if you don't mind, I can come and pick you up on Friday, so we may have a one-on-one.'

'Friday?' asked Samantha, pretending she wasn't sure she would be free that evening. But she was free and would love to be taken out for the first time. She had only delayed the call so as not to give Amanda the impression that she was easily persuaded. She had been longing to speak to him all along.

'Alright, pick me up by 6:20 I finish at 6 but will wait twenty minutes for you.'

'That's brilliant! I finish at 6 too so I'll definitely be there by 6:20. I won't keep you waiting,' Donaldson said.

Donaldson invited his two domestic workers to his living room to celebrate with him after his joyous telephone conversation with Samantha. He brought out a bottle of expensive wine and served them. 'Don't ask me what we're celebrating tonight but keep on drinking until you are no longer able to remember your names,' he said. The stupefied workers looked at each other. 'Some moments ago, our boss was barking at everyone. But now we are wining and dining with him. It's truly a strange world!' they seemed to say to each other. Donaldson didn't stay long with them before retiring to his bedroom to savour what he considered the most exciting conversation he'd ever had. After the agony of a long wait for her call, coupled with religious pestering by some sane and insane bigots, there he was – very happy at last! Should Samantha become his wife he would be the happiest man on earth. She possessed all that he wanted in a woman. She was well-educated, very beautiful and intelligent. The time had come when his friends would know that he was none of those nicknames they called him. He wasn't an *Edingo*! They would have to tell him which of their ladies could compare to his Samantha. He couldn't wait to introduce her to them. Samantha was glamorous indeed. At a height of almost six feet, she had an adoring baby-face in which were carefully planted blue eyes, each like a full moon. She had a pair of seductive lips that stood out even without applying lipstick. Her curvy torso was beautifully surmounted by a pair of long, straight legs. With her natural catwalk strides she could be mistaken for a supermodel. When she spoke, there was an insatiable urge for more by her listener; she spoke not too fast and not too slowly. When she smiled she revealed a perfect set of immaculate white teeth while the dimples on her cheeks became more glaring and tempting. Apart from the lunatic that preached to him at the petrol station, Donaldson believed that Dave was the craziest madman on earth. Otherwise, how could a man in his right mind allow an angel like Samantha to slip out of his hands? He was, however, happy that Dave's madness had paved the way for him to have an angel. He would never behave like Dave. He would keep every blessing he had. The only mistake he made was choosing a date so far in the future for their outing. He should have chosen the next day. Friday would certainly take ages to come. Oh, what a silly mistake! Anyway, he was free to call her at last. He would call her number every night before Friday. With feet still on the floor and only his trunk on bed, Donaldson fell asleep.

Before he left for work the following morning he called Amanda to tell her about Samantha's call. He then searched for one of his romantic audio cassettes which he rarely played. It was a single by David Bowie. And as soon as he started the car he slotted in the cassette, fast-forwarded to the star track *Be My Wife*, and whistled the lyrics as he drove. And when it got to the refrain, he shouted at the top of his voice, '*be my wife!*'

He wondered why some people believed that it was only Jesus who could give joy. But he didn't believe in Jesus and yet he had joy. Well, if only Jesus could give him joy then Samantha was Jesus. But he would not share her. Christians could go on sharing their dead-and-buried Jesus all over the world. But, as for him, his glamorous love existed, and she wasn't for sharing.

Everyone noticed his joyous mood as he arrived at the office that morning. It was the first time he greeted all his staff individually, mentioning their names and asking after their family members. Everyone was astounded. After he had settled down in his office Agnes came in smiling.

'Agnes, what can I do for you this morning?' he asked.

'I'm sorry sir but I've just come to ask a question.'

'Oh yes. You may ask any question if it doesn't have anything to do with religion,' he replied.

'Not at all,' said Agnes. 'You see, I have come to ask if I could share in your joy this morning.'

'What joy, Agnes?' he asked.

'Come on, Mr Weah. As you arrived this morning we all knew that you were extraordinarily happy. I am your PA and I consider it my responsibility to share in your happiness.' Donaldson laughed hysterically before asking:

'Must a personal assistant have access to my private life?'

'Not really sir. But a dutiful PA like me must find out if some Samanthas have eventually said 'yes' and stopped agitating the mind of her boss,' Agnes replied as she made for the door, leaving Donaldson gobsmacked.

He watched her until she left the office and closed the door behind. He was at a loss for words. Looking at the closed door thoughtfully, he wondered if Agnes was truly a human being. He had heard some stories about spirits who metamorphosed into human beings when he was a child. And as a child, he had been terrified by those stories. He, however, grew up to realize that they were fairy tales. But with a human being like Agnes, he was now in a state of confusion. He must find out how she got to know about Samantha. He, therefore, invited her back later in the day. And after she had taken a seat, he said, 'Agnes, did you know you surprised me this morning? How did you know about my interest in Samantha?'

'Is that why you were surprised?' asked Agnes. Continuing, she said, 'I knew you were in love with someone called Samantha the day you mistakenly called me by that name. You made the same mistake once or twice after that. I'm a woman – an experienced woman for that matter – and I know when men are in love. I overheard you blaming yourself the day she turned down your call. And I also heard when you spoke to Amanda about her not calling you on Friday. You left here on Friday very moody, and this morning you came back radiant and exchanging pleasantries with everyone. I don't need a degree in psychology to know that Samantha is finally in your net.'

'My net?' he asked, laughing. 'How do you mean? Am I a fisherman?' he asked, still laughing. 'Agnes, please go back to your office before you break my ribs with laughter,' he added, satisfied she didn't possess mystical powers after all.

At the British Embassy, people couldn't stop wondering about Samantha's changed attitude as she now smiled and exchanged pleasantries. Since she was closer to Amanda than anyone else, it was believed by some that Amanda's Christian zeal had eventually worked on her. And ever since her telephone conversation with Donaldson she had started to apply her make-up. The first time she applied it she became the centre of attention at the embassy. Some, as a matter of fact, couldn't recognize her! One of those people was the head of the consular department.

'Good morning sir,' said Samantha as she approached him.

'Good morning madam. What can I do for you this morning?'

Samantha was surprised at his response. Looking into his eyes, he immediately realised that he didn't recognise her,

'I'm Samantha. Samantha Collins,' she said.

'Oh, Miss Collins, I'm so sorry but I couldn't recognise you. You are more beautiful this morning,' said the man.

'That's alright sir,' replied Samantha, smiling.

Samantha and Amanda had suddenly become very close friends and confidants. They visited restaurants together and patronised same beauty salon. She had taken Amanda home on the Thursday before her date with Donaldson. And Amanda had helped her rearrange her living room and bedroom. It could be observed that things were carelessly arranged due to her former state of mind. 'Samantha, you shouldn't have put your dressing mirror here. Let's put it there and see the difference. You see, it reflects more rays of light here. That reading table shouldn't be there. Isn't it better here?' She also helped her clean up. Before she left she asked Samantha to lead in a Christian praise song before praying together. But Samantha shyly replied that she didn't know any Christian songs. As they prayed together, it was the first time Samantha closed her eyes in prayer.

Amanda prayed, 'Father, I thank you for the life of your daughter. I thank you for your promise of giving her double portion instead of her shame. I also thank you for her glorious future. I sanctify this flat in the name of God the Father, God the Son and the Holy Spirit. I sprinkle the blood of Jesus all over the place. Father, open Samantha's eyes to your salvation and move in and live with her for-ever-more, in Jesus' name. Amen.'

The long-awaited Friday finally came. The previous evening, Donaldson had invited his two domestic workers to help him choose the best among his numerous suits. He understood that the appropriate people to do that for him were his friends. But as he had decided to keep the matter secret from them for the moment, he had to rely on these two men. And after some moments of disagreement, they eventually arrived at a unanimous choice. It was a very expensive, shimmering black Italian suit with barely noticeable white pinstripes. The suit was one of the seven most expensive of his numerous suits he had reserved for special occasions. A plain, turquoise silk shirt and a flowery tie with wine background were selected to go with the suit. Donaldson couldn't wait for the day to break. He kept checking the time. He would stand on his feet and give a long yawn and then walk to the living room for no specific reason. He would just stand there staring at the wall-clock. At one point, he decided to rehearse his meeting with Samantha. He dressed up and stared at his image in a full-size dressing mirror. He liked what he saw, except the tie which was not well-knotted. He liked to use a double cross knot, but he wasn't very good at it. He then applied the Windsor knot. That was better, but he would try to compare it to the plain knot. He unknotted it again and applied the plain knot. No, the Windsor knot was better! When he was fully satisfied with his dressing he put on his new black leather shoes and paced the living room, staring at his image as he did. Oh, the new after-shave he bought yesterday! It was in the car. Should he go downstairs and fetch it? That would wake the guys up and they would see him rehearsing. That would be embarrassing as it was just two o'clock.

He was very happy when the living room clock chimed five times. He hurried to the bathroom. And by quarter to six he was already starting the car. The music this time was Bob Marley's *Turn Your Light Down Low* from the 1977 album – *Exodus*. He had, however, reserved another cassette which he intended to play when Samantha joined him in the evening. That was Shalamar's *The Second Time Around*. The song was spot on, he had remarked. Yes, Shalamar were right! 'You can't keep running away from love just because the first one let you down. No, no, no. I owe you one, Shalamar!' he said to himself as he dusted the cassette.

At the British Embassy, only two people could explain Samantha's angelic appearance that morning. They were, of course, herself and

Amanda. If she looked beautiful before that morning, she was simply magnificent now. She wore a white, sleeveless maxi gown with a purple lace edge and a tight bodice to accentuate the waist. And she matched the purple lace with purple low-heel shoes and a purple handbag. Her hair was long-worn with central parting. When she and Amanda met for the first time that morning they didn't exchange greetings. Instead, they only looked into each other's eyes and smiled. With that, they had spoken a language which none of their colleagues around could understand! And around quarter of an hour before their closing time, Amanda went to her in her office and said, 'Samantha, you know what? For the past few days now, people in this place have been talking about your charm. Your metamorphosis has really amazed everyone, including myself. This is not natural – it is supernatural. I really bless God for His change in you. I also thank Him for restoring your happiness. But remember this: Donaldson is neither your happiness nor the source of it. There is something great that God is currently brewing in your life. And to allow Him to complete the brew, you must give your life to Him. He wants you to become His so you may affect Donaldson's life as well. In other words, He wants to use you to bring Donaldson to Him so the two of you might have perfectly matched destinies.'

'Samantha, what exactly is delaying giving your life to Jesus Christ? You should be aware of the trick of the devil. He doesn't want you to enjoy the peace and joy of the Lord. You must resist him and decide for Jesus now.' Biting her lower lip, Samantha stared at the ceiling for some moments before finally fixing her gaze on her newly manicured nails. Scratching her forehead slightly with one of them, she said, 'Thank you very much, Amanda. I've heard all that you said but I still need some more time to think about it. You know….'

'Hey, Samantha,' Amanda cut in. 'I want to ask you two questions. If you can answer them correctly then you are right to delay longer. First, do you know when you are going to die? And, second, do you know exactly what time it will be?'

'Nobody knows all that, Amanda,' Samantha replied.

'Yes, so anyone who delays salvation is playing a dangerous game. Hell is a real place where fire torments sinners for eternity. Why are you postponing a free offer of salvation, Samantha? Why are you playing hide-and-seek with the One who can guarantee your peace and joy here on earth and then, everlasting life when you die? It is important you give your life to Jesus before having this outing.'

'Why is that important?' asked Samantha.

'So as to put your relationship with Donaldson on a solid foundation,' she replied. 'If you are both children of God He will work through that relationship to bless you both. And if Donaldson is not the man for you He will let you know before you go into the relationship and then connect you with His perfect will.'

It was twenty-five minutes past six. The two ladies were the only officials still left in the premises. A security guard came in to inform them that a man in a yellow Mercedes was waiting for Samantha. Samantha looked at her wrist-watch.

'Oh, Donaldson must have arrived five minutes ago! I told him that I would be waiting for him by twenty past six,' she said, picking up her handbag and ready to dash out. With her lips pouted, Amanda quipped, 'Samantha, be very careful. Allow God to lead you.'

'Alright *mum*,' Samantha replied jokingly.

CHAPTER 5: SORROW MAY LAST FOR A NIGHT

It was lunchtime at the British Embassy on Monday after Samantha's date with Donaldson. She recounted the events of Friday night to Amanda. Donaldson had treated her to a royal dinner at the expensive Hotel Africa. She liked the hotel, its environment and above all, its culinary prowess. She had given him a call the following morning to express her gratitude. She talked of the beauty of the hotel and the calibre of the patrons. Donaldson had felt so proud to be appreciated by his 'angel.' He replied, 'You ain't seen nothing yet, angel!' Samantha had noticed something very important about Donaldson. He didn't seem to talk too much – just like herself. Another thing she noticed was, throughout their more than three hours together he didn't touch her. Unlike most men that evening, he didn't even hold her hand as they left the hotel and walked to the parking lot. And, unlike most men of his age and calibre, he wasn't 'only looking for one thing.' There were lots of men out there who saw the first date as an opportunity for inordinate expression of passion. To these men, chivalry was long dead and cremated with its ashes thrown into the sea of forgetfulness. But to Donaldson, chivalry was very much alive and enthroned in the beautiful palace of his heart.

Another incident which confirmed her opinion of him was when he dropped her off at her home that night. As she got out of the car and walked towards her flat, Donaldson asked, 'Hey angel, are you going to say good night?' Looking back, she was surprised to see him still leaning against the car. She thought he was coming home with her. Most people would normally like to come with you after dropping you off at home for the first time, depending on the level of intimacy. Some would even wait some moments to have a coffee or drink. That was what Samantha thought.

'Oh, I thought you were coming with me. Won't you come in and have some coffee?'

'No. Not tonight, angel. I don't like to bother an angel after such a great evening. At a suitable time, I will pick you up and then come back with you, for coffee and several bottles of champagne,' he replied. Hiding her amazement, Samantha walked back to him, looked into his eyes and smiled.

'You're so funny,' Samantha replied. But that wasn't why she smiled. The smile was rather an expression of her approval of his attitude. 'You're my type of man!' she seemed to say. And as they bade each other good night Donaldson didn't hug her. He only took her hand in his, squeezed her fingers gently and whispered into her ear, 'Samantha, I want to thank you for making today one of the best.' Samantha went straight to the full-size mirror in her bedroom, looked at her reflection and smiled. As she removed her necklace and earrings she said to herself, 'This guy is suave and intelligent. He's a complete gentleman.'

When she finished recounting the events, Amanda asked if Donaldson told her how he got to know about her birthday. He had told her that he got the information from someone who wanted to be anonymous for the meantime. And she didn't want it to look as if she was pressing the issue.

'But who did you think that could be?' Amanda asked.

'Not the slightest idea, Amanda. But I don't want to be in a hurry. I will surely find out someday.' Amanda considered unmasking at that moment, but she quickly controlled herself. That should be done with Donaldson's consent, she thought. She then changed the topic and went back to the issue of giving her life to Jesus Christ.

'Samantha, as you currently hinder God's move upon your life, do you realise you also hinder His move upon Donaldson's life too?'

'How?' asked Samantha.

'Because you are the instrument that God wants to use to save him. And your refusal or postponement also affects him.'

'Wait a minute, Amanda. What is so special about giving my life to Jesus Christ? I have already abstained from all that He doesn't like. I do not commit sins. The only thing is that I don't go to church. And as for Donaldson, he's tremendously blessed already. As a young man, he has a fledging career with amazing prospect. He's very rich with abundant connections. He's a perfect gentleman who hasn't spoiled himself with women, unlike men of his calibre. I believe Donaldson and I have already met God's criteria. To me, it doesn't really matter if we don't go to church; people who go to church are those who struggle to meet those criteria. They are those who need Jesus' help to meet them.'

'That's wrong, my dear,' replied Amanda. Continuing, she said, 'The Bible says: But we are all as an unclean thing and all our righteousness are as filthy rags; and we all do fade as a leaf; and our iniquities, like the wind, have taken us away. You see, we were all born into this world with a load of inherited sins. But the moment we gave our lives to Jesus Christ those sins – both inherited and committed – are gone. As for Donaldson, the Bible says: What shall it profit a man, if he shall gain the whole world, and lose his own soul? Or what shall a man give in exchange for his soul?

Listen to me, Samantha: There is no material of this world that will go with us when we die. Right here, before we die, we have the privilege of choosing where we are going to spend our eternity. The Bible says: For God so loved the world, that He gave His only begotten Son, that whosoever believeth in Him should not perish, but have everlasting life. In the same chapter it says: He that believeth on Him is not condemned: but he that believeth not is condemned already, because he hath not believed in the name of the only begotten Son of God. Listen again: In the time of my favour I heard you, and in the day of salvation I helped you. I tell you, now is the time of God's favour, now is the day of salvation. Samantha, that refers to you. Now is your day of salvation. Are you now ready to give your life to Jesus Christ?'

'Amanda, just keep on praying for me,' she solemnly replied.

Ever since their first telephone conversation Donaldson and Samantha never missed a night speaking on phone. It was always at bedtime. And on a Saturday, three weeks after their date, Donaldson brought her to his home. He had instructed his houseboy to put extra efforts into arranging the apartment. He also invited his five closest pals without telling them about Samantha. He simply told them that he would like to give them a weekend treat at his home and they should come with their ladies. However, he had already told Samantha about his friends and the nicknames they gave him.

The pair arrived at his home around 5 p.m. waiting for their guests. She was conducted around the property after she had been introduced to Donaldson's domestic workers. It was a huge duplex with two living rooms and five bedrooms – two upstairs and three downstairs. The property was one of the numerous owned and maintained by the Wuteve Bank PLC which was one of the most successful conglomerates in Africa. Apart from his official Mercedes, Donaldson also had a Honda Civic which he seldom drove. That was the car he had chosen to bring his 'angel' home that evening. Samantha loved the car and the way he drove. She had noticed the way he drove since their first date. He never seemed to be in a hurry nor felt offended when his traffic right was infringed by other motorists. And when someone apologised, all he said was 'that's alright.' He was very cool and gentlemanly. That was unusual in Monrovia, where every motorist was in a hurry and reckless driving and swearing were the order of the day. These particular features of Monrovia road traffic had discouraged Samantha from driving. Ever since her arrival in Liberia she was driven in official car. And when she needed to go out at weekends (she rarely did, anyway) she informed the chauffeur in advance. However, Donaldson had promised to help build her driving confidence. She didn't always need to be driven, he had told her.

Donaldson had ordered some European delicacies together with a lady server from a catering company along the government secretariat road. The company, which specialised in both European and American delicacies, had been in operation ever since Liberia was an American colony. The guests could also choose indigenous delicacies, as his houseboy had prepared pounded yam with delicious beef and fish soups. All sorts of drinks, both alcoholic and non-alcoholic, were made available. In addition to these, two bottles of Irish cream were also bought in honour of Samantha. He had noticed that she liked it during their first date. It had to be a royal banquet in honour of his angel.

While they waited for Donaldson's friends and the contracted server, Donaldson served Samantha some Irish cream as she flipped through a voluminous photo album. The album began with Donaldson's university photographs, followed by those taken at various social and professional events. The latest photographs in the album were those taken at the Trade Department's end-of-year party. There was a photograph in which Samantha appeared at the background holding an empty tray. She didn't like it. 'Why did you include this one?' she jokingly asked. She saw another one where she danced with him. She smiled.

'But when did they snap these pictures? I didn't see any photographer that night,' she asked.

'Of course, photographers and video cameramen were there. How could a server know everything that was going on at a party?' he teased.

'Shut up!' she replied, smacking him lightly on the shoulder. And they both laughed. There were two particular photographs that also caught Samantha's attention: those of Donaldson as he received a certificate of award from the governor of Central Bank and a group photograph with President William Tolbert, Jr. Donaldson explained that the group was the executive committee of the Association of Liberian Bankers of which the president was the life patron. While they chatted, Bob Marley's song *One Love* was playing at the background, one of Donaldson's all-time favourites.

It was the server who first arrived around 5:35 p.m. And about ten minutes later, sounds of cars were heard from downstairs. As planned, Samantha vacated the living room and hid in one of the bedrooms. The five men and their ladies met their host upstairs and pleasantries were noisily exchanged using boyish slangs and nicknames. Four of the men were Donaldson's university mates while the other was a colleague at work. After the men's tumultuous pleasantries, Donaldson turned to the ladies and apologised for acknowledging the men first. He then offered them his hand and gave them a hug in turn. Four of the ladies were familiar to him. Their men had severally brought them to the clubhouse and some other social gatherings. But it was his first time meeting the fifth. Her boyfriend was Richard, a senior mechanical engineer and executive at a Monrovia-based American automobile assembly plant. Richard was never known to keep a lady for more than three months. For that reason, he was nicknamed *Mr Carjack* as he changed women as quickly as a jack changes tyres. Although he didn't like the nickname, his friends never stopped calling him by it. None of their ladies, however, knew the reason behind the nickname. The men had lied that Richard was nicknamed after one of his tools as a mechanical engineer. And after Richard had introduced his new lady, Donaldson teased him by calling him the abhorred nickname twice. Everyone was taken aback by Donaldson's unusual boldness, considering that he never wanted to get involved in nicknaming for fear of retaliation. Looking into his eyes, Richard then asked:

'Did you just call me Mr Jack, Donny?'

'Yes. Is that not your name, Mr Jack?'

Hysterical laughter and noisy clapping greeted Donaldson's 'bravery.' And Richard replied in retaliation:

'Ladies and gentlemen, on behalf of the MC of today's occasion, I have the pleasure of welcoming you all to *Mr Edingo's* home!' That was greeted by pandemonium. One man laughed until he dropped on the floor and three of the ladies, who knew what *Edingo* meant, could not stop laughing. There were lot of screaming. When the noise had subsided, Donaldson asked, 'Richard, why do you guys call me *Edingo*?'

'Because you've never had a girlfriend and each time we try to get you one, like the *Edingo* that you really are, you cook up an excuse!' replied Richard.

'Alright, would you stop calling me *Edingo* if I took a girlfriend?'

While two of the men replied in affirmative, Richard added, 'How can an *Edingo* ever take a girlfriend? Look at yourself; you have invited us for a treat without a lady of yours to meet ours.'

A fresh round of hysterical laughter was generated. And when everyone thought Donaldson had been provoked, he turned towards the bedrooms and whistled very loudly. His guests could only watch with mouth agape as glamorous Samantha took natural catwalk steps from an adjacent bedroom into their midst. They were so dumfounded that seconds elapsed before they could respond to her salutation. With his arm around her shoulders, Donaldson turned to Richard and asked, 'Mr Jack, am I still *Edingo*?' Richard could only watch in bewilderment. After that, Donaldson turned to the rest of the group and added, 'Ladies and gentlemen, meet my angel. Her name is Samantha. She is deputy business coordinator at the Department of Trade at the British Embassy. As a matter of fact, I have arranged this get-together to welcome her to my home for the first time. She is the one I've been waiting for all these long years!' A protracted round of applause, screaming and whistling rented the air. He, thereafter, introduced his friends and their girlfriends to Samantha.

It was an evening never-to-be-forgotten as everyone was treated to expensive drinks and luscious delicacies. It was Gabriel, a versatile lawyer among them, who gave the toast. Gabriel, a university mate of Donaldson, was the president of the Liberia University Students' Union who led a revolt against increased tuition fees during their university days. He was known to be brave and highly outspoken. Because of his amazing command of the English language, coupled with his ostentatious use of strange synonyms, he was nicknamed Mr Lexicon by his friends. Sometimes when he spoke English his friends would jokingly beg him to come down to their level of English. 'Hey, Mr Lexicon, we are lost. Could you please come down to our level?' they would tease. It was rumoured that the jury had to appeal for simpler English on his first legal representation at the law court. And that evening, as he rose to give the toast, all his friends were already bracing themselves for grammatical thunderbolts!

'Ladies and gentlemen, here's a toast to the resplendent beginning of this impervious connubial peregrination, and to a successful excortication, by our dear host, of a stigmatic sobriquet which only beseemed a true *Edingo* that he never was!'

Everybody laughed and chanted his nickname. As Samantha laughed away, Donaldson whispered into her ear, 'He's the only crazy one among us!' Despite being the only white among them, Samantha blended very quickly. She chatted and joked with everyone, especially, the ladies. And one thing further endeared her to Donaldson's two domestic workers; she personally invited them to join in the fun. As the men were reluctant, she rose from her seat and walked over to them. Holding their hands, she brought them in and served them herself while everyone marvelled at her humility. But Donaldson turned to his two workers and joked, 'Now that you have become a threat to me over my angel I think it's time for me to sack you both. It doesn't really matter if you helped me select the best suit on my first date with her.' It generated another round of hysterical laughter.

Donaldson fulfilled his promise of coming with Samantha as he dropped her off at home that night. Her home was one of the ten three-bedroom apartments on an estate occupied by staff of various foreign missions and organisations. Her neighbours were Americans, Germans, Spaniards, Norwegians, Swiss and two fellow Brits. The estate was owned and managed by an American property firm – J. Cameron Properties Ltd. The firm was in the business of building ultra-modern estates which were let out to expatriates. The atmosphere on the estate was foreign in its entirety and its serenity could be likened to that of a highly revered African shrine. Within and without the estate was a team of security operatives comprised of officers of the Liberia Police and a private security company. As Donaldson had to drive in, the security men stopped him at the entrance and searched his car, using both manual and electronic devices. As his car was passed, a senior police officer waved to them. Donaldson responded with a grin. As soon as they entered the flat, a black lady in her early twenties came out of a room and rushed towards them. She took Samantha's handbag, looked Donaldson in the eyes and said a greeting in local dialect. Donaldson returned the greeting and asked her name in the same dialect. Still speaking the dialect, he then asked if the girl took care of his angel very well, to which the lady only smiled.

As he was being conducted around the apartment, Samantha asked, 'What were you and Theresa talking about as we came in?'

Donaldson laughed before replying.

'I bet you are not jealous of your housemaid, angel.'

'Donny, we live in a cruel world of mistrust, backstabbing and backbiting where your cousin sleeps with your fiancé, let alone housemaids.'

Although she pretended it was a joke, but it was obvious that she was still haunted by the Dave-Bridget memory. So Donaldson fired a salvo, 'You're quite right, angel. But as for me, I have waited long enough to have my perfect desire and dream realised. During my long period of waiting I remained focused on my choice of woman; neither digressing nor going after any substandard. Would it not be insane to go after

49

substandard now that I've attained my long-awaited desire? Only a stupid Dave could do that.'

'I beg your pardon?' said Samantha, in utter amazement.

'I said only an idiot could throw away a long-awaited desire like you,' repeated Donaldson.

'Did you mention Dave?'

'Oh, that's just my friends' slang for a man who sleeps with his fiancée's cousin,' replied Donaldson.

'And have your friends got a slang for a treacherous cousin as well?' she asked.

'Oh yes. We call her a Bridget,' he replied.

Samantha was thrown off balance.

They returned to the living room which was modestly decorated with framed paintings, most of them landscapes. And on the wall right opposite the door was a very large portrait of an elderly woman. Donaldson didn't have to be told that it was her late mum. As he sipped his beer Samantha remained unusually quiet, casting furtive glances at him. She wondered how he knew everything about her. First, it was her birthday. And now it was Dave and Bridget. Slang? No! It was obvious that he knew about her past. Donaldson, however, knew what was on her mind but decided to enjoy the game while it lasted.

'Angel, you seem withdrawn. Is anything the matter?' he asked.

Suddenly looking very serious, she replied, 'Donny, you must let me know who told you about my birthday. You know that suspense agitates the mind. And agitating someone you claim to love leaves much to be desired. If you truly love me, you will place my interest above that of your informant. Otherwise, you don't love me.'

'Don't talk like that, angel. You know I really love you. I will surely let you know but give me more time,' pleaded Donaldson.

'You must tell me tonight when you are going to reveal your informant.'

Pleading piteously, he said, 'Please, give me till tomorrow to confirm the date with my informant.'

'Okay. But you will also tell me what you know about Dave and Bridget. Huh?' asked Samantha surprisingly.

'What about them? They are only slangs!' declared a red-faced Donaldson.

'Liar! Look into my eyes and tell me you don't know anything about Dave and Bridget!'

'I'm sorry, angel. Please, let me give you a call tomorrow to fix a date for this discussion.' Samantha didn't respond. Instead, she stared thoughtfully at him. 'Samantha, believe me, my allegiance in this regard is to you and not to anyone else. Whatever I did or said was for the sake of love. There are things I will say here tonight that you won't understand until that person is present.'

'Okay, who's that person? I can wait to have the details but can't wait another minute to know who the person is!'

'Samantha, the person has helped both of us in some ways and it's not proper for me to make them look evil. Please, give me just a little time more,' he passionately pleaded.

'Alright, I must have all the information next week,' she snapped.

'Sure,' said Donaldson with a sigh of relief. They hugged for the first time as they bade each other goodnight.

Samantha went to bed very late. She sat on the sofa all night wondering what sort of wizardry had dug into her past which she thought was long buried away in faraway England. When she thought she had started a life as a brand-new creature, the horrible and tear-soaked past had come staring her in the face. How on earth did Donaldson know? Did he consult voodoo practitioners because of her? No. A person of his social status couldn't do that. It was true that there were voodoo practices among Africans, but it was only the illiterates who indulged in those acts. A knowledgeable person like him would never do that. How and where did he obtain the information from? It was a great puzzle. No, it was a mystery. Although he didn't directly admit knowing about Dave and Bridget, his evasive answer had, however, given him away.

'Madam, it is half past three. Won't you go to bed?' That was Theresa the housemaid. She had painstakingly served Samantha for three uneventful years. Although her boss never complained about her service, she neither smiled nor chatted with her. She always scribbled her commands on a sheet of paper and placed it on the dining table. Few things, however, kept Theresa that long. One, the salary was very attractive. With the salary, she was able to take care of her widowed mother and the education of her two siblings. Another thing was

Samantha's generosity. Ever since she started working for her she never bought dresses or shoes with her salaries. Samantha always gave her all ladies' items, such as dresses, shoes, and handbags that were considered obsolete by her. Happily for Theresa, those items were all she needed to be the centre of attention for all eyes as she went out on her weekly day off. For some time now, she had noticed a tremendous change in her mistress. She now smiled and chatted with her. She had stopped scribbling her requests and, they now sat together in the living room to watch telly. But since that man came into the house about three hours ago her mistress' sadness had returned. Just when she had started believing that at the end of a dark tunnel there was a light, there came a devil who wanted to put the light out! Only God knew what he did or said to her mistress. Had she known that he was a devil on rampage she would not have welcomed him warmly!

CHAPTER 6: GOD IS REAL

The revelatory meeting was scheduled for the following Saturday at Samantha's home. Donaldson arrived fifteen minutes ahead of schedule, to Samantha's surprise. His informant would be joining them soon, he had told her. A few moments later, there was a message from the security post: a lady would like to see Miss Samantha Collins. Samantha had thought it was the informant they had been waiting for. But she was disappointed when the security officer said that it was one Miss Amanda Wilberforce. Oh gosh, it wasn't the informant! Amanda came in and exchanged pleasantries with Donaldson before engaging her friend in some conversations relating to certain events which took place at work the previous day.

'Amanda, but you didn't inform me you would be visiting this morning,' said Samantha.

'But Dr Weah did,' she replied.

'How do you mean? Don't tell me you are the informant we've been waiting for. This must be a joke!' said highly disappointed Samantha.

After she had composed herself, Amanda started, 'Samantha, your demeanour for almost three years was a source of worry to me. I knew in my heart that it wasn't your natural self, so I decided to find out what brought about a change in you. I found out in your employment dossier that you previously worked at the London headquarters of the John Lewis Partnership. And, through my brother who manages their Manchester retail outlet, I found out about the heartache you were subjected to by Dave and your cousin Bridget. I also learned about your mother's death around the same time. As I realised that no man could ever repair your badly bruised heart, I resorted to praying for you. I prayed to God that you might be connected to the right man that would heal your wound. At our last December party, however, I discovered that you were the only lady that Dr Weah wanted to dance with. I also noticed that you refused to dance with anyone until he came forward. I, therefore, took those incidents as an important signal regarding my prayer. But I must first investigate him. I then contacted one of my female converts, who had dated one of Dr Weah's closest friends, for certain information about him. It was that lady who told me all that I needed to know about him. She simply described him as a perfect gentleman who, unlike men of his age and calibre, doesn't lust after women. Convinced that Dr Weah was a caring and affectionate man, I then swung into action. I invited him for a chat where I told him about Dave and Bridget as well as your birthday. Samantha, your happiness was all I was after and I was ready to do anything to have it returned to you. But I'm sorry I intruded on your privacy. Please, forgive me.'

Samantha looked at Amanda thoughtfully for some moments. Why would Amanda go to so much trouble for her? She decided Amanda was the angel that God had used to bring her and Donaldson together. What mattered to her wasn't her privacy but her joy and peace which she now had. What privacy was she even thinking of, when her story was all over London and Manchester? She should rather be glad for having such a reliable friend in Amanda and a loving boyfriend in Donaldson. Donaldson and Amanda sat quietly with their head bowed as they awaited Samantha's outburst. But she stood up, walked over to Amanda and squatted in front of her. She then stretched forward her hand and lifted Amanda's chin. As the latter looked into her eyes, she said, 'Amanda, I will always be indebted to you. You are a friend in need and a friend in deed.' The two ladies rose and hugged each other. After that, Samantha walked over to Donaldson and simply said, 'Donny, I love you!' Donaldson looked into her eyes and replied, 'Samantha, I love you too. And I will always do until I breathe my last.'

Amanda had intended to seize the opportunity to preach to Donaldson, but he pretended he was in a hurry to keep an appointment somewhere. And as he left the flat he wondered why everyone was talking about Jesus – even a highly enlightened Amanda who should know better! He hoped she didn't infest his Samantha with that madness. After he had left, Samantha made a coffee for her friend. And as she drank, Samantha suddenly gave a long sigh.

Smiling, Amanda asked, 'What are you thinking about?'

'Jesus,' she replied.

'What about Jesus?' Amanda asked.

'Amanda, I think I need what you have. I always consider you and your way of life. There is evidence of abundant love, peace and joy in your life. They are so enormous that they do spill out massively from within you. I want to be like you, Amanda. I'm ready to give my life to Jesus Christ.'

'What?' Amanda almost exclaimed out loud in utter disbelief. 'Oh thank you, Jesus!' she said instead.

And so Samantha was led to Christ. After praying with her, Amanda offered her some advice for new Christians. She must pray and read the

Bible daily, and she must fellowship with other children of God so as to increase her faith. Most importantly, she must abstain from sin and any form of sexual immorality. Certain expressions of passion while still in courtship were not allowed by God. And sexual relations before being joined together as husband and wife annoyed God greatly, she had told her.

'And can you pick me up for church tomorrow?" asked Samantha.

'Sure, I'll be glad to,' she replied.

Donaldson and Samantha had a long telephone conversation regarding her new-found faith that night. He had questioned her allowing herself to be bamboozled by a colleague who wasn't as intelligent as she was. He argued that Jesus was just an attention seeker who used religion to achieve his objective. According to him, Jesus' corpse was stolen by his disciples so as to deceive everyone about his resurrection. When Samantha spoke about life after death, he replied that there wasn't any life after death and that there was neither a heaven nor a hell. Asked how the earth came into being, he said it was formed about 4.6 billion years ago by collisions in the giant disc-shaped cloud of material that also formed the sun. According to him, gravity slowly gathered the gas and dust together into clumps that became asteroids and small early planets. Asked how man was formed, he said it was by evolution from apes. But when he was asked how the ape was formed, he could only give an evasive answer.

'Look Samantha, how can you explain the existence of a God who is said to love the whole world when, as a kid, I lost my both parents and had to go through untold hardships of starvation and cruel abuse? Let me tell you a story tonight – a story of neglect and abuse. At the age of ten, after losing my both parents and siblings, I was to work at a vegetable farm of a man who took me into his home. But I didn't know that the man and his two grown-up sons actually dealt in marijuana and not vegetables. The farm where I worked was, actually, a marijuana farm. Our agreement was a dollar per week with three square meals provided. But he stopped my wages after two weeks, requesting that I join his sons in the sale of the 'vegetables.' He told me that I would henceforth be paid on a commission basis. But he didn't pay me a farthing! And, to ensure that I didn't abscond, he set me up with his police officer accomplices. About three weeks before Christmas, as I was going to supply 'vegetable' to a regular customer, I was apprehended and detained by the police. I was in the police custody for three days before my master eventually showed up, pretending he had been looking for me. As a condition for my release, I had to sign an agreement to refund a fine of one thousand dollars said to have been paid on my behalf by my master. Not only that, I must also agree to do anything he asked me to do. Otherwise, I faced a ten-year jail sentence. When I asked him where he expected me to get that kind of money to repay him, he said I had to keep on working for him for as many years as would be enough to offset the debt. You can see that I had literally become a slave!

'But it was a few days later, on Christmas Eve, that I took my destiny in my own hands and absconded. Everyone thought I was still asleep in the little room I shared with his four hunting dogs, but I had already covered several miles, running in the cold. I arrived at a city about fifty miles away in just four days! Virtually in rags, I roamed the city markets helping buyers to carry their wares for a few cents. And at nights I went to a public toilet, locked myself in and slept. I did that for two months before I was taken in by a widow. Like any child in a similar situation, I had an option of joining a criminal gang for sustenance, but I made up my mind to make it through formal education. But I faced hostility from the woman's envious children because of my brilliance. After two years of staying in the house, my benefactor suddenly took ill and was hospitalised for several weeks. One Saturday morning, as I returned from the hospital where I waited on her overnight, her eldest son said to me, 'Donaldson, I have contacted some spiritualists over my mother's protracted illness and was told that it is your bad luck that is affecting our home. And for my mother to get well, you must leave this home immediately.' I looked at the sky and tears rolled down from my eyes. I asked myself: where do I go from here? Do I go to the hospital and inform mama; for that is what I called the woman. That would be stupid as her condition was so critical she didn't seem to recognise anyone. I then turned to the boy and asked him to give me just two days to think of where to go. But he blatantly refused. And before I could say 'please,' all my belongings, including my books were flung out by the children as they chanted, 'Leave our home, wizard. Leave our home, wizard!'

'I picked up all my stuff, packed them in a bag and went straight to the hospital to see mama for the last time. I held her hand and told her that I appreciated all that she had done for me. I also whispered into her ear that I really loved her, even though she neither recognised nor heard me. I left the hospital and roamed the streets until the darkness of the night when I went to my school. My plan was to appeal to the school night watchman to allow me to sleep in the classroom until I had somewhere else to stay. On seeing me approach the school in the dark, the man swiftly took up his gun and yelled, 'Who are you?'

'I'm Donaldson, one of the students of this school.'

'The man knew me very well and recognised my voice. I told him my predicament and he was sympathetic. He took me home in the morning and introduced me to his family members – his wife and two younger boys. I lived with this family for about seven years until I gained admission into the university in Monrovia. Meanwhile, as I got a very lucrative part-time job and lived on the campus, I seldom travelled home. I only sent letters and enclosed some money in postal orders. During one of our long holidays, however, I decided to spend few days with the family. I had bought lots of gifts for the couple and their two sons. But I was gobsmacked when I arrived and saw the house totally razed down. The coupled and their two children had died in an inferno a few days earlier, during one of the land-cum-political disputes which characterised the early part of the 1970s. Their home had been torched at night while everyone was asleep. The people, who integrated and gave me a sense of belonging, were completely wiped out! I nearly went mad as I wept every day for many months! Now, Samantha, consider my story and justify the existence of your so-called God. Consider my situation and those of the people who had chosen to help me. The widow whose children drove me out eventually gave up the ghost, rendering her children orphans as well. The man who should be reaping the fruits of his kindness to me by now had his entire family wiped out with him. How then should I believe in existence of any God of creation if such evil could befall me and numerous other poor children? How should I believe that God exists if a kind family was wiped away just like that? If God truly exists, he must be very cruel and, therefore, doesn't deserve to be given my life. Samantha, go ahead and give him your life and what have you. But as for me, I refuse to be fooled.'

Samantha could only give a deep sigh. As a new convert, she became totally confused. And after they had bidden each other goodnight she just lay in bed thinking about the pathetic story. So, Donny went through such a horrible ordeal as a child. When she thought life was cruel to her, there was someone who fought the battle of life. 'But does God really exist? If he does, why are there so many tragedies? And why are there so many orphans? And how many of such orphans will be able to make it in life like Donaldson? Many will surely lose their lives; perpetually impoverished or become jailbirds. And the family who deserved God's reward for being kind to an orphan was wiped away! I think Donaldson is right. He's absolutely right! There are more arguments against God's existence than for it.'

She had to present Donaldson's case before Amanda and hear what she had got to say. If her answer wasn't convincing enough she would have a rethink on the so-called 'salvation of her soul.' A God who is unable to save here on earth shouldn't be trusted with life after death; if after all, there is life after death. 'That will be an issue for discussion at lunchtime tomorrow,' she concluded as she turned off the bedside lamp.

Amanda decided to speak to Donaldson at Samantha's home the following Saturday. She asked her to invite him without disclosing the purpose of the invitation. But as soon as Amanda came in Donaldson knew what her mission was: Samantha had invited him to be preached to by her friend! 'There's no problem. We shall see who converts who this morning,' he said to himself. After exchanging pleasantries, Amanda went straight to the business of the day by first saying a brief prayer.

'Dr Weah, I've come here because of you. I'm so sorry I didn't inform you of this meeting beforehand. Samantha told me a rather sad story of your childhood. And with that story, I see why you've argued against God's existence. But those who believe in His existence have evidence for that too. Some catastrophes are the result of the free will that the Creator gave us, the result of negligence, weakness and the deliberate wrong doing of human beings.

God gave us free will. If he had not, it would be impossible for Him to know those who loved, appreciated and reverenced Him. God does not intervene when we misuse our body, we shouldn't expect Him to prevent the negative consequences of that action. When men set your benefactor's home ablaze, they exercised their God-given free will in a sad way. But if God prevents one horrific action, then He must always stand in the way of every evil action. The principle of total free will upon which creation was based would be destroyed. God is not happy about our sin. Although we have free will, God has given us an adviser, our conscience, to warn us from evil. Yet very few of us yield to the advice of our conscience.'

With his left thumb on his chin, Donaldson stared bewilderedly at Amanda as she spoke.

'God does not fold His arms when we suffer as a result of an evil action. Through every bitter experience He still demonstrates His power and love. That applies to you, Dr Weah. God was the one who helped you overcome all the evils you came across. People talk of your brilliance, humility and kindness. Those are some of the things He intended to achieve in you. But He's still waiting for a major achievement. And that is your acknowledging Him as the Creator, Lord and Saviour. God loves you and I think it is His love which has brought you through all your experiences.

Sometimes God trains those He loves in the act of battle. And no matter how fierce a battle is, they will always come out victorious. Dr Weah, I strongly believe that God has a special interest in you. He said in Jeremiah 29:11, 'For I know the plans I have for you," declares the Lord, "plans to prosper you and not to harm you, plans to give you hope and a future."'

After her speech, neither Donaldson nor Samantha had any questions. They were dumbfounded. To Donaldson, it was a kind of tutorial which he should have recorded. It was a great speech! She had spoken with the boldness and conviction. Where did she get this stuff from? Was it in the Bible? For close to half an hour she had held him spellbound and made him look like a new student attending a lecture for the first time. He never expected that. He had expected a chain of meaningless biblical quotes which he would have vehemently contested. But instead he sat still and subdued. He was particularly expecting the popular *'for God so loves the world'* which he could himself quote. In fact, he did quote it regularly under the influence of alcohol! And if any of those 'Jesus people' quoted it he already had an answer for them, 'Yeah. I believe your God loves the world. But my name is not 'the world' – my name is Donaldson. So you can see that he does not love me. Good day!' When he expected a sermon, the lady had dazed him with a lecture! And, like a real lecturer, she was now ready to field questions!

'Thank you very much, Amanda. Although I don't have any question for now, I will need plenty of time to examine your facts and then get back to you,' he replied.

'Shall we then pray together before we disperse?' asked Amanda.

But he rose and replied, 'I'm sorry, Amanda. I'm not ready for that. Let me think over what you've said.' Tapping Samantha on the shoulder to signify that he was ready to leave, he made for the door.

'Won't you have some coffee before you leave?' asked Samantha.

'No, angel,' he replied, 'I should be on my way to office for a special assignment. I'll speak to you later.'

Samantha was resolute in her decision to follow Jesus Christ. She assured Amanda of her determination to join in praying for Donaldson. The knowledge displayed by her friend that morning was very great. She knew that the process of melting down Donaldson's stony heart had begun. She could observe that he had taken in the gospel truth and his walls of defence, as far as that issue was concerned, had begun to crumble. He had been devastated by Amanda's powerful combination of straight rights, left hooks, jabs and uppercuts, and a knockout was imminent! She felt like carrying Amanda shoulder high and singing a ring chant. She loved God more. The two ladies prayed and studied the Bible together that morning. The lesson was drawn from the first chapter of the Gospel according to Saint John. It was awesome how the Word of God became a man and came here to set people free. Awesome was an understatement, Samantha thought. She had started to catch the fire of the Holy Spirit! And as Amanda prepared to leave in the afternoon, she remarked, 'Amanda, you are a gift to the Kingdom of God.' But Amanda smilingly reversed the statement, saying, 'Samantha, the Kingdom of God is a gift to us.'

CHAPTER 7: THE YOUNG ACHIEVERS' CLUB

More than a year after he was preached to by Amanda, Donaldson still refused to give his life to Jesus Christ. He had appealed to Samantha to leave him to make a decision on his own. But despite their different beliefs their relationship grew splendidly. There was, virtually, nothing to argue about. Donaldson had proved to be the perfect gentleman that Samantha considered him to be at the beginning of their relationship. She had seized the opportunity of his marriage proposal to let him know that her new-found faith frowned against premarital sex. Donaldson had complied, saying that the basis of their relationship should not be premarital sex but a happy home in the future.

The marriage proposal had taken place on her birthday. He had booked a popular American restaurant where friends and colleagues were treated. And later that evening, the duo sat in her living room appraising the event.

'I never knew that the turnout would be that high,' said Samantha.

'You see, I didn't invite many of those people in the first instance. They got to know through those I invited, and they accused me of being partial. I had to apologise to them and invite them verbally,'

'Donny, I must confess that today was one of my happiest days ever since my arrival in this country. Thank you very much.'

'But I'm the one that's really indebted to you. Ever since you came into my life the flame of joy and fulfilment has been kindled in me and is burning tremendously through all nooks and crannies of my life. Samantha, you have made me a different man; I know it and so does everyone who is close to me. But there is one thing I daily think about and I'm sad because I'm not sure if this metamorphosis isn't just a mirage.'

'What do you mean, Donny? And what is it that you think about?'

'I've got a big question on my mind and a possible answer to it is what daily scares me.'

'Come on, Donny! Stop the cryptic talk and speak to me plainly. You know I'm not good at decoding. What question agitates your mind so much?'

As Samantha still spoke, Donaldson thrust his hand into his breast pocket and brought out a carefully-wrapped object. Getting down on one knee, he unwrapped a beautiful diamond ring and said, 'Samantha, will you marry me?'

Samantha could only stare at him with mouth agape. She was dazed. There was a great silence as both stared at each other without saying a word. After a few moments Samantha rose and replied in affirmative as she stretched out her left ring finger. And after Donaldson had slipped the ring on, she held his hand and helped him to his feet. Still looking into his eyes, she moved closer, and they were locked in an embrace. But as she opened her mouth to speak, emotion took better of her; tears of joy rolled down from her eyes.

'Donny, you have eventually asked me a question that I had been expecting for some time now! Among all men, you obviously stand out. And I'm confessing today that it's a great honour for me to be your fiancée and I eagerly look forward to becoming your wife.'

They really had a nice courtship. Although he didn't attend church service with her, he happily dropped her off at church on Sundays and went back to pick her after service. Once or twice Samantha had appealed to him to attend the service with her, but he didn't utter a word as he reversed the car and headed back home. Samantha and Amanda understood that he didn't like to be persuaded. So, they kept on persuading the Lord instead. Amanda had told her friend that God never gave up on anyone. But the main thing was that they must not give up their faith-induced prayer concerning his salvation. However, Samantha couldn't stop wondering what else could be hindering giving his life to Christ. He was such an upright person – very honest and a great keeper of time. Unlike some of his friends, he didn't eye other ladies and never uttered vulgar words. He never attended social activities alone ever since they started dating. And he wouldn't persuade her to come with him if she wasn't willing. He would rather not attend too. The two of them would then stay indoors watching movies. Sometimes she would beg him to tell her funny jokes. And he had lots of them, mostly campus jokes.

There was one particular joke he told her about a researching professor who visited some riverside villages. As he was being paddled across a river by a young local boy, the professor asked if the boy knew anything about Ecology. When the boy replied that he didn't, the professor exclaimed, 'What? You mean you don't know anything about Ecology? My friend, nothing kills like illiteracy; I'm afraid, a quarter of your life must have burnt out!' As they proceeded, the professor turned to the boy again and asked if he knew anything about Biology. With sombre look, the boy replied that he didn't. 'My goodness!' the professor exclaimed. 'Even you don't know anything about Biology! My boy, I have no doubts that two quarters or half of your life must have burnt out! The poor boy became very sad. And after a while, as they still proceeded, the professor said to the boy, 'Accepted you don't know anything about Ecology or Biology, but don't tell me you don't know anything about Sociology.' Almost crying now, the boy asked, 'What is Sociology sir?' 'My goodness!' exclaimed the professor. 'Yours is the worst case of illiteracy and I'm afraid, three quarters of your life must have gone!' And the boy wept bitterly as he paddled. Not long after that, there came a tempest which threw the canoe upside down. The boy, remembering that he had only a quarter of his life remaining, swam desperately to the shore. But the obese professor was drowning.

'Hey young man, please help me. I'm drowning!' he cried out. But the boy replied:

'Professor, what do you know about Swimming-*ology?*'

'There's nothing called Swimming-*ology*, you dunderhead!' the professor furiously replied.

'Professor, if you don't know anything about swimming-*ology*, I'm afraid, your whole life is gone!'

Samantha laughed so much that she had to take some painkillers before going to bed.

He also shared a joke of a very shy man who gave a beautiful lady a ride in his car in a bid to woo her for love. But his courage failed him each time he looked into her eyes. Each time he looked into her eyes the lady would smile and say to him, 'Matthew chapter seven and verse seven.' Thinking she was one of those hardcore born-again ladies, the man changed his mind and dropped her off. But he decided to find out what was in the quoted verse when he got home. He then took a Bible and opened the quoted verse. He was greatly surprised to discover that the lady had meant that he should 'ask and he shall be given; seek and he shall find; knock and it shall be opened for him!' What a missed opportunity!

Richard Menakor, aka Mr Jack, started as a Production Manager at an American automobile assembly plant – Automobile Americas. His immediate boss at the production department was the American Production Director – Mr Walter Brandon – who was the sole interviewer of applicants for the post of Production Manager. Mr Brandon had shown great interest in Richard, even before the interview.

He had been enticed by his academic and professional achievements at such a young age. And, apart from his intimidating academic and professional records, his performance at the interview was superlative. Out of a group of six applicants which included two expatriate engineers, one of them a German, Richard was selected without any hesitation. The job attracted a chauffeur-driven state-of-the-art, four-wheel drive and posh residential duplex. The remuneration, which was in American dollars, went with various astronomical allowances. And ever since he joined the company he was annually sponsored on a holiday trip to the USA as part of the job's fringe benefits. Richard's father had eloped with an Ivory Coast-based Nigerian wealthy business woman when he was just a baby, but his mother never remarried. She worked very hard to provide him with quality education. And he didn't disappoint as he graduated with a second-class upper division Bachelor of Science in Mechanical Engineering. He went back to the same university to obtain a master's degree in the same field. He worked briefly with the Federal Ministry of Works and Transport where he qualified as a member of Liberian Society of Mechanical Engineers before his mouth-watering employment with the American automobile company. He so loved his mother that he carried her photograph about in his wallet and regularly showered her with expensive gifts. In his living room were expensively decorated photographs of him and his mother.

During the trauma of her husband's elopement, his mother – Mrs Leah Menakor – was preached to by some Christians who also helped her financially. She was told that it was only Jesus who could turn her husband's heart back to her. For that reason, she started to pray and attend church services. But after several years of waiting in vain, she lost hope and stopped going to church. After all the efforts of the pastor and elders of the church to have her back in church had failed, they resorted to regularly visiting her home to pray for her and her child. On one of their visits, the pastor had prophesised that Richard would be distinguished in his chosen career and financially blessed. However, he had to be shown the way of the Lord right from childhood so that the devil might not use worldliness to truncate the plans of God for his life. The elders then appealed to Mrs Menakor to allow him to come with them on Sundays.

Little Richard loved to attend the church basically because of music. He loved to sit near the instrumentalists and watch them play. At the end of the service he and other children would rush to the instruments and start drumming. A senior member of the choir once tried to stop them, but he was restrained by the pastor, who posited that the children were the future of the church and that they needed to learn everything about it. At ten years of age, Richard was already drumming to the admiration of the members of the congregation. He was also a talented member of the drama team. He received overwhelming applause at a New Year's Eve programme, when the juvenile drama group presented a play in which he acted the part of a demon. Wearing a black costume which had full-size human skeletal system painted in white, he tricked his victims into committing various sins. And when they died he was one of the demons who ushered them into hell, beating them mercilessly as they proceeded. Some members of the congregation wept while many of them applauded the group. It was crystal clear that Richard was destined to be an important instrument in the hand of God.

On completion of his elementary education, he was awarded a scholarship to study at the famous St Patrick's High School, Monrovia. Admission to St Patrick's High School was based on excellent performances in both oral and written examinations, with a scholarship awarded to the highest scorer. Richard was the first child from his village to gain admission to any school in Monrovia as well as the first scholarship recipient. His admission was celebrated by the entire village while the church held a thanksgiving service for him. One of the happiest people in the village was his headmaster, Mr Nehemiah, through whom the letter of admission was sent. And at the thanksgiving service, Mr Nehemiah reiterated his belief that Richard was the one to put the village on the national map.

Because of the distance of Monrovia from the village, Richard could only come home during the holidays. And each time he was around, his home was daily filled up with friends and well-wishers. His mother had, however, noticed that most of the friends who stayed late were girls. She had particularly noticed two girls from the youth choir who always left last. She also noticed that the two girls didn't walk together when they left. It appeared they weren't on good terms. She always remembered the prophecy about his bright future and danger of promiscuity. One evening, after all his friends had left, she called him into her room and asked, 'Richard, why do Lydia and Esther always stay behind after everyone has left?'

'They wait behind because they like to ask me questions about their school subjects and —'

'No, Richard!' his mother cut in. 'You always speak in English each time you are alone with them and I always hear you mention the word 'love' repeatedly. Accepted I don't understand much English, but I do understand the various meanings of the word. Which of them are you in love with? Listen to me, Richard: You are a thirteen-year old, junior high school final year student who has still got a very long way to go. You shouldn't allow girls a place in your heart for now. It is detrimental to your envisaged bright future. Henceforth, those girls must leave at the same time as the others. Otherwise, I will report the three of you to the pastor. Have I made myself clear?'

Apart from Lydia and Esther, there were other girls who didn't come to Richard's home but met him at various secret places. Some of these girls always invited him to their home whenever their parents were not around. An incident, however, took place which prompted him to stop attending the church. The rivalry between Lydia and Esther had started having negative effects on the performances of the choir and drama teams. Most of the girls no longer attended choir or drama practices punctually. The two groups had been divided into factions, with some supporting Lydia and some Esther. The behaviour among the young girls, however, reached a crisis when the two rivals and their supporters resorted to physical confrontation after a church service. It was so horrible that finger nails, teeth and pebbles were among weapons used by these unruly girls. And before the church officials could arrive at the scene many of the girls were already stripped half-naked. The culprits were taken to the pastor's office where the weekly meeting of the church leadership was in progress. All the leaders were dumbfounded to learn that the cause of the disturbance was fifteen-year old Richard. According to Lydia, Richard had proposed to her before Esther wrote to express her love for him. She found the letter in one of Richard's books which she had borrowed. It wasn't Esther's shameless request that infuriated her, but that in the letter she had called her a whore. All the girls involved were suspended from their respective groups. They were also reported to their parents and schools for disciplinary actions. As for Richard, he would be summoned to the church disciplinary committee when he arrived for holidays. But, having got wind of the incident, he never returned to the church. And as bad habits are said to die hard, his behaviour went downhill, together with his academic study.

Realising that the old prophecy about her son was nearing fulfilment, his mother returned to church so her son may be continually prayed for. The first step, according to the pastor, was to genuinely give her life to Jesus Christ. It was then that heaven would reckon with her prayers. Mrs Menakor returned to church with renewed zeal, serving the Lord and praying for redemption of her son. When Richard discovered that his mother had returned to church, he no longer came home during holidays.

He chose to hang out in Monrovia with his rich schoolmates who enticed girls with money and expensive gifts. His recklessness continued unabated when he got to the university. Sometimes, when the campus girls were not available he and his rich friends would cruise about the city at night in expensive cars.

As soon as he secured the lucrative American job he sent for his mother and expressed his desire to take her from the village.

'Mum, I want you to leave the village and live with me here in Monrovia,' he told her.

'No, Richard. I prefer to stay in the village.'

'Why mum?'

'I just don't want to live in the city.'

'Mum, I still want you to think about it. You see, I want you to be where I am, so I can take care of you every moment.'

On Mrs Menakor's return to the village she went to her pastor and discussed her son's intention.

'So why don't you want to go?' asked the pastor.

'The main reason is,' replied Mrs Menakor, 'all the churches in Monrovia speak English. And that will make it difficult for me to blend or participate actively in the church,' she added.

'That's not correct,' said the pastor. 'Not every church in Monrovia conducts service in English. And where it is conducted in English I'm sure there is adequate provision for interpretation. Now, think about this: your presence in Monrovia will help you monitor Richard and continually witness to him the Word of God.'

Much as Mrs Menakor was happy over her son's success she always remembered the prophecy. She saw his success as fulfilment of the first part of the prophecy. But the second part was scary. 'O Lord Jesus, You said that the heart of a king is in Your hand. Please, twist Richard's heart to Yourself,' she always prayed in tears.

There were six well-to-do young men in Richard's group which was named as the Young Achievers' Club. And the oldest among them was Lloyd who was just twenty-seven years old. Others were between twenty-four and twenty-six.

Gabriel Beyan Francis (Lexicon) was born with a silver spoon in his mouth. He was the youngest of his parents' three children – all boys. His parents were both legal luminaries. While his father, who was a product of Harvard University, had a private chamber, his mother was a judge of the Liberian Supreme Court. It could be said that legal profession ran in their family as his two siblings were also legal practitioners working at their father's chamber – Samuel Francis and Sons (Solicitors and Advocates). A staunch member of the True Whig party, Gabriel's grandfather was a cabinet minister from 1947 to 1969, during President William Tubman's regime. Stepping into his father's political shoes, Barrister Samuel Francis – Gabriel's father – was also a member of the True Whig party and a cabinet minister from 1971 until 1980, when President Tolbert was assassinated in a military coup. Unlike his siblings, Gabriel decided not to walk in his father's shadow but carved a niche for himself. After working at a private chamber for three years he registered his own law firm – Gabriel Francis and Co. Within a very short period of its establishment he won lucrative contracts and became solicitor to many companies and wealthy individuals, both indigenous and expatriate. As young as he was, his popularity rapidly grew in the profession. Apart from his legal charges, he also received numerous expensive gifts from his wealthy clients who were eager to show their appreciation to a young barrister who had helped them win cases which had appeared impossible. He had four state-of-the-art cars in his garage, three of which were gifts from his clients.

Although he was brought up a Catholic, he never saw Christianity beyond social activities and wasn't very sure of existence of God. He began to distance himself from church activities after he graduated from university, and later stopped attending church altogether, although he sent money whenever there was a church event. His parents and siblings, who were active in church, had tried to persuade him but he was adamant. On Sunday morning, after reading almost all the Sunday newspapers with the meticulousness of a graduate researcher, he retired to his study where he buried his head in his voluminous law books. Once in his study, no reason was important enough to draw him out when he wasn't done. None of his domestic workers dared come in. The only person who sometimes interrupted him was his fiancée – Lisa – who always spent weekends with him. With pyjamas on, she would enter the study and just stare at him. And as soon as he saw her in this posture he understood that she longed for his presence. He would smilingly look into her eyes and plead for more time to round off. Without saying a word, she would turn around and leave the study. Lisa, like her fiancé, was the youngest in the family of four children. Her father was one of the wealthiest rubber and diamond exporters in Africa, with assets scattered all over Europe and America. She was a product of the University of British Columbia, with a master's degree in International Relations. She was employed by her father to manage his exports business.

Silvestre Abrahams studied Computer Engineering at the University of Liberia before enrolling in the Liberian army. His father, retired General Matthew Abrahams, had served under the aborted regime of President William Tolbert. As a member of some paramilitary organisations, Silvestre had shown great interest in military career right from his high school days. His father had closely monitored his paramilitary activities and deduced that he was cut out for military career. And as soon as he finished his degree, he was enrolled for a cadet course at the Liberian Defence Academy. At completion, he was among fifteen officers who were sent to the US for a ten-month training course. At just twenty-two years of age, he became a Lieutenant. And within the next three years he was promoted to the rank of Major. Muscularly built and standing at six feet three inches, Silvestre carved a picture of a very strict military officer. By merely looking at him when in full military uniform, he could be mistaken for one of those 'no-nonsense' officers. But the only things that were military about him were his physique and military uniform. He was a soft-spoken and knee-slapping guy. Anytime he was teased by his friends over his career he would respond by calling them 'a bunch of bloody civilians.' And when he was asked why military officers were paid for doing nothing, he would reply, smiling, 'Sure, we're working very hard to prevent your fart-loaded bums from being riddled with the enemy's bombs and bullets. We also impose corrective government to save our nation from the clutch of good-for-nothing, God-forsaken bloody civilians like you.' There would then be hysterical laughter over the word, 'corrective.' Of course, everyone knew that there was nothing corrective about the military regimes. They were worse than the civilian governments which they claimed to correct. What good had dictators got to offer?

Apart from their huge salaries, Silvestre and lots of young officers like him regularly had large but inexplicable amounts credited to their bank accounts by the military junta. The amounts, Silvestre had confided in his friends, were bribes to prevent them planning a counter-coup. And so, he and his military colleagues were super rich at a young age! His father, who had also benefitted from the corrupt system while in service, had ten properties scattered all over the country. He also had one in New York and another in London, with fat foreign bank accounts. Though polygamous, he was made a deacon by one of the orthodox churches where special seats were reserved for him and his family. Wearing overflowing native attire and flanked by his two gorgeously dressed wives, he continually grinned as the priest eulogised him in his 'sermon.' Silvestre was the fourth of his father's seven children and second of his mother's three. And he was his father's only male child. It was believed that his father had married his mother as the first wife was unable to give him a boy. His father was never converted, and he hated being preached to about giving one's life to Christ. 'What am I doing in church every Sunday, and why do I spend so much to meet the church's needs if I haven't given my life to Jesus Christ?' he once asked a team of Pentecostal preachers. But he failed to understand that attending church and giving generously were quite different from being born again. He didn't understand, too, that God wasn't interested in the gifts of a sinner. Attending church and giving without accepting the lordship of Jesus Christ were merely acts of religion. When he was confronted with these facts, he warned the evangelists never to come near him again! After all, his church priest, who was more knowledgeable than them, socialised with him and had even been invited to bless a property he bought for one of his numerous concubines. Why were those Pentecostal Christians presenting God as a ferocious beast looking for humans to devour? They should go to blazes with their rotten doctrines! Silvestre had taken after his father in this regard. He never listened to any preaching about holiness or being born again. He only attended the family church on Sundays so as share in his father's accolades. Besides, attending the church was one of the responsibilities he believed he owed his father. Like his father, he dated many ladies behind his fiancée's back.

John Maxwell obtained a first-class Economics degree from the University of Liberia. He then proceeded to University of Washington where he obtained Master's and Doctorate degrees in the same field. He was the eldest child of his parents who were wealthy cocoa farmers. On his return from the US, he was employed by the University of Liberia as a Senior Lecturer. However, he didn't complete a year on that job before he was appointed as a member of the Liberia Economic Planning Committee with an official residence allocated to him at the presidential villa. As a member of the committee, he was entitled to two chauffeur-driven official cars, a personal assistant and various allowances in addition to his huge monthly salary. At the age of twenty-six, he was the youngest member of any governmental body in Liberia. And he was already being tipped for the next Minister of Trade. John invested heavily in shares, purchasing major shares in top businesses in the country. Unlike most of his friends, he believed in the existence of God but didn't believe in hell. He had grown up with the notion that the concept of hellfire was just a ploy by some moralists to scare people off evildoing. This concept, according to him, was later hijacked by religionists. 'If those Christians were not insane, how could God who 'so loved the world' throw His creatures into fire?' he once asked. And, claiming that he wanted to enjoy life to the fullest, he didn't have a fiancée or a regular girlfriend; he had a fleet of them.

Lloyd Nimely was the eldest son of the Chairman and Chief Executive of the Wuteve Bank where Donaldson worked. He was the only one among the group who didn't graduate from Liberia University. He had a degree in Accounting from Liverpool University, and was a member of the British Institute of Chartered Accountants. He worked briefly at the tax office in London before being recalled by his father to join the Wuteve Bank as an assistant Head of Accounting Department. About two years later, he became the Head of the department and was designated as the Accounting Manager. Lloyd had liked Donaldson the very day he was presented to the Management Board. He was the first head of department to pay him a complimentary visit in his office that morning. They chatted about the banking business and current state of industrialisation in the country. They also talked about the environment and people, and then lunched together. Within weeks, they had started visiting each other's homes and socialising together. And maybe because Donaldson jokingly introduced him to his friends as 'my young chairman' or because he was the oldest among them, he was nicknamed 'chairman.' Like his parents, Lloyd was a nominal Christian who would attend Sunday services provided they did not clash with 'more important' social activities. Being a wealthy young man, he had many ladies flocking around him.

CHAPTER 8: SATAN IS CRAFTY

Mrs Menakor's fiftieth birthday was a few weeks ahead, and Richard had decided to celebrate it with pomp and pageantry. It was an opportunity to show his love for her. At first, she had objected an idea of elaborate celebration, but her pastor opined that the celebration would provide an opportunity to preach to her son and the other blasphemous members of the Young Achievers' Club. Pastor Isaac would be arriving from the village, together with some elders, to conduct a special birthday service at celebrant's home. The following day would be thanksgiving service at the Monrovia church. In his mother's mind, that gave two separate opportunities to fire gospel missiles to the profane hearts of the highly affluent youngsters, who failed to recognise the hand of God in their lives. But before then, some spiritual preparations had to be made. After all, the Bible says, 'No man can enter into a strong man's house, and spoil his goods, except he will first bind the strong man; and then he will spoil his house.' Those young men were indeed an abode of the strongman and their hearts were the goods to be spoiled. And only divine intervention, through fasting and prayers, would provide the chain and fetters to bind the strong man, so a seven-day fasting and prayer programme was, therefore, declared in advance of the celebration. (The plan was, however, kept secret from the young men.)

The birthday programme itself was drawn by Richard and Donaldson. Two venues would be used: a large expanse of land in front of the celebrant's home would be canopied to host all guests, including friends, relatives, church members and neighbours during the day, while a high-class American restaurant would host invited dignitaries at night. Two local music stars had been contracted to entertain guests at the open venue and the restaurant. And, through Major Silvestre, security would be provided at the two venues by men formerly of the Liberian armed forces. Richard had secretly acquired a brand-new car for presentation to his mother. The car was kept hidden in Donaldson's garage. It was an opportunity for him to openly honour his mother and appreciate her unfailing love.

The birthday invites were printed and distributed about four weeks earlier. They were expensively designed cards with a beautiful picture of Mrs Menakor in front. The six members of the Young Achievers' Club had obtained matching traditional outfits to be worn at the open venue, and fine French suits to be worn at the restaurant. Interior and exterior decorators were contracted by Richard to give his sprawling duplex a facelift. The entire building and its environment were repainted; grasses and flowers were trimmed, and all carpets and rugs replaced. When all work was completed, the property looked like a newly built palace! Richard looked around on the eve of the celebration and was very happy. Beaming, he asked his mother if she loved the new look of the house. His mother replied, 'Richard my son, many people called me names when I decided not to remarry and have more children after your father deserted us. But you didn't make me regret that decision. Richard, you are more to me than a hundred children. Even my detractors are aware of this. The only thing is….' 'Hey mother, I just remember that I must meet some workers at the restaurant. Please, excuse me,' cut in Richard, on aware that his mother was about to bring issue of salvation into their discussion. It wasn't the first time his mother had tried to change the subject of their discussion; she always did. But as clever as he was, he always had one excuse or the other to jump the discussion. There was a day when he was successfully 'pinned down' by his mother for a biblical discussion. He had told his mother that there was neither heaven nor hell anywhere. But when his mother asked him how he would feel when he died and discovered that there was hell, he retorted, 'Mum, how would you feel when you later discover that heaven is just a figment of the erratic imaginations of some idle minds, having deprived yourself of enjoyment here on earth?' He then picked up his car keys and left, leaving his mother despairing.

The party organisers and all the personnel contracted over the ceremony arrived on Friday night, the eve of the ceremony. Mrs Menakor's friends, relatives and few in-laws had started arriving too. There were enough rooms for all the guests to sleep in. There were three bedrooms upstairs and six downstairs, including boys' quarters. Apart from his bedroom and that of his mother, the rest could be shared by guests. About ten fat cows were booked for the ceremony. (In Africa, the enormity of a celebration was measured by the number of cattle slaughtered.) On Saturday morning, all guests and organisers were treated to a breakfast of bread and fried eggs with a cup of coffee or tea, while Mrs Menakor hopped around to express her appreciation. She had changed into one of the three expensive outfits bought for her for the occasion. The birthday programme would commence around midday with prayer and a sermon. Richard wasn't aware that the sermon was going to be given by Pastor Isaac whom he had been avoiding for a long time. He had thought it would be given by her mother's Monrovia pastor. He had initially tried to remove the item from the programme, saying that prayer and a sermon would bore the guests. But his mother had replied that, since the party was organised to honour her, she should be allowed to dictate the items of programme. He then burst into laughter as he put his arm around her shoulders. 'If it pleases my mother, then it is OK!'

'And all your friends must be present at the opening prayer. Okay?' his mother added as he was about to leave her bedroom.

'I will try to convince them, but I can't guarantee that,' he replied.

But his friends had already made up their minds not to miss any of the items of the programme. A few minutes of listening to fallacies would not make them fallacious, they had said. But it seemed the Lord was ready to grant the request of the interceding church. Richard was, however, surprised when his mother told him that the religious aspect of the programme would only be attended by relatives and close friends. She explained that it was restricted to relatives and close friends since others would still be joining her at church, the following day, for thanksgiving service.

Richard's friends arrived in their posh cars around 11:45 a.m. followed by a fully-loaded army truck. They were soldiers who were to provide security at the venues of the event. Everyone in the compound was awestruck. As Silvestre pulled up, two fierce-looking soldiers jumped down from the truck, opened the door of his car and gave a military salute. There wasn't any doubt that, as from that moment, everyone in the compound wanted to be a military officer! The affluent young men were then ushered upstairs by Richard. On sighting Mrs Menakor in the living room, they all removed their local caps and bowed in greeting. 'My children, it is well with you all. I really appreciate all you've done for me. Thank you very much. I pray in Jesus' name that your children shall honour you,' she responded ecstatically. While the men joked with Mrs Menakor, Donaldson went to the wine bar and brought two bottles of *Haut Brion* and served himself and his friends. As they drank, a woman came upstairs to inform Mrs Menakor that a pastor and four other men were waiting downstairs. The young men looked at one another and then at their cups of wine in a manner suggesting, 'We hope the pastor will not cast us straight to hellfire for this!'

'Bring them here,' replied Mrs Menakor.

'May the peace of the Lord Jesus Christ be upon this house,' said Pastor Isaac as he led a team of his church elders into the living room.

'What!' exclaimed Richard. 'Pastor, are you the invited minister? You … you … are … welcome sir.' He stuttered. 'Elder Mark, Deacon Moses! You are all welcome to my home. Please, have a seat!'

'Thank you, my son,' replied the pastor.

Although it was more than ten years since the pastor saw him last, he didn't behave as such. He wanted to make Richard feel that the old incident was long forgotten. And after he and his entourage had had a seat, Richard introduced his friends one after the other. After that, he introduced the pastor as a God-sent father who stood by him as a child. He joked about how he grew up in the church and how he loved to play the musical instruments. He also recalled his days as a member of the choir and drama teams. But he never said anything about the circumstances that led to his absconding. Shaking his head in approval, the pastor confirmed that he was a talented drummer and actor. He was an undisputable gift to the church.

After discussing the pleasant parts of Richard's past, they settled down to the business of the day. And after the opening prayer, followed by praise and worship songs, the pastor explained the spiritual importance of a birthday celebration, citing Psalm 90 with emphasis on verse 12. *'Teach us to number our days that we may gain a heart of wisdom.'* He then praised Richard's obedience to the commandment of God, by honouring his parent. He added that, by honouring his mother, he had honoured God. When a child honoured their parents, they would receive from God all the blessings that they desired. There would also be additional blessing of long life which was needed to enjoy those blessings. With intensive prayers, Pastor Isaac had devised a meticulous way of arriving at his main sermon – that of winning the souls of the young men. And it seemed the gentlemen were enjoying every bit of it, as they could be seen nodding their heads in affirmation each time the pastor made a point. It was evident that their earlier disposition towards the birthday service had tremendously changed. And as the sermon progressed, Mrs Menakor ceaselessly prayed within her heart that her son and his friends might begin to embrace Jesus Christ.

But as the forces of darkness weren't sleeping either, the sermon was to be rudely interrupted. While the sermon was on, one of Richard's domestic workers came upstairs to inform him of the presence of three elderly men from the village. As the service was meant for relatives and close friends, he didn't have any objection inviting them upstairs. But it was only two of the guests who came upstairs. They were Richard's paternal uncles whom he didn't think he had ever met before. But as soon as they came into the living room, Mrs Menakor jumped out of her seat and embraced them. Beaming, she introduced them to Richard as his uncles – his father's elder brothers. The men's presence at that time was purely a coincidence. As none of them lived in the family village, there were no chances of their being informed of the celebration. They had travelled all the way from Ghana where they traded. That was where they lived since their youth, even before their eloped brother got married. The last time both of them saw Mrs Menakor was at Richard's christening – when he was just a week-old baby! Their brother had informed them, via telegraph, of a gift of a bouncing baby boy. And coming quickly from Kumasi, where they were based, they brought all sorts of gifts for the baby and its mother. But two years later, when their brother eloped with a secret lover, all Mrs Menakor's efforts to locate them in Kumasi proved abortive.

Although Richard wasn't happy about their presence, he was able to conceal his feelings. Bowing very low in greeting, he had offered them a seat next to his mother's. But they didn't sit down. Instead, one of them walked over to the pastor and whispered into his ear. The expression on the pastor's face, though incomprehensible, was noticed by everyone. The visibly disturbed pastor then made an excuse and left the room with the two men. On his return, a couple of minutes later, he requested a private talk with Mrs Menakor. Both of them then withdrew to the guestroom, leaving everyone wondering what was amiss. But not quite five minutes after they withdrew, Mrs Menakor could be heard protesting almost at the top of her voice, 'No, Pastor. That's not possible.' Fed up of the suspense, Richard rose and stormed into the guestroom. Seeing his mother in tears, he queried, 'Mum, what's really going on? What have the so-called uncles told the pastor?' When none of them responded, he stormed out of the room threatening to get the two intruders arrested by the police. The pastor and his mother rose and ran after him, appealing for calm. Richard's friends rose from their seat and calmed him down. But Donaldson said, 'Pastor, we all know that today is supposed to be a very happy day. And it had been until those two men came here some minutes ago. If they were sent here to spoil our fun, we shall not stop our friend from taking any action against them. I want to request, with due respect, that the three of you go back to the guestroom and tell our friend what is really going on.' But Mrs Menakor snapped, 'No! There is nothing confidential about it. Richard, your uncles have brought your father here to apologise to us after twenty-three years of abandoning us. But I will never have him back. I mean never!'

'Whose father did you say he is?' Richard angrily asked. There was uneasy calm in the whole compound. Continuing, Richard said, 'Pastor, tell him and his brothers to leave my compound immediately. If I go downstairs and see anyone of them, I will have them beaten up by soldiers before handing them over to the police for trespassing.'

'Mrs Menakor, I want you to remember that you are a Christian – a new creature. Please, let's forgive and seek after peace and reconciliation,' pleaded Pastor Isaac.

'Hey spare us, Pastor! Christianity my foot! My mother and I are not ready to welcome a cruel deserter here,' said Richard as he made for the stairs, followed by his mother and friends. Arriving downstairs, he barked, 'Which of you here claims to be my father? If you are still here after the count of ten, you should consider yourself lucky to be alive.'

At that moment, a grey-haired man in his early sixties came out of the portal's post and prostrated piteously before Richard and his mother.

'Leah, I have sinned against God of heaven and against you and Richard. I'm daily tormented by the sting of my sin. I know that it is too late for me to come back begging. I have been going about with this terrible guilt all these years until I met with the Lord Jesus Christ. Please, forgive me and don't allow me to die in this horrible state of my heart!' the man sobbed. The atmosphere was palpably charged. Emotion ruled the air. While men shook their heads regrettably, tears could be seen rolling down women's faces. Breaking the silence, Pastor Isaac said, 'Mrs Menakor, the Spirit of God tells me that this is a golden opportunity for us to achieve the purpose of the birthday service. This is the last hurdle – a mountain erected by the enemy against achieving the desire of our hearts. The Bible asks us to resist the devil and he shall flee from us. Please, forgive your husband and make Richard see reason. Remember your prayers that the Lord might bring him back to you. Now that the Lord has eventually answered your prayer, please forgive and let the devil and his cohorts be ashamed.'

'That's not possible, pastor! Never! Why should I forgive a man who put me in untold hardship and shame for many years? Why should I forgive a man who repaid my faithfulness, respect and loyalty with unfaithfulness and betrayal? Pastor, you mention hurdles and mountains? I'm not ready to cross any of them. All I know is that Richard and I will never forgive this traitor. We don't even know how to forgive monsters!'

'Yes, Mrs Menakor. But the Spirit of God will intervene and teach you how to forgive,' replied the pastor.

'That's enough pastor,' cut in Richard. 'I've had enough of this nonsense. Soldiers! Please, throw these three intruders out of here.' And turning to the pastor, he said, 'Pastor, we've had enough of the birthday sermon too. If you'd like to continue the rest of the programme with us, you are welcome. Otherwise, I would like to say good bye and wish you safe journey back to the village!' He then headed upstairs together with his mother and friends. But as six hefty soldiers grabbed the elderly men, the pastor pleaded, 'Hey gentlemen, I'm Pastor Isaac. Please, don't treat them roughly. Allow them to leave by themselves.' The soldiers obeyed. While the pastor's entourage went upstairs with their hosts, the pastor went to have a chat with Richard's father outside the compound.

Richard's father – Andrew Menakor – grew up with a dangerous lust for riches. His first job was as a sales clerk at a rubber company until he was sacked for financial misappropriation. He later got another job as a hotel manager, which he did until he got married. While working at the hotel, he got acquainted with a wealthy Ivory Coast-based businesswoman who was a regular lodger. Their relationship, however, became so passionate that anytime the lady was around Andrew would place himself on the nightshift, so they could spend the night together. And at the end of her stay, the lady would offer him an envelope which contained wads of new notes. After a few months, the woman proposed marriage to him. She told him that she wanted them to get married and live together in Ivory Coast where he would be a partner in her business. It was pleasant news to Andrew who had already coveted her luxurious life. And about three weeks later, he lied to his wife that he was being transferred to Monrovia to manage a new branch of their hotel. He would arrange for her to join him after some weeks, he had told her. But two months after his departure, when she didn't hear from him, she contacted his former office. But she was told that her husband had resigned his appointment and that the hotel had no branch in Monrovia. His secret affair and elopement were, however, revealed to her by one of the hotel cleaners. All her efforts to locate him since then had proved abortive.

Throughout his first year in Ivory Coast, Andrew didn't engage in any job whatsoever. He, however, lived like a king in the lady's palatial house. Although she was seldom home, there were lots of houseboys and maids to attend to him. His breakfasts were served while in bed and there were state-of-the-art cars and chauffeurs to take him around. As he was an orphan and had lied about his marital status, he had no reason to visit Liberia. What else did he even want in Liberia? Here was a woman who was not only beautiful, she was stupendously rich. As for his son Richard, when his new wife started producing babies for him, he would have another son who would be much better off than Richard. He didn't even like to think of Leah and her child, as both of them were an impediment to his astounding destiny. With a wife like Madam Rita whose destiny matched his, the sky was the limit. A soothsayer had once told him that his destiny was like a flame. Hence, he needed a woman whose destiny was like air, so he could become greatly prosperous. According to the soothsayer, no fire could burn in the total absence of air. And as the air tended to become a terrible wind, the flame tended to become an inferno. An inferno needed a terrible wind to rage on, the soothsayer had asserted. Now Rita's destiny was the wild wind needed by his destiny to become an inferno, whereas Leah's destiny was nothing but a vacuum. And destiny, like a sound wave, could not travel in a vacuum. Now that God had rescued his destiny from a vacuum, he dared not go back! 'Good bye to Leah and good bye to Richard! Welcome to my world!' he said to himself as he lay in bed one particular night, after a delicious dinner with his new wife.

Andrew didn't have a clue about Madam Rita's business. When he eventually summoned up all his courage to ask, she simply replied, 'I deal in diamonds, Andrew. I travel about to buy and sell diamonds.' And when he asked when he would be joining her in the business, she replied, 'When you feed well enough and become attractive and presentable to our wealthy international customers!' But something he didn't understand was the fortnightly meeting which took place behind closed doors at the mansion. The night meeting was attended by ten very rich men and women. Andrew always wondered why a business meeting should be that secretive and why he wasn't allowed to join them if he truly belonged to the group. He was becoming worried. But precisely a year after his arrival, Madam Rita invited him for a chat in her bedroom. Ever since his arrival at the mansion they had been sleeping separately, except occasionally when he was invited for some reason. 'Andrew,' she began, 'It's time for you to join me in the business. You see, the business is a kind of partnership and I'm a senior partner. Tomorrow is the next business meeting and I will be formally presenting you for initiation. So, make sure you are in your best attire for the initiation ceremony.' But she didn't allow him to say a word before asking him to go back to his room.

Andrew had wanted to ask a question about the word 'initiation.' He was puzzled. He only knew of being initiated into cultism. An 'initiation ceremony' into a business organisation sounded rather strange to him. Madam Rita had only entertained a very few selected questions from him ever since his arrival at the mansion. And after a few months, their relationship looked more of 'mistress and servant,' except occasionally eating or sleeping together. Andrew, however, knew what he wanted. As soon as he got what he wanted he would disengage himself from the so-called marriage. He would continue to play a monkey for now. After all, there was an old African adage, 'He who will catch a monkey must act as a monkey.' But he was to discover to his chagrin, some twenty-four hours later, who was the monkey and who was its catcher.

It was 11 p.m. The members were already seated before Madam Rita went to fetch Andrew. It was his first time of entering the lavishly decorated special living room. The switchboxes, sockets and lamp holders were gold-painted. The walls were painted in glittering white, while the sofas and rug were in a perfectly-matched wine colour. The combination of red and mercury fluorescent tubes on the ceiling provided a mixture of lights which partially obscured faces of members but brought about exaggerated beauty of everything in the room: clothing, shoes, furniture, bottles of wine and the decor. As Andrew reached a sofa, Madam Rita suddenly exclaimed, 'Stand up!' And the rest of the people replied in unison, 'For sheep must remain standing while goats are seated.' Then a very large man rose from his seat and walked over to Andrew. Putting his left hand on Andrew's left shoulder, he asked, 'Who is this sheep?'

'He's my sheep, president,' replied Madam Rita. 'I've brought him here to feed among goats that he might become a goat himself.'

Andrew was visibly shaken. He would have bolted had the door remained open. But it was firmly locked. Besides, he wasn't sure he remembered where the exit was.

'Are you truly ready to become a goat?' the man asked. Andrew was hesitant. The man repeated the question.

'No … y-e-e-s sir,' he answered as he nervously released a gentle, smelly fart. Everyone took out their handkerchief and covered up their nostrils.

'What kind of farting sheep is this?' asked the president angrily.

'I'm so sorry, president. He is nervous,' replied Madam Rita who took a bottle of air freshener from a nearby drawer and sprayed the room.

'That's alright,' said the president. Turning to Andrew, he asked, 'What is your name?'

'Andrew sir,' he replied, almost sobbing.

'Stretch out your left hand,' said the president. Andrew obeyed. Both his thumb and index finger were then lacerated, with the dripping blood collected in a large calabash which already contained the blood of the rest of the group. After some incantations by the president, the calabash was given to Andrew to drink from. Andrew collected it and hesitated. 'Please, I don't want to drink … please.' he sobbed.

'Come on, drink!' barked the president.

And after Andrew had drunk everyone in the room took turn to drink. When the process was completed the president turned to Andrew and said:

'Andrew, as from today you are no longer a sheep but a goat. You may have a seat now.' And after he had sat down, the president explained that he had just been initiated into a secret cult. But Andrew rose immediately and held his head in both arms as he sobbed:

'But Madam Rita told me you were business partners. Oh my God, oh….'

'Keep quiet, you idiot,' Madam Rita cut in. 'Has anybody told you that we are not? Why don't you listen and find out what businesses we engaged in?'

Continuing his speech, the president listed their business units as kidnapping, drug peddling and currency counterfeiting. Andrew was given till the next meeting to decide which unit he would like to work in.

'Please, I don't want to join your group. I want to go back to Liberia,' he sobbed

'You are a fool,' retorted the president. 'Nobody quits after being initiated. You will either go insane or drop dead if you try it!' he added.

'President, don't mind my husband,' began Madam Rita. 'I will speak to him. And I assure you that, come next meeting, he will be more of a goat than a sheep,' she added.

The exaggerating lights were turned off to give way to bright white light, while foods and drinks were served. It was only Andrew who didn't go to the dining room. But as he still sat down sobbing, the president walked over to him and said, 'Andrew, the opportunity we've offered you is what many are looking for. Membership of this chamber involves lots of stringent requirements, all of which we waived for you. We currently have many men and women all over the sub-continent working for us with the hope that they would be invited to this inner caucus someday. But here you are, without any experience of the job, you have been made a member. If you realised that as from this moment you have become a multi-millionaire, you would not be weeping. Maybe you are thinking of the risk involved. Don't be childish, Andrew. The principle upon which our operation is based can be found in the Bible, in the book of Mark chapter three and verse twenty-seven – *'In fact, no one can enter a strong man's house without first tying him up. Then he can plunder the strong man's house.'* How did we tie the strongman? By buying up people that matter in government, including top security agents. It may interest you to know that among us in this room are top government functionaries and police chiefs. So, Andrew, grab your opportunity with both hands.'

And as he turned around to leave, he added, 'Lest I forget, I would like to give you a taste of what awaits you.' And he dropped a fat wallet on Andrew's lap. Andrew was surprised to discover that the content was cash of one thousand US dollars, an amount equivalent to hundreds of thousands of Liberian dollars. He almost screamed for joy! And the following morning, in consultation with Madam Rita, he joyfully made up his mind to belong to the narcotic group.

As expected, things became rosier for Andrew as he became a member of the crime ring. Within a year of his membership he had acquired his own home and several cars. Although he had split from Madam Rita, he had fleet of girlfriends. And sometimes too, he did sleep with her. But like any interesting movie which must surely come to an end, his joy was short-lived. The crime ring was broken by a new incorruptible Inspector-General of police. The criminals and their accomplices were handed various jail terms while assets were frozen, and properties confiscated. Andrew was given seventeen years. And it was in his eleventh year that he was led to Christ by a team of visiting prison evangelists. On his release, he was advised to look for his family and apologise to them, even if his wife had remarried.

That was the story related to Pastor Isaac by Andrew outside Richard's home. Trusting God for reconciliation, the pastor advised him not to go back to Ghana with his siblings. He wanted him to stay with him at the village while God melted down the stony hearts of his family members. There was, however, a price to pay. He must prepare to weather the storm of jeers and insults from villagers who still remembered him as someone who deserted his family at a crucial period of their lives. Knowing the thought on his mind, the pastor had quoted Hebrews chapter twelve and verse two, *'Looking unto Jesus the author and finisher of our faith; who for the joy that was set before him endured the cross, despising the shame, and is set down at the right hand of the throne of God.'*

CHAPTER 9: A FRIEND IN NEED

Years after Mrs Menakor's talk-of-the-town birthday party, God's grace still abounded on the rebellious group as they continued to blaze the trail in their respective professions. Richard was made the Regional Director of Automobile Americas. Gabriel became solicitor to people that mattered in the country and beyond, including the military Head-of-State. Silvestre gained rapid promotions and became a Lieutenant-General. John was sworn-in as Minister of Trade and Economics while Lloyd became an Executive Director at the Wuteve Bank. Having taken a number of career-boosting courses both at home and abroad, Donaldson had coveted a World Bank job. He had sent his application through the Central Bank of Liberia. But while he was still awaiting a decision, he was appointed as the Deputy Governor and member of the governing board of the Central Bank of Liberia. His appointment coincided with his thirtieth birthday and took place just two months after his wedding to Samantha. Although it was a court wedding, a thanksgiving service was held at Samantha's church. As much as they tried to make the wedding a low-key event, his friends had seen it as another opportunity to display their affluence. It was attended by all the staff of the British Embassy and graced by the British Ambassador, the Chairman and Chief Executive of the Wuteve Bank, the Governor of Central Bank of Liberia, some federal ministers, regional governors and banking executives. Samantha shone like a million stars in an expensive wedding gown. She was given away by the Embassy's Director of Trade, Mr Carlton Oswald while Amanda's mother, who had arrived two weeks earlier with Amanda, had perfectly played her mother. Amanda had secured a transfer back to Britain a year earlier and got married the same year. Her wedding, which took place in Manchester, was attended by both Samantha and Donaldson.

Donaldson and Samantha drew tears from the eyes of every guest as they gave an emotional speech of thanks, paying huge tributes to their dead parents. Samantha had recounted her mother's last words concerning her 'good man.' She then turned to Donaldson and said, 'I always knew since the beginning of our courtship that my mother's prediction about you was true.' And folding her arms around his neck, she added, 'My husband, thanks for all your love.' And the whole hall erupted!

Donaldson loved Samantha even more after they got married. To him, she was the epitome of peace and joy. They never had confrontations over any issue as he was always ready to concede. He literally allowed his wife to make decisions on virtually every matter, including finances.

Samantha, however, never abused this gesture. She remained as humble and submissive as ever. She had a clever way of calling her husband's attention to his errors. And as soon as the latter realised this, he quickly apologised and they both laughed it over. Based on criteria such as love, faithfulness, and honesty, Samantha was convinced that her husband was the best in the world. He had dazed her on their return from Florida where they honeymooned, when he presented her with copies of bank documents required to grant her joint ownership of his bank account. To return the loving-kindness, she instructed her employers to subsequently pay her salaries into the joint account. She also made sure that all the cash in her old account was transferred to the joint one. Donaldson was very surprised when he discovered this. 'Oh no, darling!' he exclaimed. 'Your personal account should have been kept for your sundry expenses. I have a responsibility to provide for our home,' he argued.

'Yes, darling,' replied Samantha. 'But I also have a responsibility to assist my husband,' she concluded.

With a husband like him, she had every reason to thank God for being disappointed by Dave. She could now realise what the Bible meant by having double portion in place of one's shame. However, as much as the couple loved each other, each had a specific area they wouldn't want their partner to try to influence. On the part of Samantha, she didn't believe she had to go and see her aunt – Bridget's mother – as suggested by Donaldson. She had told him several times that what really mattered was forgiving her and her treacherous daughter. And to her, the idea of travelling to England just to convince them of her forgiveness was weird. Donaldson's insistence on meeting her aunt, who was her only surviving relative, wasn't just to convince her of Samantha's forgiveness; it was premised on the African tradition which didn't recognise marriage until the groom met the bride's parents or relatives. Such marriage was culturally invalid without a bride price paid to the parents or appropriate relatives of the bride.

It was two years after their wedding before Samantha eventually yielded. That was after the birth of their first child, a beautiful girl named Natasha. Their trip was futile, however, as the aunt was deceased and all efforts to locate Bridget or any of her siblings proved abortive.

Donaldson still maintained his stance on Christianity. Although Amanda's preaching had removed some scepticism, like most unbelievers, he still deliberately hardened his heart. Nevertheless, he still dropped his wife off at church every Sunday and during the week. And at the end of service he was always on time to pick her up. Samantha had long stopped trying to persuade him to come in. She had resorted to prayer, in collaboration with her pastor and members of the church.

Only Richard remained a bachelor in the group of friends. He had decided to remain single to enjoy life to the fullest. He didn't want any 'daughter of Eve' restricting his activities in the name of marriage. According to him, when it was time for him to have children, he could impregnate some women and then father their children without having to accept the mothers. That was the best kind of life to live to have peace and long life. He was of one those sexists who believed that the word, woman, was derived from the phrase, 'woe of man.' He always told his friends that after God created man on the seventh day the Bible said that He rested. But since He created woman He never rested! And if the book of Genesis was accepted as the true account of creation, then, all the problems the whole world was facing were due to a stupid or covetous woman, called Eve. As for him, he didn't need a woman. He didn't want any woes! His only 'wives' were alcohol and cigarettes which he neither drank nor smoked responsibly. His lust for the duo had long transcended enjoyment. They had become an addiction. But that was one thing he would never accept. Addiction? No, he wasn't addicted. He could never be addicted to anything, he always boasted. He always told his friends that he could drop any habit anytime he liked, although he had never tried. For an incomprehensible reason, however, none of his friends were able to make him understand that he was very close to alcoholism. There was little his mother could do either. She knew her son's addiction to women, alcohol and cigarettes, and she felt an impending doom. The old prophecy about him always kept ringing in her ears. And the last time she reminded him of the prophecy, all he could say in reply was that there wasn't any repercussion more tragic than death, which was inevitable for everyone.

His mother no longer looked as happy as she used to. Sometimes she would instruct the housemaid not to prepare any food for her throughout the day. She had stopped wearing the beautiful and expensive dresses bought for her. When asked why she preferred to wear her old abandoned dresses, she simply told her son that beautiful dresses didn't correspond to a sad heart. After all, the Bible had said that no one put new wine in an old wineskin. Her problem was, however, compounded by the fact that she could no longer speak to Pastor Isaac about moral and spiritual degeneration of her son. After what had happened at her birthday party, she had refused to pick the pastor's calls. The pastor had eventually stopped calling; he had retired to intercessory prayer. Once in a week, early in the morning, Andrew would go before the pastor and thank him for all his efforts. 'Pastor, thanks for all your efforts, both physical and spiritual,' he would say. 'I believe more than before that the Lord will surely use you to restore my family.' The elated pastor would then reply, 'That's the spirit, Brother Andrew! That's the spirit! I'm so glad for your faith. The Lord has done it in the spirit. And it's just a matter of time for its physical manifestation. Hallelujah!'

At the time Andrew arrived at the village the church needed a sexton. And the church leadership didn't have any objection giving him the job. From the first week of his arrival Andrew had taken to solo evangelism. He would walk from village to village, preaching Jesus Christ to people going to or returning from market. It was more of a joke at the beginning, as most villagers knew his story. 'Look who's preaching,' the villagers would whisper among themselves and then burst into laughter. 'After he has been thrown out by his millionaire secret wife he thinks he can return to us by pretending to be a Christian preacher. Don't mind the good-for-nothing old fool. If every preacher is like him nobody will go to church.'

But after about two years of his relentless solo evangelism, the people realised God's presence in his ministry and his dignity and pride were restored within and without the village.

He was preaching along the road on one market day when he saw a woman crying for help as she cuddled a tot. He stopped preaching and watched a crowd gather to revive the dying child. The boy, who was the only child of the widowed woman, had been ill for days. That afternoon, after everyone had gone to market, he convulsed severely and then fainted. The woman's efforts to revive him alone had proved abortive. All the men in the neighbourhood gathered around the child, applying both traditional and western medicines. But Andrew could see them shake their heads in regret as the five-year-old boy lay on the bare floor. The woman ran into the house, took a knife and was about to kill herself when a group of men grabbed her. 'Please, let me die. Leave me alone. Why am I still alive?' she wailed. Andrew was filled with compassion. He turned his face to heaven and prayed, 'Lord Jesus, I currently feel the same way you felt when you visited Lazarus' home and saw everyone crying. The Bible says you also wept. But your compassion didn't end at weeping – you raised Lazarus! Lord, I want you to raise this child that these people may believe that you are the Lord. Thank you for not putting me to shame.' He then walked briskly to the crowd and asked, 'Is the boy dead?' But the people looked at him indignantly. One elderly man walked over to him and rudely asked if nobody had ever died in his presence before. But Andrew boldly replied, 'Yes, I have seen lots of people die.

But I assure you that I will not see this boy die today. My Jesus is here to raise him.' He then left the elderly man at the spot and walked over to the corpse. Bending over it, he laid his right hand on its forehead and said, 'My little friend, you've had enough sleep. I command you in Jesus' name to rise!' The boy immediately opened his eyes. And holding his both hands, Andrew helped him to his feet.

There had never been such commotion in the village since its inception. The crowd stared at Andrew in awe. Somebody said he had only heard about miracles in the Bible, but he never believed they still existed. The news spread so quickly throughout the village that within a few minutes an unprecedented crowd had gathered at the place. And after Andrew had waited until the boy finished the food served him by his mother, he began to speak. 'My people stop looking at me as if I raised the boy. I didn't. The Lord Jesus did. You all know my story in this village; I was a wretched sinner and a family deserter. But Jesus Christ never casts anyone away and He never deserts. He forgives all who repent of their sins and makes use of as many as are ready for Him. After the Lord forgave me of my terrible sins I decided to make myself available for his service. When I made this decision, the Lord saw my heart and provided me with His grace to fulfil it. You have just seen the least of what the Lord can do today. And you know what? The Lord did it because of two reasons: one, because I was grieved in my spirit seeing the boy dead, and two, because He wanted to prove his existence to remove your unbelief. With what you have seen the Lord do here today, if there is anyone here who still refuses to give their life to Jesus Christ, such a person is deliberately declaring for Satan. But if you are now convinced of the existence and ability of God and you want to give your life to Jesus Christ, could you please raise your hand that my pastor may pray with you.' Amazingly, almost all the people raised their hands while Pastor Isaac, who also came to witness the miracle, prayed with them. After the prayer, all the members of the church who were present helped in writing down the names and addresses of the new converts. On the following Sunday, the church auditorium was filled up to its capacity while canopies were erected outside, to accommodate twice the number of people in the main auditorium! Andrew was officially announced as the church evangelist and head of the evangelical team. But the news of the Lord's doing in his life didn't change the hearts of his family members – they still refused to accept him.

Mrs Menakor was sitting alone in her bedroom one Monday afternoon when the bedside phone suddenly rang. It was an emergency call from Richard's company. He slumped while on duty that morning and was taken to the John F. Kennedy Medical Centre, one of Liberia's foremost hospitals. She neither allowed the speaker to finish nor hanged up before bursting into tears, screaming loudly. Her screaming attracted all the domestic workers. And as they rushed to her bedroom they found her sitting on the bare floor, wailing. After some moments, she asked her chauffeur to go start the car. And, without covering her unkempt hair, she made for the car.

At the intensive care unit of the hospital, she was prevented from seeing Richard who had just been revived and was still receiving oxygen therapy. 'Is he alive? Please, let someone tell me the truth,' she said as she paced the corridor. Three officials of Automobile Americas, one of them black, emerged from an administrative room of the hospital and saw her weeping. Recognising her, they stopped and exchanged greetings. The black official then spoke in the local dialect, 'Madam, the boss is not dead. He's recovering rapidly. His situation may be because of stress but he's getting better. Please, stop crying.'

'If that's true, why didn't they allow me to see him?' she queried.

'Because he's currently being attended to,' replied the black official. 'Okay, I will ask a doctor to speak to you,' added the man as he dashed back to the administrative room. He came back few moments later with a doctor who allayed her fear.

'Madam, Mr Menakor collapsed at work this morning and was rushed here. We've been able to revive him, but we must run some tests to know the cause.'

Mrs Menakor expected that her son would be discharged the same day, so she became apprehensive when she was advised to go home later in the evening. She had refused to leave the hospital without seeing her son. They should let her know if he was dead, so she might join him as soon as possible. After some deliberations by a team of medical personnel, she was allowed to see her son. The nurses in charge had tried to allay her fear by saying that his ailment wasn't too serious and that he only needed some rest. But when her weeping could no longer be condoned by them she was asked to leave. After all her entreaties that she might be allowed to stay with him had failed, she reluctantly left.

The home was sour. There was air of apprehension as everyone wore a sombre look. Mrs Menakor went straight to her room confused over what to do. She couldn't pray. It had been so long since she prayed. In fact, she hadn't since her encounter with her estranged husband years ago. Much as she would like to call Pastor Isaac, she didn't possess the boldness. She remembered a Bible verse that said, '*but the righteous are as bold as a lion,*' and wept all the more. What exactly should she do now?

She couldn't contact her Monrovia pastor either, for she had shunned him since her birthday party. She had stopped attending the church service regularly. And each time she attended, she avoided the pastor until she eventually quit the church. So many times, the pastor had sought an audience with her, but she declined. Now, realising that her son's problem was more spiritual than medical, she was at a loss over what to do. What about the prophecy? She feared to think about its fulfilment. She wept at the top of her voice and roared like a lion each time she remembered the old prophecy. The thought of losing her only child kept tormenting her. Although all the domestic workers were gathered in her room, nobody was courageous enough to utter a word of consolation. The only lady among them also wept while the men shook their heads regrettably.

It took three days before the cause of Richard's ailment could be established. It was diagnosed as renal failure. The consultant had explained to his colleagues at Automobile Americas that renal failure was a medical condition in which the kidneys failed to adequately filter waste products from blood. According to the consultant, there were two main forms of renal failure. These were acute kidney injury, which could be reversed with adequate treatment, and chronic kidney disease, which may not be reversed. The hospital, however, needed more time to establish which of the two cases applied to Richard. Further tests conducted on the fifth day, however, pointed to the second case of the renal failure – chronic kidney disease. It was discovered that he naturally had only one kidney which had become grossly defective such that a kidney transplant was urgently required. Without it, according to the consultant, he might be spending his last few days alive.

This was a massive problem, as organ donation was not common in Africa in those days. Flying him abroad was out of the question as he still had to travel with a donor – someone with two perfectly functioning kidneys. It was a huge impediment. Even with the very huge financial compensation promised by his company, no donors came forward. His true medical situation was initially kept from his mother. But when all efforts to find a donor had failed, the truth of the matter had to be revealed to her. However, much as she was willing to donate to her son, she had only one kidney. She even appealed to the hospital to allow her to donate her only kidney, but she was told that hospitals would never kill her to save her son. That evening, she contacted all her relatives and narrated her ordeal, but no one was ready to donate their kidney.

Richard was still in hospital after two weeks, frail and pale. The news had travelled around the city, and his friends spent plenty of time with him at the hospital. But none of them came forward to donate. Instead, they jointly placed an advert on both print and electronic media, promising a very handsome financial reward for a potential donor. But nobody came forward.

One particular morning, as his friends and mother's relatives assembled around him, Richard called his friends' names one after the other and sluggishly spoke, 'Friends, I find it extremely difficult to believe that none of you has made an attempt to spare me a kidney that I may live. That's alright. I know that I don't have much time left with you. But may I make a request please? Can you all promise to look after my mother when I'm gone? Although I am leaving enough for her to live on, please ensure that she is not lonely and ....'

'No, Richard! You're not going to die. You shall not die but live to declare the goodness of the Lord in the land of the living. I'm here to donate my kidney,' interrupted Andrew who burst into the room with Pastor Isaac. Everyone was startled. No one knew how he had found out about Richard's situation. Unknown to Richard and his mother, Pastor Isaac had an informant among Richard's domestic workers. His name was Enoch. Enoch, a committed Christian, was one of the people that saw Andrew prostrate before his son on the morning of Mrs Menakor's birthday. His heart had become heavy and he had rigorously fought back tears. And when the pastor and his entourage were about to leave, Enoch secretly slipped a note into the pastor's hand:

'My name is Enoch, and a child of God by His grace. The address of this house is as follows: 23C Sekou Toure Avenue, GRA, Monrovia. If you need me to do anything to help, I will be more than ready to do it. And if you provide me with a phone number or contact address I will keep up communication with you.'

There was a graveyard silence as Andrew and Pastor walked over to Richard. And as the pastor spoke, everyone stared at him in awe, 'Good morning everyone. Friends and well-wishers, Elder Andrew is here to prove that he still loves his only child. He's also here to demonstrate Christ's love which death or threat of it cannot overcome. Now instead of wondering how we got to know about this matter I think the most important thing now is to introduce us to the doctors-in-charge so the transplant process may commence; we've got no time to waste.' Mrs Menakor, Donaldson and Gabriel then rose and led Pastor Isaac and Andrew to the office of head of nephrology. And after some administrative procedures, a bed was allocated to Andrew in the same ward.

The tests conducted on Andrew revealed that, although he had two kidneys, only one of them was in perfect condition. The state of the other kidney implied that he would need kidney treatment with regular check-ups after the transplant. The head of nephrology had invited him together with Pastor Isaac and Mrs Menakor to his office where he explained to them. 'If the donor wants to go ahead he has to append his signature to a statement in this form,' he said. Andrew collected the form, read through it and appended his signature without hesitation. There was another portion to be signed by his next-of-kin. The doctor looked at the pastor and asked, 'Sir, are you his next-of-kin? You need to sign this portion too.'

'No, doctor,' the pastor replied. 'His wife is here. She is his next-of-kin. Please, pass the form to her,' he added.

Mrs Menakor looked at the pastor and then her husband, and tears began to roll down her cheeks as she collected the paper.

'Madam, that's alright. You've got nothing to fear. Everything will be done perfectly,' said the doctor who misconstrued her emotion.

After the pre-surgery formalities, Mrs Menakor took Pastor Isaac and Andrew to a private room which was adjacent to the waiting room. There, she knelt down before Andrew and held his legs as she pleaded, 'Pastor, please help beg Andrew to forgive me. Andrew, I'm so sorry.' But Andrew got hold of her arms and lifted her on her feet. As both of them broke down in tears, Andrew said, 'Leah, I'm supposed to apologise to you and Richard. None of you has offended me in any way.' And while the couple embraced in tears, the pastor quietly left the room. He was later seen in the waiting room flipping through a medical journal. The two of them approached him and asked in unison:

'Why did you leave us alone in the room, pastor?'

'Oh, Mr and Mrs Menakor, I'm so sorry. But my parents have taught me that I should always leave whenever emotion and passion flow between two lovers.' The couple laughed hysterically at the joke. But all of a sudden, the woman knelt down while the man prostrated before the pastor.

'Sir,' beginning Andrew, 'I want to apologise on behalf of myself, my wife and son for the embarrassment and ordeal we had subjected you to.'

'What embarrassment? What ordeal?' the pastor asked. 'C'mon rise and let's give all praise and glory to God who has turned an unpleasant situation to a means by which His name must be glorified,' he added.

Andrew and his son were placed in the same room. That was at the request of the family. And at night, when all relatives and friends had left, Richard muttered, 'Dad, I never imagined that you would be the one to save my life. I have sinned against God and against you. Maybe what I'm currently passing through is because of my terrible transgression. Dad, please forgive me and pray for me.'

'Richard my child,' began Andrew, 'you don't have any blame whatsoever – I caused the whole problem. As for praying for you, sure, I do that every day. But there is one thing that is more important for now. Although we know that God can bring us out of this place safely, we still must consider the possibility He might want to use this circumstance to call us home. As for me, I have nothing to fear about death. My mansion is secured in heaven and is continually tended by angels in anticipation of my glorious arrival. I never looked back ever since I gave my life to the Lord. I have worked prolifically in His vineyard with great passion for perishing souls. But your own case is different. I was told of your zeal and passion for the things of God when you were very young and how you later pitched your tent with haters of God. You allowed the enemy to blindfold you. But God is a farmer who allows us free harvest from His farm. Yes, we all reap free harvest of mercy every moment of our lives. Tonight, you have another round of harvest placed before you and it's up to you to receive or refuse it. Listen to the Word of God in the book of Deuteronomy chapter thirty and verse nineteen, *'This day I call the heavens and the earth as witnesses against you that I have set before you life and death, blessing and curses. Now choose life, so that you and your children may live.'*

Again, listen to the Word of God for backsliders in the book of Jeremiah chapter three and verse twenty-two, *'Return faithless people; I will cure you of backsliding.'* Listen to the response of the backsliders in the same verse, *'Yes, we will come to you, for you are the Lord our God.'* Richard, are you ready to say the same? Are you ready to return to the Lord your God now? Weeping profusely, Richard was led back to Jesus.

CHAPTER 10: WHAT SHALL IT PROFIT A MAN?

The Lord really demonstrated His power, and both nephrectomy and transplant went without any hitch. Initially, there were symptoms of side effects from the immunosuppressant, but they miraculously fizzled out. The patients' recoveries had amazed the surgeons. The Lord totally removed all post-operation pains or complications so that within a few days Andrew had resumed his normal activities. As for Richard, he was discharged after three weeks, though he had to keep once-a-week appointments for three months. Amazingly, resumption of full activities, which should take up to twelve months, only took five months. The new organ, against all odds, started working immediately! Before the operation, Pastor Isaac had arranged seven-days of fasting and prayer among his prayer team. The team was moved to Richard's home in Monrovia where they were joined by Mrs Menakor. It was during the seven-day programme that the Lord revealed that the enemy had planned to use the ailment to take Richard away. But He had glorified Himself by giving His children victory – victory over sin and death. Hallelujah!

Mrs Menakor wasn't aware that Richard had rededicated his life to Christ, and so was stunned when he asked one of his domestic workers to buy him a copy of the Bible. That was a week after the operation while he was still recuperating. Mrs Menakor looked at her husband in astonishment. Andrew smiled and nodded repeatedly, a gesture that could mean, 'Yes, he's back to the Lord. All glory to Him.' Mrs Menakor then fell on her knees. Lifting up her both hands, she began to sing praises unto the Lord with tears of joy rolling from her eyes. She was joined in her songs by her husband. Richard also mumbled along. The trio was later joined by Pastor Isaac and two members of the prayer team, who had been shuttling between the village and Monrovia. The three men joined in the praise and worship without bothering to exchange greetings. Two nurses who had come to carry out examinations on Andrew and Richard shrugged their shoulders and turned back. They would have to come back later.

The worship continued unabated for almost half an hour! The Spirit really moved, as He always does whenever and wherever His lordship is acknowledged and openly confessed. As they worshipped, one of the members of the prayer team who came with Pastor Isaac raised his hand. When they all stopped singing he told the pastor that the Holy Spirit had just dropped a scripture in his heart for Richard. It was Isaiah chapter forty-three and verse twenty-five. It read, '*I, even I, am the one that blots out your transgressions for my own sake, and will not remember your sins.'* Again, Richard burst into tears as he worshipped the Lord.

At that moment, the two nurses returned with a doctor. The three of them were surprised to see Richard weeping.

'What did you do to him?' the doctor asked. 'You should allow him to recover fully before discussing family problems,' the doctor concluded almost angrily.

'Doctor, no one has upset me,' replied Richard as he wiped his tears. 'I wept because of the enormous time I have wasted without God.'

'Wasted?' the doctor asked, surprised, 'Richard, I want you to realise that no amount of time spent on one's treatment or recuperation is a waste.' The doctor clearly hadn't got Richard's point. As the Christians looked at one another, Richard was first to laugh. The others joined him. The two nurses looked at each other. The doctor, though hugely embarrassed, put on a brave face, 'Can every visitor excuse us for a few moments,' he said, 'we need to examine the patients. And we shall no longer tolerate any act that will prevent our team from carrying out their responsibilities. We appreciate that this is a VIP ward, but we have a single rule for all our patients in this hospital.'

None of his friends knew about his new-found life throughout his stay at the hospital. The only thing they noticed was a Bible which was always placed beside his pillow. That wasn't really a clue, as it could belong to one of his parents. He had decided to keep everything secret from them until he was discharged. He really wanted to invite all of them to his home and have them preached to by Pastor Isaac. He always remembered the golden opportunity which his mother's birthday had afforded and how it had been spoiled. The meeting had to be reconvened! He would seize the opportunity to confess to his friends that he never doubted God's existence all those years; he deliberately hardened his heart to enjoy life to the fullest. He would tell them that it was total stupidity to think that life was better outside Christ. Life without Christ was make-believe; it was a life embroiled in the sweet enticements of the devil. But any gifts offered by the devil must eventually be paid for. Nobody ever won when they served the devil, and nobody ever lost on the side of the omnipotent God. He would tell them that in Jesus Christ was life and the everlasting life. In Him were righteousness, peace and eternal joy. He rehearsed his speech almost every day while in his sickbed. If they accepted Jesus Christ, they would still be friends. Otherwise, he would only be their friend from a distance, not living as they did. As a church boy many years ago, he had recited the whole of first chapter of the book of Psalms at one of the church's special events, to the admiration of the congregation. He still remembered the first two verses, in the old-fashioned version they had used then, '*Blessed is the man that walketh not in the counsel of the ungodly, nor standeth in the way of sinners, nor sitteth in the seat of the scornful. But his delight is in the law of the Lord; and in His law doth he meditate day and night.*' That settled it, he concluded.

The meeting was scheduled for the Saturday which preceded Richard's long-awaited return to work. He had invited all his friends to celebrate his total recovery. The meeting, which began with wining and dining, had Pastor Isaac, Mr and Mrs Menakor and a member of the village church in attendance.

After everyone had finished eating, Pastor Isaac rose and said a brief prayer. He then reminded his listeners of the scuttled birthday sermon, adding that it was God's plan that they gathered again despite the devices of the enemy. He added that the Lord had an unequivocal interest in the lives of the young men. That was the reason He had given them another opportunity to listen to Him. But it wasn't enough to listen to Him – they had to allow the Spirit of God a chance in their lives. Quoting from the Bible, he asked, 'What shall it profit a man if he should gain the whole world and lose his soul? Or, what shall a man give in exchange of his soul?' He also explained that man, in his wickedness and ungratefulness, was using the free gifts of God without worshipping God. These free gifts included life, free will and intellect. Instead of man using the gifts to honour his Maker he decided to use them only for himself.

The pastor revealed that the botched birthday sermon was specifically arranged to preach Jesus Christ to them because, as a group of blessed young men, it was very important for them to know the source of their blessings. It wasn't because of what they did but what Christ did, that they were blessed. He was the one who lifted up, and if one proved haughty He could bring them down. Quoting from the book of Ecclesiastes, he said, 'Don't let the excitement of youth cause you to forget your Creator. Honour Him in your youth before you grow old and say, "Life is not pleasant anymore."' With a grimace, Donaldson turned to John, who was sitting next to him, and whispered something into his ears. John then made an eye contact with every member of the group, except Richard. And every one of them, except Silvestre, subsequently made a grimace or pouted their mouth. Pastor Isaac paused and looked around.

Continuing, he said that the greatest idiot on earth was the person who denied the existence of God and His Son Jesus. Unfortunately, education or material possessions had blocked many people's God-given sense of reasoning. The poor claimed that their financial situation prevented them from serving the Lord while the privileged attributed their status to their ability. The problem with man was that he always looked for reasons to hate God or deny His power. But believing in Him or not believing in Him didn't change anything about Him. Whatever He asked man to do was for man's own good. He so loved the world that He gave His only begotten Son.

The pastor then asked, 'How many of you guys can release your son to die in place of your enemy?' And after pausing for a while, he continued, 'When it came to donating your organ to your friend to save his life, you all remember what happened. It wasn't your fault that you didn't come forward; it's because man's love is finite and conditional whereas God's love is infinite and unconditional. Some of you may be citing appalling or terrible circumstances as evidence against God's existence. But do those evidences change anything about God? No! The only thing they do is move you closer and closer to the lake of fire! And I like to stress that anyone who denies the lordship of God through His Son Jesus Christ is already in fire; it doesn't matter if they wine and dine with the kings of the earth. All of you young men sitting before me here today are basking in immeasurable grace of God. Please, don't attribute your success to your ingenuity. Lots of people are out there who are more brilliant and educated but with nothing to show for their ingenuity. There is nothing any man has that he didn't receive from God. Do you appreciate Him and give Him the glory? Young men, it will interest you to know that your friend – Richard – has rededicated his life to Christ about three weeks ago. He's now a child of God. And, as an interlude, I will like him to rise and speak to you all.'

Richard's friends looked at one another in shock and then at him. 'Richard? This can't be true,' they seemed to say. And, as he rose and made a very low bow, they all gave him a long look.

Richard began by thanking the pastor. He then thanked his father for helping him to retrace his steps. He also thanked his mother for being there for him, both physically and spiritually. Lastly, he thanked his friends for their companionship and the exciting moments they had shared together. He then began by narrating his early childhood story, including how he grew up in the church serving the Lord. He went on to reveal the strange dreams of heaven and hell he had at the age of twelve and another one in which an unknown man warned him about his lifestyle when he was at the university. He had kept those dreams to himself, even though he was continually haunted by them. But the most frightening was the one he had in his sickbed, three weeks ago, in which a fearful-looking man was pulling him away by a long metal chain tied around his neck. That was the same day he was led back to Christ by his father. Calling his friends by their full names, he told them that it was the deceit of Satan not to believe in existence of God. The devil stole peace and joy, destroyed destiny and killed the individual! But the good news was that the Son of God had come to give life in abundance.

He told them that being young and living a life of affluence wasn't an indication that they had everything, as the life of a man didn't consist in the abundance of what he had. He added that life without Christ was already in crisis. Any blessings given by God must be used to glorify Him by acknowledging Him and keeping His ordinances.

Turning to Donaldson, he said, 'Donny, you're the most brilliant among us. I have reached this conclusion because, while we all had parents to lean on as we climbed the ladder of success you had none. And while we had parents who did our thinking for us you did yours all alone. Although He loves all of us, to some of us he reveals his love in a special way. If we have no one else to care, God loves and cares for us. I want to urge you to give your life to Jesus the Son of God and allow Him to rule over you. That is the only way we can have the real peace and joy here on earth. And whenever we die we can be sure of a place of rest with Him. Thank you.'

Richard's speech was followed by perfect silence. The speech was loaded with emotion and surprises. 'Jack has become a preacher,' they all seemed to say. Here was someone who dated many ladies at a time, drank like an old sailor and smoked like old Indian locomotive. And here was someone who always claimed to be the most gregarious among them! The world was full of wonders. Donaldson sat glued to his seat. He was lost in thought and seemed to be oblivious of things around him. He held his forehead in his left hand and wineglass in his right. But his palm suddenly gave way and the wine glass fell off. 'Oh, I'm so sorry,' he said. Richard called a lady worker to clean the floor and offered his friend another glass. Although he collected the new glass, he never had it filled with wine. None of them had any more to drink after the speech.

After studying their countenances for some moments, the pastor rose again and asked, 'Is there anyone here who has decided to give his life to Jesus Christ? Let him raise his hand.' There was another round of graveyard silence as everyone looked around to see if someone else had raised his. 'This is not supposed be a collective decision,' the pastor added. 'Salvation matter is personal, and please don't wait until someone else raises their hand before you raise yours.' His words had an effect! Silvestre Abrahams didn't only raise his hand; he rose and walked across the large living room. And, standing before the pastor, he said, 'Pastor, if you're sure Jesus can still accept me I am ready to give my life to Him.' If Richard's speech was a surprise, Silvestre's decision and his corresponding attitude were more than that. A military heart melted before Jesus! It was, obviously, something out of this world.

'May I know your name sir?' asked Pastor Isaac.

'I am Silvestre – Lieutenant-General Silvestre Abrahams.'

Turning to the rest of the group, the pastor said, 'Is there anyone who will like to join General Abrahams here before we begin to pray? Please, make up your mind quickly. Do not defer your salvation. The Lord Jesus is here this hour!' After repeating the appeal twice without anyone else coming forward, the pastor prayed with Silvestre. He turned to the rest again and told them that they could still make up their minds. And if they did, they should contact him through Richard. Before Silvestre went back to his seat, Richard rose and walked over to him. He shook his hand rigorously for some moments before giving him a long hug. 'Welcome to the Lord's side,' he whispered in his ears as they hugged.

Donaldson couldn't sleep that night. As he relaxed on the sofa, he kept wondering why everyone was turning into a religious maniac. The incredible aspect of it was, this cancer was now eating up the minds of highly educated professionals like Silvestre. And, like a numskull, Richard had buttressed his religious conviction with dreams! Dreams? One didn't need a degree in psychology to know that dreams were merely activities of the subconscious mind. If you thought about a matter for too long there was tendency for such matter to take root in your subconscious mind when you slept. Sure, if you allowed religious bigots to stuff your mind you probably will dream about heaven and hell!

His two friends had joined the team of gullible followers of that dead-and-buried, attention-seeker of the Roman era called Jesus. And the pastor too was trying to spread his dragnet towards the rest of them! What did he take him for? Another fool? He was only just able to restrain himself from being rude to the elderly man – but he better not try to preach at him again!

Samantha woke up in the bedroom and noticed that her husband wasn't in bed with her. She looked at the wall clock. It was a quarter past eleven. She rose and walked over to the living room. He didn't even see her standing behind his sofa and was visibly startled when she spoke.

'Darling, what are you thinking about?' she asked.

'Jesus,' he snapped a reply.

'What about Jesus?' she asked.

'Why do some people think it's normal to pester others with their beliefs?' he asked almost angrily.

'Calm down, honey. Please, tell me precisely what happened.'

He then narrated the events at Richard's home that afternoon, including Silvestre's conversion. Although Samantha was elated, she was able to conceal her emotion. 'Darling, that's alright,' she said. 'Don't allow that to spoil your bright working week ahead. Whatever anybody said to you in the afternoon was just a piece of advice. And advice, unlike a decree, is not enforced. It is either taken or refused. Once you have refused their advice you shouldn't allow that to affect you mentally. Come on, let's go in and sleep.' Donaldson was relieved. Samantha always had soothing words for him. Her words were always like chilled water obtained after hours of deathly thirst. He rose from the sofa, grabbed her by the waist and they were locked in a long kiss.

Three people were conspicuously missing at the clubhouse the following weekend, two of whom were Richard and Silvestre. The duo had decided to stop going to the clubhouse after their conversion. Pastor Isaac had told them to avoid gatherings where Jesus Christ wasn't honoured. Much as there was nothing wrong in exchanging visits with their friends, it was spiritually wrong to be engaged in their merry-making; for sins like adultery, fornications, lies, idle talks, pride and drunkenness couldn't be separated from their former gatherings.

The pastor was spot on. The two men remembered those scantily dressed women who always crowded over them at the clubhouse. They also remembered the immoral activities that rent the air when the lights were dimmed. At one time or the other, women had been paid to dance nude. Oh gosh! They remembered those horrible events with disdain.

Richard remembered those nights when, after he had decided to sleep alone, he would suddenly wake up after midnight with a great urge for women. He would pick his car, head to one of the nearby brothels and bring a prostitute home. 'Lord, I thank you for saving me from that way of life,' he muttered.

The third person that wasn't present at the clubhouse was Gabriel Beyan (Lexicon). Although he didn't come out to accept Jesus Christ, the seed of salvation had been sown in his life. He was really caught between conviction and confusion. However, everyone in the group had a closest pal, and his closest pal was Silvestre. He knew Silvestre inside out. He knew him not only as a brilliant university mate and fine soldier, but as an intelligent individual who believed in testing hypotheses before making vital decisions. Therefore, for him to have decided for Jesus, he believed that Silvestre must have come out with a convincing reason to reject the alternative. And that evening, as his friends were at the clubhouse sipping their beer, he sat alone in his chamber office ruminating over the Jesus matter. He loved to stay late at his chamber to have uninterrupted meditation.

But as he was lost in thought that evening, he suddenly became aware that someone was in the reception area. It couldn't have been his secretary or any of his other staff, as they all left the office almost two hours earlier. Was it a mere imagination? But he heard footsteps!

'Who's there?' he yelled.

'Good evening sir,' a male voice responded.

'What can I do for you, and how did you come in?' he asked as he came out of his office.

'We are sorry sir,' began the man, 'I'm Dr Samson Song and here's my wife – Cynthia. Coming from our midweek Christian fellowship, as we drove along the street, the Spirit of God instructed me to drop a tract with anyone found in this office. But as we came in through the open door we didn't see anyone here. We just heard your voice as we turned around to leave.' Gabriel was gobsmacked. 'Can I have the tract, please?' he managed to ask. The man opened his big preacher's Bible, brought out a white tract and handed it to Gabriel. And right in their presence, he regarded the caption in absolute bewilderment. *'Now is the accepted time; behold now is the day of salvation.'*

'Excuse me … did you say the Spirit of God asked you to give this to anyone found here?' he asked with a shaky voice.

'Yes sir.'

'Alright, thank you very much,' he said. But as the couple turned around to leave, the man added, 'Sir, I can perceive in my spirit that the message of the tract is specifically meant for you. If I'm right and you want us to pray together, here is my card.'

Gabriel collected the card and looked at it after they had left. It read, 'Dr Samson Song, Consultant Neurologist, University of Liberia Teaching Hospital.' Gabriel was surprised that such a medical guru also followed Jesus. He then retired to his office, highly perplexed. He was once again lost in thought. Some strangers had brought him a tract which precisely addressed his subject of meditation. What a coincidence! Perhaps it was a supernatural coincidence. Without deceiving himself any further, Gabriel knew that Jesus was really interested in him. He picked up his phone and rang Silvestre and Richard. That evening, heaven recorded yet another victory over the pit of hell!

CHAPTER 11: POWER TUSSLE IN LIBERIA

Rejoice, Africa.
For death's been ousted via a coup,
And his deathly power he has lost.
Hurrah, we must live forever!
Rejoice not, Africa.
For he's succeeded by greed,
Whose rule is just as deathly!

The nation of Liberia, which began as an American colony, came into being in the year 1822. It was because of the efforts of the American Colonisation Society to settle freed American slaves in West Africa. Liberia became independent in 1847 and became the first African republic. Up until 1980, the country was dominated by the small minority of descendants of the first black colonists, known collectively as Americo-Liberians. Liberia's first president, Joseph Jenkins Roberts, was born free on March 15, 1809 in Norfolk, Virginia, United States. He emigrated to Liberia in 1929 where he later became active in politics. He belonged to the Republican Party but contested the 1848 presidential election as an independent candidate. Roberts ruled from January 3, 1848 to January 7, 1856 and was succeeded by another Americo-Liberian, Stephen Allen Benson, who ruled until January 4, 1864.

The True Whig Party, however, won the election in January 7, 1878 and continued to dominate the political scene up till 1980, producing one president after another. Notable among them was William Tubman who ruled from January 3, 1944 until his death on July 23, 1971. Regarded as 'father of modern Liberia,' Tubman opened the door for massive foreign investments as a means of modernising the economy and infrastructure. During his regime, Liberia experienced a period of massive prosperity. He was succeeded immediately after his death by William R. Tolbert, Jr. However, the noble history of the country was rewritten in human blood on April 12, 1980, when Tolbert was assassinated in a bloody coup-de-tat. One of the plotters, Master-Sergeant Samuel Kanyon Doe, who later ruled as an executive president, became the chairman of the People's Redemption Council and de facto military head of state from April 12, 1980, having slaughtered many members of the True Whig Party. Doe suspended the constitution and ruled with military might until 1985 when he ordered an election, which he contested and won. On assumption of power, he sent other ethnic groups, including Americo-Liberians, to jail. On accusation of corruption, all the cabinet members of his predecessor were tried through a highly flawed legal process. The accused were neither allowed to be legally represented nor appeal to a higher court. All of them, but one, were eventually executed by firing squad.

On his first anniversary as a military dictator, Doe promised to return the country to civil rule as soon as possible. But four years after he had tasted power, like a fly which tasted the sweetness of palm wine, he made up his mind not to quit. Instead, he formed his own political party and ran for civilian presidency. As expected, the election was rigged in his favour. And when he appointed his cabinet members, they were mostly his tribesmen. The rigged election and abysmal level of corruption and nepotism informed the formation of a rebel group led by Charles Taylor. But soon after its formation, the rebel group split into factions with Prince Yormie Johnson heading a prominent one. The assault against Doe and his regime started in 1989. And on September 9, 1990, he was captured by Yormie Johnson's group and taken to a solitary place where he was subjected to excruciating tortures before he was killed. But that wasn't the end of the trouble, it was the beginning of one of the world's worst ever genocides. Instead of Doe's death ushering in peace and tranquillity, the nation was plunged into political imbroglio which resulted in a terrible tribal war, as leaders of all the notable rebel factions were desperate to rule. And between the years 1989 and 1998, the country had witnessed the most atrocious civil war in Africa.

A few days after Samuel Doe was captured and killed, there was a prophecy about the cloud that was about to engulf the nation. At the village church, the prophecy came through Pastor Isaac during the bi-monthly convention of the church. The Lord had spoken about the impending impasse and its attendant genocides. He wanted His people to get closer to Him in prayer and holiness. Those who relied on His saving grace would never be disappointed, He had assured. And after the prophecy the pastor spoke, 'Brethren, we are bracing up for a situation where many homes and churches may be destroyed, children orphaned, and spouses separated. Many of us will be wondering why God didn't intervene and stop the impending doom. The answer is in the book of Proverbs chapter fourteen and verse thirty-four. The Word of God says righteousness exalts a nation, but sin is a reproach to all people. The Bible also says that the wages of sin is death. Although the calamity is not God's doing, He allows it so He may glorify Himself in the lives of those who fear Him. According to the book of Genesis, when He destroyed the earth He still chose to save a handful of people – Noah and his family members. When He burned down Sodom and Gomorra he saved Lot and his family members, except Lot's wife who disobeyed. Although in the impending war, tens of thousands shall lose their lives, many unbelievers shall still have opportunity to come to the Lord. But the big question is: how many of us will still be able to say that God is good and merciful despite the loss of their loved ones? How many of us will still come here and worship with us? How many of us will encourage themselves that their loved ones have gone home to be with the Lord? The writer of the book of Second Thessalonians says we should *'encourage one another with these words.'*

'Despite the prophecy, we shouldn't be discouraged from praying for the peace of the nation at all times. God is still able to avert the crisis or shorten its length because of His beloved. The Bible says we should pray for the peace of Jerusalem. This country is our Jerusalem, so we must pray for its peace. Beloved, this is the time we need one another more than before. Let us live as a true body of Christ that we are. Economy and commercial activities will soon be hit very hard while money will disappear from circulation so that only few people will be able to eat. A time will come too, when armed robbers will invade homes and farms. Hunger, starvation, hyperinflation, malnutrition, desperation, rape, murder, robbery and epidemics are some of the attributes of civil war. These are weapons of Satan against nations that disregard God. But as children of God, we must share the little we have with our brethren and never renege in our responsibility to stand in the gap to pray for our country. God's Word says that God has not given us the spirit of fear, but of love and of power and of sound mind. Let's also remember that for us, to live is Christ and to die is gain. We shouldn't forget that our Father cares about us. We shouldn't allow the enemy to make us doubt His faithfulness. And at the end of the impending trial we will be able to pass through the gate of praise, come into His presence in His sanctuary and look joyfully upon his countenance and see the fullness of His grace.'

When Samuel Doe seized power in 1980, he retired lots of top military officers from the rank of captain and above. But, surprisingly, Silvestre was not only spared but got promoted twice within two years. And in 1989, a year before he gave his life to Jesus, he became a Lieutenant-General and garrison commander. One remarkable event, however, took place the year after. As he arrived in his garrison office one Monday morning, he received a call from the office of the president. The president would like to have a private talk with him that morning. He rose immediately, got into his chauffeur-driven, bullet-proof Mercedes with his aid-de-camp and headed for the presidential mansion. He was received at the reception of the sprawling mansion by the president's aid-de-camp, a colonel, who was already waiting at the reception some ten minutes before his arrival. After a brief exchange of military salutation, he was set to escort Silvestre and his aid-de-camp to the president's office. The walk wasn't a straight or short one. They had to walk a considerable distance within the mansion, turning the corners, negotiating the bends, alighting from elevator or escalator until they arrived at a large, sparkling corridor which led to the office. Security at the mansion was beefed up to an uncommon standard. It had to be, considering the rebellious activities going on within and without the government at that time. Besides, the advancement of Charles Taylor and his group towards Monrovia was a major threat. Hence, there were high-class security operatives at every entrance, corner, turning or corridor of the mansion. And at every facet of Silvestre's journey, different entry passes were issued by heavily-armed, stern-looking military officers who never forgot to give a military salute as soon as they sighted him and his entourage. Though walking with military rapidity, Silvestre never missed acknowledging any of those salutes.

He was received by the president's civilian protocol officer whose expansive office was adjacent to that of the president. The protocol officer was a very tall man in his late forties, and the president's tribesman. As Silvestre and his escort entered the room the man rose and offered him his hand, bowing at the same time. After exchanging pleasantries in vernacular, Silvestre was offered a seat. But he went to shake hands with all the people he met in the room before taking his seat. There were five people already seated in the lavishly decorated room which had the Liberian coat of arms and president Doe's large portrait hung on one of its walls. Each of the men in the room had an appointment with the president slated for that morning. Two of them were cabinet ministers while two were military officers from Economic Community of West African States' Monitoring Group (ECOMOG), a West African military contingent organised to monitor the crisis. The fifth person was a Lebanese multimillionaire businessman, Bilal Chagouri, a close pal of the president. After Silvestre had sat down, his escort stood at attention in front of him and gave military salute to signify his readiness to leave. Silvestre rose immediately and returned the salute before they rigorously shook each other's hand. Everyone in the room marvelled at the humility displayed by the young general.

Barely three minutes after he had taken his seat the protocol officer went to him and whispered that all the other people in the room were there to submit some confidential documents to the president and would not stay long. About five minutes later, one of the phones on the officer's table rang. It was an intercom. And after the protocol officer had had a brief conversation with the caller, he gestured to the ECOMOG officers to proceed to the office of the president's Chief Security Officer for onward journey to the president's office. It was a very cumbersome process to see the president. The administrative bottleneck at the mansion was second to none.

After all the security checks to which visitors were subjected right from the entrance of the mansion to the reception, and from the reception to the office of the protocol officer, they still had one more hurdle to cross. Every visitor, new or old, must pass through the final check at the office of the president's Chief Security Officer, a Lieutenant Colonel, another of the president's tribesman. As a matter of fact, every one of the president's staff members, of high or low rank, was the president's tribesman. And they all communicated in their own tribal dialect, *kru*. Fortunately, Silvestre spoke this dialect fluently, even though he didn't belong to the tribe.

The ECOMOG officers returned after about ten minutes, signed off and bade everyone goodbye. Bilal Chagouri was next, but within five minutes he was back to sign off. After him were the two cabinet ministers. When it was Silvestre's turn, the president's ADC came back to fetch him. On arriving at the office of the president's Chief Security Officer, he was received with military accolades. Although it was his first time at the mansion, Silvestre was well-known among all officers as most of them had one time or the other attended the training sessions he had given for them. As he acknowledged their salutes he still had time to crack a few jokes. He prompted laughter among the staff when he asked one pot-bellied officer, 'Major, last time we met you weren't pregnant. How old is your pregnancy?'

He was received with a broad smile and warm handshake by the president. The president's sprawling office had within it a large conference room and a leisure room which contained a beautiful suite of sofas and an exquisite dinning set. The conference room contained expensive conference chairs and a massive round table. On the table was placed a few flower vases, each holding a small Liberian national flag.

Silvestre was ushered into the leisure room. Gesturing to him to have a seat, the president himself took a seat directly opposite and asked, 'General Abrahams, what can I offer you? I've got all sorts of African and foreign drinks in that fridge and there is also a professional wine-mixer here too.' And before Silvestre could say 'no thanks,' a man in white party suit with white shirt and black bow tie to match, came in and bowed very low before the president. 'General, please don't hesitate to tell him your choice. He knows mine already,' said the president. Looking at the man, Silvestre said, 'Please, can I have some fruit juice?' The president was flabbergasted. And he waited until the mixer completely vacated the room before he began to explain the reason for inviting his guest. He started by asking if he fancied being the next Chief of Military Staff. And before Silvestre could say a word he added, 'You see, General Abrahams, most of the people around me are traitors. I have been having a series of negative security reports about the current CMS. It's very hard to believe that the people I have helped to attain military or political heights are the same that stab me in the back. For the past few years I have put you under surveillance. But I've never heard of your meeting with my enemies or any of those hypocrites. You're not one of those sycophants that litter our barracks and political terrain. You know what I mean – those professional bootlickers. I have found you to be a soldier of unique professionalism. You are well-liked and respected by mates, juniors and officers of higher ranks. That explains why I put you under surveillance in case you intended to use your popularity to do something funny.'

The president paused for a while, cleared his throat and continued, 'Before you answer my first question I want to add one more. The second question is, are you on my side? If you are on my side, what can we do to thwart all these rebellions? And if you are not, what can I do to have you on my side? I don't want the questions answered today. I want you to go home and think about them and then come back here next week.'

Despite his relatively low level of formal education, President Doe was astute. He was a very clever speaker who knew how to put words in people's mouth. When you engaged him in a dialogue your brain must be at the highest point of its efficiency. Otherwise, you would leave the venue wondering if you had not dug your own grave. He was like the proverbial devil. Anyone invited to share a drink with him must use a very long straw. 'The devil has no permanent friends. As you drink with him he might suddenly lose his temper and pounce on you. But, since you have a long straw which enables you to drink from afar, you have a chance of bolting before being attacked.' That was the analysis that was going on in Silvestre's head as he listened with rapt attention to the president and commander-in-chief of the Liberian armed forces.

The first person Silvestre spoke to, apart from his wife, was Richard.

'What do you intend to say to him next week?' asked Richard.

'What do I intend to say? Had he not suggested next week I would have given him my answer right away. My service is unto my country and not an individual. I do not belong to any side. But, as my commander-in-chief, I only have an option if given an assignment which I'm not willing to do. For instance, unlike some of my colleagues, I can't be used to terrorise innocent civilians. Neither can I be used as a member of any kangaroo military tribunal to court-martial innocent officers. Never! But that doesn't mean I will team up with his opponents. The only option I have is resignation.'

Despite his usual stance on religion, Richard opined that the matter be discussed with Pastor Isaac for counselling and prayer. To Richard, a blood-thirsty boss like Doe might not be satisfied with a resignation; it was obvious how far he could go to rid himself of any perceived opposition.

Fortunately, the following Sunday was the bi-monthly convention of the church. Although the three converts – Richard, Silvestre and Gabriel – attended a Monrovia church, they never missed the bi-monthly conventions of the village church. The three men had cooperated to give the church auditorium a modern look and furnish it with sophisticated equipment. They also bought a luxurious bus for the church and a beautiful car for the pastor. After all, the Bible says a labourer is worthy of his wages. Those who preach the gospel should be allowed to make a living from the gospel if that living is neither solicited nor ill-gotten.

Richard, Gabriel and Silvestre met with Pastor Isaac at the vicarage after the bi-monthly service. Deacon Andrew and his wife were also present. They had long since returned to the village after Richard's recovery from the kidney transplant. Their son had renovated their village home to Monrovian standards and bought a Mercedes for his father, in addition to the one he presented to his mother on her fiftieth birthday. After they had been treated to a lunch of rice with chicken stew, Silvestre began to narrate his meeting with the president.

After the pastor had prayed a brief prayer, he began by thanking Silvestre for the confidence reposed in him and the others. He added, 'You see, Brother Silvestre, our God is so merciful He never wants any sinner to die but come to repentance. God wants the president to receive His free offer of salvation. He has ordained that he listens to the Word of God, and it's you that He has decided to use. When God wanted to use Moses to lead His people out of Egypt He exalted him before Pharaoh. He also exalted Elijah before King Ahab. God has exalted you before the president. This is evident by the fact that, rather than been retired like many of your colleagues, you keep on reaping more and more promotions. Not only that – He has filled the heart of every officer with your love and respect. And rather than seeing you as a threat, the president has chosen to ally with you. Brother Silvestre, you must confront him with the truth about his administration and then preach the gospel to Him. Don't be worried about how to present this. The Lord said He will fill our mouth with words. He surely will fill your mouth with words and your heart, the abundance of boldness you need for the task. I want to assure you that while you are having a meeting with him tomorrow the prayer team will be on their knees interceding.'

Silvestre met with the president the following morning. After exchanging pleasantries, the president went straight to the business by requesting answers to his last questions.

'Your Excellency,' began Silvestre, 'as a trained officer of the Liberian army, my service is unto the Federal Republic of Liberia and not to an individual. However, as executive president of this nation and commander-in-chief of the Liberian army, you always have my loyalty and respect. Sir, as much as I will never side with any rebels against you or your administration, I will like to be left to concentrate on my military career and not be dragged into politics. Regarding the Chief of Military Staff appointment, I want to thank you for your great trust. I, however, regret to inform you that I'm not able to accept the appointment. In this heightened climate of political stalemate and military disintegration, there is little or nothing a CMS can offer the military or this country at large.' Silvestre paused at this juncture to clear his throat. Looking the president in the eye, he noticed that he rhythmically struck his upper tooth with a gold pen in his hand. That was his usual posture whenever he was perplexed.

'May I ask you a question, sir?' asked Silvestre. 'Of course,' replied the president nonchalantly. Continuing, he said, 'Sir, I know that you are a Christian by birth and I know that you were born into Baptist denomination, but my question is do you still believe in God? Do you believe in His Son Jesus Christ? Do you believe in heaven and hell?' The president remained silent. After waiting for some moments, the president pulled a face, and replied, 'Well, I believe in God and Jesus Christ. I also believe that there is heaven. As for hell, I believe it only exists in the dilapidated mind of scaremongers.'

'Sir, do you believe in the Bible as the words of God?'

'Yes.'

'Good,' said Silvestre, 'Now have you ever read chapter sixteen of the book of Luke and chapter twenty of the book of Revelation? In chapter sixteen of Luke, Jesus talks about a rich man and an impecunious Lazarus. When both of them died, according to Jesus, Lazarus went to Abraham's bosom while the rich man went to hell. Jesus Christ Himself confirms in that story that hell does exist. In chapter twenty and verse fifteen of Revelation, however, we learn that those whose names were not written in the book of life were thrown into the lake of fire.'

'Lots of innocent blood has been shed in this country, sir. I quite believe that your ascension to the highest administration in this country was God's doing. But since the day you came to power blood has never ceased to flow in this land. God wants you to repent of all evil and give your life to Him. Please allow peace to reign at any cost, even if you have to sacrifice your office. The Bible says, 'Seek peace and pursue it ...'

'Excuse me, General Abrahams!' the president cut in angrily. 'Enough of this nonsense!' he barked. 'Are you a soldier or a priest?' Silvestre remained calm, looking the president in the eye. But the president fumed, 'You haven't answered my question! Are you a soldier or a priest?'

'I am a soldier, Your Excellency – a sanctified and regenerated soldier!' Silvestre replied.

'Whatever that means, Silvestre Abrahams, I want you out of here immediately, otherwise ...' barked the president who didn't have to complete his statement to be comprehended.

Silvestre rose immediately and stood at attention before him before making for the exit. And as he was about to close the door behind, he looked back and said, 'Your Excellency, I like to inform you that since I became a child of God more than a year ago I didn't spend a dime from the mysterious funds regularly credited to my bank account, including that of last week. I shared them among orphans and widows who are victims of your bloody administration. I have an up-to-date record of this. Good day sir.'

CHAPTER 12: DARKNESS EVERYWHERE!

One Sunday evening, as Silvestre was studying the twentieth chapter of the book of Luke, the Holy Spirit highlighted a particular verse. That was the twenty-third verse which reads, *'But he perceived their craftiness, and said unto them, why tempt ye me?'* Much as he desired to read on, the Holy Spirit kept referring to this verse and it kept ringing in his ears until he was totally stuck on it. He tried to figure out the message without any success. After he had prayed about it and the message remained incomprehensible, he retired to his room for a siesta. As he lay in bed he wondered if it was the Holy Spirit who highlighted the verse or if it was just a mere thought. He was confused. Just then his phone rang. It was one of his military guards who called to inform him of the presence of three top officers at the entrance. One of them was Lt General Silas Roberts, his close pal for many years. He was surprised by their unannounced visit. Although he hadn't got any reason to suspect Silas, he always adhered strictly to the military maxim – at the time of war trust your colleagues but at the time of anarchy only trust yourself. Although he had known the guy since their days at the Defence Academy, they had travelled together to the US for a further training, the only thing that was constant in life was change! A highly principled man of today might become an instrument of corruption and nepotism tomorrow. Human beings!

Though he didn't know the purpose of visit, he had to be at the top of his wits. If Silas had come alone, even unheralded as it was, it wouldn't have been a source of worry to him. But three top military officers paying an unannounced visit at that period of insecurity called for scrutiny. As he headed to the living room he took along a small object which he carefully hid in the flower vase on the centre table. The three officers were later ushered in by the guard. And as they met Silvestre in the living room, they all stood at attention. After exchanging military salutes, Silvestre shook their hands one after the other and offered them a seat. At that moment, his wife who had gone out with the kids came back home and exchanged pleasantries with her husband's guests. She then went to the bar and brought a bottle of aromatic schnapps and four wine glasses in a silver tray. Beaming, she placed the tray on the centre table and jokingly asked, 'What will my lords have for lunch?'

'Oh, thank you, madam. We are okay with the drink,' said the three in unison.

Mrs Abrahams didn't have to be told before vacating the living room as the top military officers sipped their drinks. As soon as she left, Silas cleared his throat and began, 'Silvestre, I know that you are very surprised to see us this evening. We have come here in connection with the present situation of our country. I have thought carefully about men to discuss this matter with and I could only come out with just three of you who are trustworthy, principled and highly patriotic. I first went to Josiah this morning. The two of us then went to Parker. When I mentioned your name to the two of them they both agreed that we needed you for a successful mission.' He paused briefly to have a sip. And as he held the glass to his mouth he looked in Silvestre's eyes above his eyeglasses. It was a clever way of deciphering the latter's mind before going ahead to hit the nail on the head. After returning the glass to the table, he cleared his throat once again and continued. 'As soldiers, we all signed an oath of allegiance to our country and not to an individual. We also vowed to give anything, including our lives, to protect it. But, unfortunately, we have reneged in our vow, leaving some greedy sons-of-bitches to ravage our nation and subject innocent citizens to untold anguish. Without mincing words, we all know that the main problem is the president. Remove Samuel Doe, then the problem is removed. However, to have him removed doesn't need to involve firing even a single shot – it is very easy for us since we all hold strategic positions in the military. And as soon as he's removed we can install a civilian interim government. That will convince the people that we don't have a selfish agenda. But that depends on our collective view. With Doe removed, all the rebelling factions could be invited to a round table talk to forge a new course to national reconciliation and political development. Colleagues, we must put an end to this bloodbath before it becomes uncontrollable.'

'There is no question of who is going to head the government among us as we have pencilled down three civilians to choose from as soon as Doe's regime is toppled,' added one of the other two guests.

'But considering General Abrahams' intellectual gift and his popularity within the military, we might prefer that he head the transitional government. But that depends on his view,' added the other.

As they all remained quiet waiting for Silvestre's response, he held his chin in his left hand as he meditated on the proposal. The men were right, he thought. As top officers who had the wherewithal to stop Doe, they truly had an obligation to save their country from his bloody fangs and usher in a true democracy. The process of removing Doe was truly simple as every noble-hearted soldier was already disenchanted with his governance. But wait a minute! He had promised the president not to team up against him. Wasn't it sinful to get involved in the mission after he had given the president his word? Was his posture not directly opposite to that of David when he was being pursued by King Saul? David had an opportunity to kill Saul, but he made up his mind not to lay his hand upon God's anointed. When Saul's time was up it was God Himself who took care of that. But He still used someone! There were no other people who could remove Doe and stop bloodshed in the land than the highly placed top officers like him and the three colleagues. But did God specifically instruct him to go ahead? Although he was a soldier, the Bible said that as many as were led by the Spirit were empowered to be children of God. No, he would not do anything without receiving a nod of approval from God.

Silvestre broke the long silence by asking the men to give him seventy-two hours to think about the mission. They shrugged. They were convinced that his decision would be positive. The main issue of the day was then suspended for that of the cancelled independence parade. It was generally believed that the parade was cancelled by the president for his personal security purposes and not to reflect the nation's mood as he wanted the nation to believe. They cracked a few jokes afterwards before they rose to leave. But as Silvestre rose to see them off, the Spirit of God reminded him of the Bible verse, '*But he perceived their craftiness, and said unto them, why tempt ye me?*' 'Oh, blessed Holy Spirit, I now get your point,' he said to himself. And being highly charged by the Spirit, he suddenly stopped the men and echoed the biblical phrase, 'Why tempt ye me?' The men looked at one another pretending they didn't understand what he was talking about. But he repeated the question in modern English, 'Why are you tempting me? And what have you got to gain from my destruction? What have I done to deserve this evil?'

Mrs Abraham, who was alerted by her husband's raised voice, came to the living room and stood with her husband while their guests stood at the other side of the living room, separated by the centre table. As the men continued to feign ignorance, Silvestre called in three of his armed guards and asked them to watch the exit. Turning to one of the officers, he said, 'Brigadier Parker, would you honourably bring out the recorder in the inner pocket of your jacket before I ask the boys to do it for you. And I warn every one of you not to do anything funny here, otherwise….' Without bothering to complete his statement he put his hand in one of his pockets and brought out a hand grenade. Placing a finger on its safety pin, he looked at his guards and barked, 'Search his jacket!' Turning to his wife, he said, 'Honey, take the children and vacate the house through the kitchen exit.' After she had left, he said, 'Now if anyone among you tries to be clever we shall all knock at the gate of heaven or hell in a jiffy!'

Since Brigadier Parker didn't want to be searched by subordinates, he quietly brought out a very small tape recorder and handed it over to one of the guards. Silvestre took it, rewound the tape and listened to the playback. 'Good,' he said. 'Now we can compare notes,' he added as he dipped his hand into the flower vase and brought out his well-hidden recorder. They all listened to the playback, leaving his guests more awe-stricken than gobsmacked. 'Nothing different,' he said. 'So, I keep the two,' he added tauntingly. Turning to General Silas, he said, 'Silas, you know you can be a CMS without having to rope your friend in a phantom coup?' Silas' mouth was agape. He couldn't just understand how he got to know about the ploy to make him the CMS. There were, in fact, lots of things he didn't understand. Among them was how he found out about Brigadier Parker's hidden tape. Who could his informant be? It could never be any of his two accomplices. And the plan to make him a CMS was strictly between him and the president. There were four people involved in all the arrangements; the president, himself and the two accomplices. Who was the traitor among the four of them?

By the beginning of 1990 President Doe was already holed up in the presidential mansion, with rebel factions gaining more and more control. It was the beginning of anarchy; the advent of liquid darkness of indeterminate viscosity engulfing a nation with, hitherto, nascent economic development. There were killings and robberies by members of the rebel factions all over the country, while the loyal group handpicked perceived traitors within the military for secret execution. Ever since his botched meeting with Silvestre, the president had made up his mind what to do about him. He was of the view that whoever that wasn't with him was against him; there was no sitting on the fence. There were two types of opponents, according to him: the conspicuous ones like Charles Taylor and Yormie Johnson, and the hidden ones like Silvestre Abrahams. More dangerous are the hidden ones, for they had access to your drawing board, logistics or game plans. They were like cobras under your bed. They, therefore, deserved to be ruthlessly dealt with.

As Silas stood motionlessly before Silvestre, his mind flashed back to the day the president invited him and expressed his desire to make him the next CMS. That was why he tried to ensnare Silvestre by roping him in a phantom coup, for which the penalty was death. He had told Silas that he couldn't afford to repeat his mistake of not getting rid of Taylor and Johnson when he had the chance of doing so. With the kind of popularity Silvestre enjoyed in the military, according to the president, it was obvious that his regime wouldn't last twenty-four hours if he decided to join one of the rebel groups. To him popularity, in whatever capacity, bred ambition. For instance, a popular member of parliament would dream of becoming prime minister, a popular vice president would think of being president. There were, however, two paths to fulfilling ambition: one of blood, the other of sweat. While diligent people worked hard to get to the top, the desperate or unscrupulous preferred the way of blood. Ambition, like a radioactive substance, had to be carefully harnessed. Unless harnessed it would become over-ambition which bred desperation. And a desperate man would take any path, including a bloody one. As the president philosophised that morning it was clear that he was making himself a point of reference.

Silas' mind suddenly returned to the reality that Silvestre had scuttled their plan! What was he going to tell the president? He had lost whatever trust the president had in him. Instead of being a clever tool, he would be a liability. He would not only lose the chance of claiming a coveted post, he would never be trusted for any others. He had lost his opportunity to be the president's right-hand man!

It was Silvestre who broke the long silence.

'General Silas Roberts, what are you thinking of? How I got to know about your hidden plan? Now listen to me: I don't have any mystical powers other than the power of the Holy Spirit. This evening, before you came here, He had revealed your intention to me. That was the smallest of what He does in the lives of true children of God. So many times I have implored you to give your life to Jesus Christ. But you prefer the lordship of Satan. The fact we are soldiers doesn't mean we should be evil. There are soldiers in the Bible who did righteously before God. Gideon was a typical example. With the current situation of our country, is it not insane to pursue personal gains?'

'Remember, the Bible says, 'What shall it profit a man if he shall gain the whole world and lose his soul?' We are already rich men. But we should still have feelings for those of our people who are poor and who have suffered most from the fighting. How can you rejoice in promotion or riches obtained through the blood of the innocent? Believe me, no one who sheds the blood of the innocent who will go unpunished by God. But the good news is that the blood of Jesus is there to cleanse every repentant sinner.'

'Since the blood of innocents is crying out for God's vengeance, I suggest you urgently need to run to Christ with sincere repentance. Silas, Jesus still loves you and your two accomplices. Drop the thought of evil and embrace the gospel of the Lord Jesus Christ now! But if you still want to hatch new plans against me you may go ahead. The Lord who overthrew this one is always there for me. But I hope you have a change of heart before it is too late. Good day.' And the three men walked out quietly with their heads bowed.

The following day, as Silvestre sat in his office, Silas came in without the normal protocol required to see a fellow officer. And without bothering to exchange formal or military pleasantries, he began, 'Silvestre, I have come to apologise. Please, find a place in your heart to forgive me. Could you please give me a call when you get home tonight? I need your help over certain matter. Thank you very much.' And he dashed out of the office without allowing Silvestre to say a word. About half an hour later, Silvestre receive a radio message from the office of the CMS asking if he had seen Silas' letter of resignation. He was gobsmacked. A few minutes later, an officer – a colonel – brought a file. It was given to his secretary at the outer office. The secretary took it in while the colonel waited outside. Silvestre opened the file and read through the brief letter twice. He then removed it from the file and asked the secretary to make a copy. The file, with the original letter in place, was then returned to the waiting colonel. When Silvestre was left alone in the office he held the copy of the letter and read it a third time.

General Officer Commanding
1st Mechanised Division,
Liberia Army,
Monrovia.

7th September 1990

To: The President, Commander-in-Chief of the Liberia Army
Through: The Chief of Military Staff
Through: The Chief of Army Staff

LETTER OF RESIGNATION

Dear Sir,

I hereby resign as GOC (1st Mechanised Division) and as an officer of the Liberia army, with immediate effect. Consequent upon lack of concessions among the warring parties, the masses whom I have sworn to protect are the ones at the receiving end, paying heavily with their blood every day. When I joined the Liberia army about twenty years ago I was happy to serve in an ever-growing, highly professionalised military. But the events which unfolded lately, coupled with ignoble tasks that I had to perform as an officer, have left a sour taste in my mouth. I still have the love of this nation burning in my heart. And if I have done anything in the past to suggest otherwise, the Lord will surely help me to make amends. I want to thank the hierarchy of the Liberia military for the opportunity given me to serve.

God bless our nation.

Yours faithfully,

Lt Gen Silas Roberts

Silvestre dropped the letter on his table, held his chin in his right hand and stared at the ceiling. He was perplexed. Had Silas contacted him earlier he would have advised him against resigning. To win a battle you must be part of it. You can't win a battle from without. However, there are battles for which you don't need firearms. Some are fought with intellect and others are spiritual. Nobody loses on the Lord's side and nobody wins on the devil's side. The first thing for Silas was to give his life to Jesus Christ. The Lord would then take charge from there. He asked him to give him a call later in the evening. What had he got to discuss with him? Perhaps he wanted to confess certain atrocities he had committed or to discuss his future plans. Whatever he wanted to discuss with him he must seize the opportunity to preach Jesus Christ to him extensively. Silas had quit the army! The army had lost a gem.

As requested, Silvestre gave Silas a call as soon as he arrived at home that night. But they didn't discuss matters on the phone as it was obvious that their phones were being tapped. They both realised that he was under surveillance as soon as he handed in his resignation letter that morning. They also realised that, while bugging could begin immediately that morning, process of stalking him would take a little longer. So they preferred to meet in person that night.

Silas arrived almost an hour after the telephone call and went straight to the purpose of his visit. He first revealed all the clandestine activities he had taken part in. He confirmed that the president was to make him the CMS on condition of successfully implicating Silvestre in a fake coup. But the main reason for his secret visit was to reveal the plan to assassinate Silvestre on the ninth day of the month, which was three days away. After thanking him for the revelation, Silvestre asked about his future plans. As he was Americo-Liberian, his immediate plan was to sneak out of the country with his family members. He would go to Dallas, where his grandparents came from. There he intended to commence a doctoral programme as he fancied a job as an academic.

'Silas, it is absolutely wrong to put the cart before the horse,' Silvestre quipped.

'How do you mean?' asked Silas.

'There is a step you should have taken before resigning.'

'And what is it?'

'It's nothing new, Silas. It's what I've been discussing with you all this while. It's about Jesus Christ. You see, you've definitely got to the stage in your life when accepting the lordship of Jesus Christ is more important than before. Jesus Christ is the way – the only way and not one of many ways. He's the way to earthly peace and heavenly abode. Maybe you didn't even have to resign your appointment if you had allowed him to order your steps. You will never realise what you are missing until you accept him. Did you notice that I wasn't stirred by the news of my impending assassination? Well, it is because of my firm belief in the words of God. Excuse me, let me show you something.'

Silvestre went into his bedroom and brought a copy of the Bible. He then sat close to his friend on the sofa and read the first five verses of the second Psalm.

'Why do the heathen rage, and the people imagine a vain thing? The kings of the earth set themselves, and the rulers take counsel together, against the Lord, and against His anointed, saying, Let us break their bands asunder, and cast away their cords from us. He that sitteth in the heavens shall laugh: the Lord shall have them in derision. Then He shall speak unto them in His wrath, and vex them in his sore displeasure.'

He also quoted from the ninety-first Psalm, *'A thousand shall fall by my side but no evil shall come near my dwelling.'* But he was quick to add that, should the enemy succeed in taking his life, he would still have nothing to lose but lots to gain. For, to him, to die is gain. But there was one thing he was very sure of: if it was true that the enemy was planning his demise, an incident would take place on the same day that would convince Silas that God did really protect His own. He had got no precautionary measures than praying and burying his soul in the Word of God.

Silas was led to Christ that night. And it was emotional departure as he left around midnight. It was to be their last time together for many years, as he left for the US two days later. There wasn't any problem regarding travel documents since all his family members had dual

118

nationality. However, his major concern as he left the Liberian shore on 9th of September 1990 was the safety of his friend. Before they left for the airport that morning his family held a prayer for Silvestre. 'Lord Jesus, you have used Silvestre for the salvation of my soul and those of my family members. Now is the time to use my prayer for his protection from the impending attack on his life. Lord, let it work for him according to his faith in your unfailing love. Protect your son and save him from the evil plan of his enemies, in Jesus' name. Amen!' The prayer wasn't in vain. Later that day, Samuel Doe was lured to his death by his deceitful allies.

CHAPTER 13: DARKNESS LINGERS ON!

The death of Samuel Doe did not usher in peace and tranquillity. It rather compounded the war. If he left behind a stream of blood, that stream quickly became an ocean after his demise. The hostilities which began in 1989 raged on until 1997, when a new democratic regime was put in place. But before then, an estimate of five hundred thousand people had lost their lives in Liberia. Most of the country's businesses collapsed, as the economy zigzagged along the negative axis. It was a mixed feeling for Silas in the US when he learned about Doe's death. He was happy because, without Doe, the process of national reconciliation and true democracy could begin. But if he knew that Doe would be removed he wouldn't have resigned – he would have stayed on to try to right his wrongs. For instance, there were two officers he had roped into a false coup. They had been court-martialled, with both men awaiting execution as at the time he left for the US. Before he left Liberia, acting on Silvestre's advice, he had held a press conference where he confessed his roles in the phantom coup. He also issued a confessional statement with a copy sent to every Divisional Commander requesting that the innocent men be released. But as it turned out, all Silas and Silvestre's efforts were unnecessary, for God himself was at work. Immediately after the death of their captor, and without any legal proceedings, the two wrongly accused officers were released and reinstated. Silas' joy was complete!

The crisis before Doe's demise was only the tip of the iceberg. His death intensified the power tussle between Charles Taylor's National Patriotic Front and Yormie Johnson's breakaway Independent National Patriotic Front, with Doe's Krahn militants launching vindictive offensives on one part and the Liberian armed forces on the other. Between 1990 and 1996, the country witnessed the most horrendous events in its history. Murder, rape and looting were the order of the day. The period also witnessed the closure of virtually all foreign missions in the country. While the British embassy, which closed in 1991, was among those which left early, the United States embassy was one of the last to leave. When the British embassy closed, Samantha didn't return to Britain with her colleagues because of her marriage. Though jobless, she stayed behind with her Liberian husband, hoping to get a new job when the political tension subsided. But she found herself mistaken. Even with the interim national government in place, the hostilities still raged on like wild fire. With the help of the United Nations and the Economic Community of West African States, peace was eventually attained in 1996 and general elections, through which Charles Taylor became the president, were held in 1997. But Charles Taylor was widely believed to have coerced the population into electing him by threatening to resume hostilities if he lost. A second but more fiercely-fought civil war, however, broke out after two years of his assumption of power. It was terrible! Genocides were committed, with human corpses littering every street. Many wealthy individuals were kidnapped and killed.

One Monday morning, around May 2000, a group of heavily-armed militants fought their way into the well-fortified Central Bank of Liberia with the aim of looting the treasury. But they were unlucky, as another group of militants had earlier raided the bank and swept the treasury clean. The disappointed militants then kidnapped five top officials of the bank, including Donaldson, and took them away to an unknown destination, demanding a high ransom. Among the five men, only Donaldson could raise the ransom before the stipulated deadline, through his joint savings with his wife and assistance from friends. Lots of valuables, including cars, were also auctioned. The other officials, though able to pay part of the ransom, were shot dead right in Donaldson's presence. Of the whole ordeal, that was the one part Donaldson wished he could wipe from his mind.

But a fresh blow was waiting for him at home on the night he was released. Shortly before his arrival, bandits had broken in and taken all that was left in the home, including a box which contained miscellaneous documents. The leader of the gang had queried why the family of a rich banking executive had no cash in the house. When Samantha explained that they had just paid a huge ransom on her husband, the hoodlum replied, 'Oh I see – the only language you understand is abduction.' Then he grabbed her oldest daughter and made for the exit.

Samantha ran after him, grabbed one of his legs and knelt before him, pleading. The man paused and asked, 'White lady, why are you still in this country when others have left?'

With tears rolling down her cheeks, Samantha replied, 'Because I love this country and my husband. And I trust God to bring back His peace to my country. Sincerely, I believe things shall be alright for this beautiful country again. I believe…' She couldn't complete the statement as she fell on her face and fainted.

She woke up later and found herself laid on the sofa, surrounded by her husband and two of his friends. The trauma she had gone through during her husband's five-day abduction, coupled with the shock of the visiting bandits, had greatly affected her. 'Oh God, they have taken my daughter away! Oh, my daughter, my daughter…' she sobbed as she gently opened her eyes.

'No, darling, Natasha is here. They didn't take her away,' Donaldson replied as he brought Natasha forward. Samantha gave a deep sigh before drawing her daughter to herself.

The leader of the gang had been moved by her expression of optimism about the future of the country. He was greatly surprised that, while he and his gang had lost hope on the future of the country and had resorted to extinguishing whatever remained of its peace, there was a foreigner whose heart continued to bleed for the same country. He had lifted the unconscious Samantha onto the sofa and left.

'Darling, they have taken everything, including our documents and the only car left,' Samantha said as she fully regained consciousness.

'Yes, I know. But they didn't take our lives,' replied Donaldson.

The two incidents and the incessant attacks on the Central Bank of Liberia had prompted the couple to begin to think about leaving the country. Why shouldn't they? For many months before he was kidnapped, Donaldson had not received his salary. No worker at any sector of the economy had. Samantha had become a full-time house wife in 1991, when the embassy was closed. Now their savings were all gone. The children had not gone to school for many months. So, it was time to decide. Much as Samantha would have loved to return to Britain, none of her family members had a passport; hers had expired long ago without any way to renew it. They were at a total loss over what to do.

One Saturday morning, as they sat in the living room thinking of a way out, their home phone suddenly rang. It was Amanda calling from Britain. It had been a very long time since she spoke with Samantha. Due to the prevailing crisis, the phone service in Liberia was not reliable. Getting through that morning was nothing but a miracle. The two ladies were elated. After exchanging pleasantries, their conversation then took a serious turn. They talked about the perilous situation in Liberia, Donaldson's abduction and the sorry state of the couple's finances. Samantha also explained what was preventing their travel to Britain. Amanda said that obviously something urgent had to be done, and she would take the matter up with her bosses at the Foreign Office where she now worked.

Amanda swung into action as soon as she arrived in work the following Monday. She presented her friend's case to the head of the

African unit, Allan Price. He was sympathetic, but although he promised urgent action, she had to give him a few days to think of what to do. It wouldn't have been a big problem if it was only Samantha or if they all had either their passports or birth certificates. But they had lost all the documents to the hoodlums. Before Amanda left Mr Price's office that morning, he collected Samantha's date of birth which he forwarded to the Home Office, so they could issue a letter of confirmation of her British citizenship. With the letter obtained, the next hurdle was obtaining a copy of her wedding certificate from the Liberian registry. That would be a herculean task as virtually all Liberian offices and establishments were closed.

Donaldson had been to the registry on several occasions, but it remained closed still. After several visits, however, he eventually met one of the security guards who directed him to the registrar's home. Recognising Donaldson, the registrar ushered him into his living room and offered him a seat. As soon as he sat, the registrar's wife brought a bottle of water and a glass on an aluminium tray. As she placed the tray on a stool before Donaldson, her husband said, 'We are sorry Dr Weah. This is the best my family can offer anyone at this time,' gesturing at the empty wine bar.

'I can understand sir,' replied Donaldson. 'I really appreciate your hospitality. Everything is upside down in the country. As you are aware, there are people in this country who cannot even afford water,' he added while his hosts nodded in approval.

After a sip from the glass of water Donaldson told his host the purpose of his visit. He needed his help to obtain duplicate copies of his marriage certificate and his children's birth certificates. Donaldson was very lucky. The head of security department had fled the country, but not before submitting the keys of the registry offices to the registrar. Without wasting time, the registrar took the keys and beckoned to Donaldson to come with him in his battered old Volkswagen beetle.

Amanda was delighted to hear that her friends had finally obtained duplicate copies of their stolen documents. The British Embassy in Sierra Leone was responsible for consular needs of British citizens still trapped in Liberia. Donaldson, Samantha and their two children made the long journey to Sierra Leone without incident, and each member of the family was issued with an Emergency Travel Certificate.

The only remaining problem was the airfare for the four travellers. But Donaldson's friends had come to their aid. Silvestre, Richard and Gabriel had provided more than enough money for their airfare. None of the three men was really affected by the on-going war. As for Richard, the American Automobile plant had temporarily relocated to Sierra Leone. And he had wanted his parents to come with him, but they wanted to continue to serve the Lord in their village church despite the raging war. As for Silvestre and few officers of the Liberia armed forces, the financial effect of the war was minimal. Gabriel's legal tentacles extended beyond Liberia, to some English-speaking ECOWAS states. And, being a cautious person, he didn't only keep local bank accounts – he had bank accounts in Sierra Leone and the USA. And, like Richard, he also bought and moved to a property in Sierra Leone as the civil war intensified.

Two days before Donaldson and his family left the country, his Christian friends organised a party for them. The motive behind the party, which was attended by all their family members, was to preach to their recalcitrant friend for the last time. And that afternoon, after they had had their meal, Richard stood up and spoke. He started by telling Donaldson how much he would be missed by all his friends. They had all benefitted from his wisdom during their various times of difficulty. But, despite all his sterling qualities and noble achievements, there was a missing factor in his life. Turning to Donaldson, he told him that the missing factor in his life was Jesus Christ. Quoting from the Bible, he said, 'In the days salvation I've helped you. Now is the day of salvation.' Recalling the incident of his abduction, he reiterated that it was God who preserved his life for the simple reason that he might turn it over to Him. He then seized the opportunity to reveal that he was the only one left among them to become a child of God. The other two friends – John and Lloyd – had by then also given their lives to Christ.

Replying, Donaldson thanked his friends for their love. Regarding giving his life to Christ, he told them that he was yet to be convinced of the existence of God. If truly there was a God, what was He doing about the situation in Liberia? The ongoing war in the country was ample evidence that God was a myth. The so-called God could afford to fold his arms while the lives he was said to have created were being destroyed in thousands. He concluded by advising his friends not to worry themselves about him as he already knew the truth. Asked what the truth was, he said, 'God is a mirage!'

The night before he travelled out, Donaldson had a very strange dream. In that dream he saw two roads before him. One of them was a very broad tarmac while the other was just a narrow footpath. He also noticed that, while the broad road was busy, the narrow one was lonely.

And as he wondered which of them he should take, a man appeared and directed him to the broad road. But just as he was about to continue along the broad road, a soft-spoken man appeared and said to him, 'Wide is the gate and broad is the road that leads to destruction, and many enter through it.' But the first man, joined by other pedestrians, earnestly urged him on. Ignoring the soft-spoken man, Donaldson joined the pedestrians and they all travelled along the broad road. But not very long after that, the broad road suddenly became muddy, and ferocious animals surrounded him. He was terribly scared. But as he turned around to run he discovered that all other pedestrians had disappeared and there were seven monsters approaching him from behind, each holding a long chain. All his efforts to scream or run were abortive as his two feet were glued to the floor. He was then bound in chains and dragged along the road by the monsters.

But a very bright light suddenly appeared in front of them. And from the bright light emerged the soft-spoken man. Donaldson and his captors remained static as soon as the man emerged. Regarding Donaldson for some moments, the man said, 'The prayers that your wife and friends daily pray for you have reached me, and I have decided to show you mercy.' The speech was greeted by terrifying lightning and thunder, after which Donaldson found himself alone and loosed from the chains.

Although he was terrified by the dream, he kept it to himself. Who was the soft-spoken man? What did all that mean? In the end, he concluded that the nightmare in his subconscious mind was due to the overwhelming stress he was currently experiencing.

As all international flights from Liberia were still suspended, Donaldson and his family members had to travel from Sierra Leone's Lungi airport which was situated in Freetown. Lungi Airport was the only international airport in Sierra Leone. The family was seen off by Richard, Silvestre and Gabriel. Shortly before the family marched to the boarding room, the three Christian friends had a last-minute chat with Donaldson over the issue of the salvation of his soul. In their final bid to convince their friend, they had asked him to take a cue from them who had all once held a similar view about God and Christianity. They told him that if they weren't convinced of existence of God's love they wouldn't have given their lives to Jesus Christ.

Although he was able to conceal his emotion, Donaldson remained haunted by the dream. He remained speechless as he thought about whether to share the dream with his friends. But the long silence was broken by the announcement, 'Passengers for Flight 2314 British Airways to London Heathrow should proceed to the boarding room immediately.'

Before the family finally departed for the boarding room, they were prayed for by the three Christian friends. Shortly after that, a British Airways Boeing 737 was seen midway into the sky. And the three friends, standing by their cars outside the airport, waved emotionally to the ascending aircraft.

Donaldson and Samantha were in a pensive mood as they sat flanking their two children on the flight. The joyous kids, who didn't notice the mood of their parents, chatted away asking their parents all sorts of questions. The couple were engrossed by the thought of starting afresh in Britain. Where and how were they going to start? Although the accommodation issue had been resolved (they would stay in Samantha's old flat), how were they going to cope financially until they were able to get a suitable job? Samantha would be entitled to apply for unemployment benefit as soon as she sorted out her passport. But how long would that take? As for the children, she wasn't sure they were immediately qualified for UK benefits. One thing she always believed in was God's unfailing love. She always knew that God was in her every situation. But she was concerned about her unbelieving husband. The Bible said that, while one person would chase a thousand, two persons would chase ten thousand. But the Bible didn't mean just two persons. It obviously referred to two God-fearing persons. The Bible even said that if two persons should agree as touching anything it would be done for them. But her husband never agreed with her on the issue of Christianity! That was where the main problem lay.

Donaldson was engrossed by the thought of his new life in Britain. He had only been to Britain twice. The first time was when he wanted to meet some of Samantha's relatives before their wedding. But now he was going there to start his life afresh, surrounded by a huge air of uncertainty. Just then he remembered the information pamphlet he picked up at the boarding room. The pamphlet, which was titled 'Welcome to London,' contained important information for visitors to the greatest multicultural city in the world. He opened the booklet, which began with a micro poem, and began to read:

LONDON

As conspicuous crumbs
Draw all manners of pests,
A large-breasted London
Daily draws all creeds and races
That, together with her offspring,
They might have their daily succour.

CHAPTER 14: WELCOME TO LONDON!

The BBC news had brought an abrupt end to Evangelist and Mrs Clooney's delicious dinner that was meant to celebrate a successful youth rally which took place earlier in the afternoon. Another boy stabbed to death in gang violence! A 15-year-old murdered by a 16-year-old! The couple had just returned from Earl's Court where they addressed a mammoth crowd of the city youths. Juvenile crime was a menace that almost overshadowed the sterling qualities of London. There was no single week without an incident of stabbing or killing. It was a situation that left the London police struggling to cope. There was the so-called postcode war among various youth gangs all over the city, with weapons like guns and machetes freely used. Postcode Confrontations took place both at night and during the day; at school or in the street. What were the major causes of confrontations? The quest for supremacy was the major cause. Another cause was desire for vengeance over issues as trivial as dating. As a result of this madness many youths were killed or maimed for life while many others grew up in jail.

The weather was very friendly with the sun surprisingly gracing the occasion (no one in London expected sun at that time of the year.) Some zealots had suggested that the friendly weather was indicative of God's approval of the rally! Well, that may not be disputed considering the absolute peace and tranquillity that reigned at the venue throughout the event. Most of the attendees were officially invited through their respective schools. Others were attracted by posters, billboards and series of adverts placed in the papers.

The spate of knife crimes in the city had informed the formation of a youth organisation called *Drop the Knife*! With government permission, Evangelist and Mrs Clooney and their team had paid regular visits to high schools where they held counselling sessions. The organisation was at the heart of a fierce battle against juvenile crime in the city. Although the couple understood the enormity of the responsibility they had taken on, they were never swayed. They had resolved that, while they were still alive, the menace was not just to be confronted, but totally stamped out. Although the police were truly doing their best, how would they understand that the problem was really a spiritual one? To the couple, it took a spiritual mind to appreciate spiritual things, a rare thing in a society where majority of the people didn't believe in God's existence? Most people believed that they evolved from apes or they were a product of a big bang! These deceptive beliefs had prompted Evangelist Clooney to write and distribute some leaflets among London commuters:

ATTENTION COMMUTERS!

Have you ever considered that there is nothing you have used today that was not made by someone? Your mobile phone, home, clothing, shoes, TV, computer, were all carefully designed and made. And, believe me, YOU are not an exception. You are not a product of any BIG BANG or EVOLUTION; you were never an ape! You were carefully and beautifully made by Someone – God. All this BIG BANG and EVOLUTION stuff is Satan's gimmick to lure you to hell with him. But God does not want you to go to hell as it wasn't originally meant for man. That is why He sent His Son to redeem you. Receive the Son of God TODAY as there is no alternative way by which man can be saved. JESUS CHRIST is the only way. Thanks and have a beautiful day at work!

In his speech at a Christian seminar, Evangelist Clooney had said, 'How can people believe in the existence of demons when they don't believe in existence of God? But the reality is that behind every criminal act there is an evil force. So the effort of the police or government towards curbing juvenile crimes is like trying to get rid of a tree by mere cutting off its branches! Sure – it will sprout new branches and the tree will live on. An unwanted tree can only be got rid of right from its root. And it is only divine intervention that can tackle crime from the root. However, for certain miracles to take place God and man must work together as partners. That doesn't mean that God is not able to work out miracles alone. Of course, He does. But He sometimes delights in partnering with us. Take examples of the lad whose lunch Jesus multiplied to feed the multitudes and the widow whose little oil was multiplied to provide jars full of it. There are so many similar examples in the Bible. It wasn't that Jesus wasn't able to feed the multitudes without the boy's meal nor the widow blessed without having a little already. But, as already stated, God chose to partner with them. That is the reason we need to take practical steps when we pray.'

And that was the reason the couple, apart from corporate and individual prayer efforts, set out specific strategies for accomplishing their goal. One such strategy was organising youth rallies. Wisdom was, however, applied in ensuring that the rallies didn't look entirely religious so as not to put many off. The only events that drew crowds anywhere were sports and social events. Religious events rarely did. Somebody once said, 'If you don't want anyone to sit next to you on a packed bus just dress in a priest's cassock, clutching the Bible.' Commuters would not like to sit next to you out of hatred for your faith or fear you might start up a religious discussion. For these reasons, Evangelist Clooney's youth rallies had to be more social than religious. To stimulate youths' interest, ballets, debates, quizzes and refreshment were among the items of the programme while biblical verses and stories were only used to drive home salient messages.

Apart from Earl's Court, other venues were hired in Brixton, Peckham and Shepherds Bush. The choice of Brixton as a venue was, however, premised on the fact of its notoriety. In the recent past, Brixton had become a sort of lion's den – a harbinger of all sorts of criminal activities including murder, racism and rape. Although the efforts of the law enforcement agencies had brought about a considerable reduction in these crimes, there were still serious crimes committed among teenagers. At Brixton, one often noticed lots of hooded teenagers on bikes and mopeds at night. Their secret mission was to supply drugs through a complicated network of patrons within the city.

Another notorious place was Peckham. Peckham was an unofficial settlement for African immigrants, predominantly West Africans. It accommodated lots of Nigerians, Ghanaians and Sierra Leoneans. Indeed, Peckham was a beautiful sight in summer time as inhabitants were dressed in their traditional attires while going about their legitimate or, sometimes, illegitimate businesses. The killing of a young schoolboy in Peckham that year had shocked and focussed the attention of the entire nation on the problem of youth violence.

The Earl's Court rally was a tremendous success. The invited youths – male and females – had engaged in debates over causes of knife crime and the means of eradicating it. The youths had pledged, that afternoon, on behalf of themselves and their friends, to allow peace to reign in the capital. And when it was time to pray for the city, the response had been overwhelming. It was widely believed, therefore, that God had indeed begun to melt down the stony hearts of the youths. The major highlight of the day, however, was Evangelist Clooney's heart-warming speech.

'Good afternoon, my young friends – leaders of tomorrow. First and foremost, I would like to thank you all for making today's event not just a reality, but a huge success. I thank all for coming. I would like to remind you why we are gathered here today. The reason we are here today is to safeguard our future. Let me confirm to you today, friends, that you are the most important people in this nation. You are the future of our nation which we must safeguard. You are the indispensable part of the population. You are more important than the Prime Minister!' A tumultuous round of applause with deafening shouts and whistling greeted the last statement. The youths were happy at being said to be more important than the politicians.

And when the noise subsided, the evangelist continued, 'You see, I really mean what I said – you are more important than the members of government. Why? Because you are the future of this nation. Here today may be tomorrow's Prime Minister. Here today are those who will break records. Here today is a generation which is going to succeed and lead. But all that great destiny could be spoiled for your life by knife crime. Don't languish in a jail cell because of violence. Don't let the enemy of your soul rob you of your God-given future.'

'In Christianity, we call destiny 'the will or plan of God.' The plan of God is perfect for all that He created. It is the will of God that we have an enjoyable present and future. But there are two things that work against the plan of God for our lives. Firstly, God has given us free will. We have human rights, such as the right to free speech. But no part of exercising our rights should ever prevent another person from exercising their rights. The courts of law exist to punish whoever exercises their rights to the detriment of others.'

'Think of smoking, for instance. We all know that smoking is dangerous to our health. But as a smoker sits with his lit cigarette, he not only endangers himself but also those who inhale his smoke. When a man has an affair, he puts the happiness of his family at risk. In the same way a knife-wielding teenager will not only destroy his life or future but others' as well. He also puts his family to shame and gives them sorrow.'

'Secondly, there is an enemy who wishes to destroy lives and divide communities. His name is Satan. He leads people to commit crime, for he knows that every crime you commit will damage the beautiful plan of God for your life – it surely will have an adverse effect on your future. Don't let the devil destroy your life and your future. Let Jesus Christ rebuild your life and lead you in the right direction. Thank you and God bless.'

The couple and all the members of the organisation were happy with the way things were going. Even the Mayor of London phoned to congratulate them for making such efforts to oppose knife crime. They were still basking in that euphoria of the rally when the kill-joy news was aired. 'Another teenager knifed to death?' repeated Evangelist Clooney after the newscaster. 'Again?' asked Mrs Clooney rhetorically. The couple were psychologically affected anytime there was a reported incident of stabbing or shooting. But this report was a bitter pill to swallow. It was as if the incident was arranged by the enemy to say 'hey, you guys are fighting a lost battle!'

The couple stared speechlessly at the television set.

'Darling, are we really making any difference?' asked Mrs Clooney.

'Yes, darling,' replied her husband. 'Nobody loses in Christ. And nobody wins in Satan,' he added. That was his slogan. He had stuck to it since his days as a new convert. He loved it because it gave him a ray of hope anytime he was confronted with a huge problem.

'You see, darling,' he continued, 'we're not just fighting juvenile crime, we are at war with the kingdom of darkness. And to win this type of war you need the vital weapons of patience and perseverance. But most importantly, you must believe in the Captain of the battle – the Lord Jesus. Do you realise that the news we have just seen was a strategy of the devil? Why must the news come at this moment when we are celebrating what God has begun to do in the lives of the youths? The reason is very simple. That we might accept defeat and quit. But the Bible asks, "Whose report shall we believe?"'

'Our Lord's, of course,' replied Mrs Clooney, smiling.

To effectively tackle the problem of juvenile crimes, root causes had to be investigated. A community investigation team was formed, chaired by Evangelist Clooney. The team was made up of Christians from various backgrounds; after all, there is only one body of Christ – one fold and one shepherd.

Among the people interviewed during the community investigation were young prison inmates, school administrators, parents of the victims and social workers. The findings were to be published for presentation to the government. It was an arduous task, but they relied on both wisdom and strength of Christ to do it. The members often met for joint prayers as they discharged the responsibility. Their goal was not just to rid the capital of juvenile crimes but to liberate the young from the clutches of blood-thirsty demons, winning them for the Lord. The battle was not theirs but God's: *'Who are thou, O great mountain? Before Zerubbabel thou shall become a plain: and he shall bring forth the headstone thereof with shouting, crying, grace, grace unto it.'* (Zechariah 4:7).

In their investigation, a random sample of knife murder victims was selected, and their families, friends and school mates interviewed. The investigation also took them to two London prisons – Her Majesty's Prison Brixton and Her Majesty Prison Wormwood Scrubs.

CHAPTER 15: A FRESH START

The children were the only happy ones when Donaldson and his family arrived in London. Samantha, though sad, had managed to hide her emotion while trying to pep up her husband. She had lots to think about too. Apart from job prospects and the education of her children, the tenants who rented her flat had been very careless. There were lots of repairs to be done in the flat, the most pressing of which was the central heating system. Their first night at the flat was nightmarish as they arrived in London during the coldest part of December. Despite their late arrival and flight fatigue, she visited some notable markets like Elephant and Castle, East Street and Dalston for portable electric heaters, without success. All the markets had closed. In the end, she made some coffee for the family and lit the gas cooker. Everyone then warmed themselves in the kitchen before going to the bedrooms to bury themselves under the duvet.

It took her only two weeks to obtain a new passport. And as soon as the passport was procured she registered at the nearest Jobcentre for job opportunities as well as to make a benefits claim. But she discovered that the benefits were too meagre to sustain her family. However, Amanda and her husband helped them financially. Although Samantha wanted to go back to the Foreign Office, she wouldn't mind any job that came her way for a start. She believed that in every circumstance God wanted His children to give thanks. Apart from her temporary financial situation, she had a load of reasons to thank God for. She had left Britain alone many years ago but returned as a family of four. God had given her a very loving husband and two beautiful, exceptionally brilliant children. Her prevailing circumstances vis-à-vis her financial situation and Donaldson's unbelief would soon become things of the past. She believed. She would always be grateful to God for Amanda who played a pivotal role in her return to Britain with her family.

The Saturday after the family's arrival, Amanda and her pastor husband paid them a visit during which they discussed her re-application to the Foreign Office. Amanda had brought a form to be completed and submitted to the Foreign Office on King Charles Street, London. That was where she worked after her transfer from Liberia. That was where many of Samantha's former colleagues worked; those who didn't want to be transferred to another country after their evacuation from Liberia. It was only Samantha who had resigned her appointment at that time.

Samantha was invited by the Foreign Office for a chat two weeks after submitting her application. First, she was asked why she resigned her appointment in the first place. And after she had explained that it was on marital grounds, the Human Resources Officer told her that the major problem was that the Office was slightly overstaffed due to the closure of several of its foreign missions. He added that the only available openings were at the foreign missions in Africa and Asia. However, if she knew of any of the Office's staff who wished to work in those continents she could swap with them.

Samantha thanked the officer and left the office dejected. Before leaving the Foreign Office that afternoon she branched off at Amanda's office to give her feedback. Amanda, who rarely looked gloomy, just gave a long smile.

'Why are you smiling, Amanda?' asked Samantha. 'Are you sure you heard what I just said?'

'Yes, Samantha. I heard you very well. I'm smiling because God has made a way already.'

'Where and how?' asked Samantha.

About ten minutes before Samantha came in Amanda had received a call from a colleague who worked at the office of the Foreign Minister. The lady, a devout Christian, had just informed her of her decision to join her missionary husband in Asmara, Eritrea. The couple had only been married for two months when the husband travelled out on missionary assignment. The man had thought that he would only be away for a few months. But when the situation of things over there demanded a very long stay he appealed to his obstinate wife to join him on transfer. Amanda had always advised that the lady join her husband in Africa as it wasn't in the interest of God that Christian couples should live separately. She had quoted the Bible verse, 'In order that Satan might not outwit us, for we are not unaware of his schemes.' But the lady had remained unyielding until that afternoon. So, when Samantha was looking for a job, Amanda could see the finger of God in the whole arrangement. She was particularly aware that the lady's transfer application would be treated urgently as personnel for Africa and Asia missions were in short supply. Without wasting time, Samantha returned to the Human Resources Officer with Samantha's colleague that afternoon. The application was hurriedly processed, and she was re-absorbed into the service two weeks later.

It took her children six weeks to obtain their British passports under the British dual nationality law. But before then they had been enrolled at nearby council schools. It, however, took Donaldson over a year to obtain the right to reside, even with the brilliant efforts of his solicitors. He had been invited for an interview at the Home Office in Croydon. And, after a marathon questioning session, he was told to prepare to be transferred to a detention camp. What for? He was dumbfounded. He couldn't believe he was to be detained despite being spouse and father to British citizens! What an insult? He fumed. Was that anything other than racial discrimination? Had he known that he would be subjected to such embarrassment in Britain, he would have applied for asylum in America.

'No, honey, don't say that. The Lord will fight for us,' Samantha had interjected.

'Okay … okay. What is the use of sojourning in your spouse's country only to be treated like a castaway?' asked Donaldson rhetorically.

He couldn't stop pondering over his negative metamorphosis as he lay in bed at the detention camp that night. Some years ago, he was a centre of attraction everywhere, including one of the British embassies in Africa. He had even received accolades from their ambassadors and high commissioners. But now he was not only being treated as persona non grata, but like a pet with contagious diseases. Imagine a former member of the governing board of a country's highest banking authority treated as a destitute. 'Such is life,' he thought. But why had the on-going war in his country singled him out for an unprecedented fall? There were his five friends who never felt any bite of the war and never had to leave Africa. Imagine him staying at a detention camp like an illegal immigrant! He never imagined he was coming to Britain to receive that kind of treatment, after all the ordeals he went through obtaining his papers. His interviewers didn't even explain why he had to be detained. When he asked them, they simply replied that his lawyer will explain to him. They then wanted to know if he had private solicitors. Otherwise, the Office would help provide one. But he told them that he needed time to contact his wife before making his decision.

Samantha was in the office when she received her husband's call. She was greatly agitated when her husband told her of the decision to send him to a detention camp. She stopped what she was doing and went to Amanda's office, sobbing. Amanda too couldn't conceal her disappointment. And for the first time, ever since Samantha knew her, she looked seriously puzzled. Amanda took her mobile and called her husband. There was an instruction from him: Donaldson should reject public solicitors as an arrangement was being made to get him private ones who were members of his church.

The two lawyers provided by Amanda's husband swung into action without any delay. They first contacted the immigration department to apply for Donaldson's bail. But they were gobsmacked when their application was turned down and the reason for Donaldson's detention stated as 'presenting fake or forged marriage certificate.' The certificate, which was the major document submitted in support of his application, had been forwarded to the embassy of Liberia for verification. And it took the embassy about six weeks to establish that it was forged. The couple couldn't believe it. Samantha had had the clue of the allegation two weeks earlier, when she was summoned for a separate interview and the interviewer asked her about the source of their certificate. But the issue wasn't raised during Donaldson's turn. He only received a letter summoning him for another interview, not realising he was being invited to be detained.

Donaldson stared at the ceiling and battled against tears when one of the lawyers requested the truth about the document. The truth, according to the lawyer, was the only factor that would determine the course to chart in ensuring that he was not deported. That only rubbed salt in his wound. So, his immigration status had made him untrustworthy? With his age and degree of enlightenment, some people still believed he could be compelled to confess to a crime he never committed? He remembered an old African adage and said it out loud, though unconsciously, in his native dialect, 'Once you are floored by a major problem the minor ones climb over you.'

'I beg your pardon?' said the lawyer as he couldn't figure out the meaning. Donaldson ignored him.

Donaldson's team of solicitors swiftly filed a motion seeking a court injunction refraining the Department of Immigration from removing him on the grounds of insufficient evidence. The solicitors claimed that, though they were already conducting their own investigation on the said certificate, they strongly believed that the marriage certificate wasn't the only evidence of their client's marriage. The certificate wasn't, therefore, enough grounds for his deportation. According to the solicitors, there was much other evidence to be considered in establishing the fact of his marriage. These included video clips, marriage photographs, testimonies from guests who attended the wedding, DNA linking his purported family members, etc. They, therefore, appealed to the judge for bail while further investigations were carried out about his marital claim.

Their request was granted, and Donaldson came back to his family after three days at the detention camp. But he was only given up to ninety days to return to court to prove his case. According to the judge, he could forward further documentary evidence to the Immigration Service who would issue notice of withdrawal once they were satisfied with the new evidence. Meanwhile, the certificate issue almost caused a domestic problem between Donaldson and his wife. So many times, she had asked her husband the same question, 'Darling, are you sure it was the registrar who gave you the copy?' But at a point Donaldson could no longer tolerate the question and he retorted, 'I'm tired of this question. And I hope you're not insinuating I forged the certificate of a marriage which really took place?' It was the first time he ever spoke to her in annoyance. But Samantha quickly pacified him by apologising in his three native words which she had memorised over the years, 'Sorry, husband, love.' Donaldson couldn't resist laughter as he could easily fathom what she really meant to say, 'I am sorry darling. I love you.' It was the first time, too, that he ever heard her say any words in his native dialect. The couple burst out laughing. Samantha had, once again, demonstrated a virtue of a Christian wife.

Donaldson and his legal representatives had a difficult riddle to unknot regarding the marriage certificate. He had explained the circumstances surrounding the certificate as much as he knew. He had also explained how all his family's documents were taken away by hoodlums, and how he later obtained a duplicate copy directly from the court registrar. However, all attempts to reach the registrar had proved abortive. It was later discovered, through Richard, that the man and his family had emigrated. Sierra Leone-based Richard had been of tremendous help in the investigation. He had shuttled between his base and the court in Monrovia, trying to check his friend's marriage record. But the whole council building, which housed the court, was locked. He had also explored other means of getting evidence to substantiate his friend's claim. He had contacted friends and relatives, asking if they kept photographs or anything that could be of help.

But all his efforts were futile until he made a great discovery two weeks before his friend was to return to court. He was lucky to find the court open on his umpteenth visit. He went straight to the new registrar and explained his mission. The registrar, also a devout Christian, confirmed receiving a message from the Liberian embassy in London requesting confirmation of a marriage certificate. However, as the marriage register was among the documents set ablaze by war hoodlums, he had to confirm with duplicate copies of certificates issued during the year in question. But none of them matched the particulars provided. 'None of the duplicate copies will ever match the particulars sir,' Richard responded ecstatically, having realised where the problem was. And after he had explained that the duplicate copy had been issued out to his friend, the duplicate booklet was brought out and a missing folio corresponding to that of Donaldson's was discovered. A letter confirming Donaldson certificate and explaining the error in the previous one was promptly forwarded to London by the registrar.

Coincidentally, Samantha had a day off work and the children too were on holiday. After breakfast that morning she and the children had an hour's prayer session praying for God's intervention. She had told the children that their father could be taken back to Africa if they didn't pray very hard. Although they always prayed together early in the morning, she had told them that that morning was special. Samantha didn't only pray that morning but fasted as well. She normally fasted once in a week. Although Donaldson never joined his family for prayer, he never complained when they sang at the top of their voices or clapped noisily. Rather, he would roll over in bed and face the wall. He never came to the living room whenever prayer was on until it ended. Much as he didn't believe in their prayer he never liked to distract them. Sometimes he would lay awake in his bedroom smiling mockingly as his wife dictated prayer items to the children. He didn't have to intervene as she indoctrinated the kids, he had reasoned. 'They will surely disengage themselves from all those illusions when they grow up,' he had said to himself as he listened amusedly to their prayer that morning. But he didn't know that the prayer was all God needed to save his situation that day.

As communications were still bad, Richard couldn't make a call to London immediately he left the registry. He had to get to his base in Freetown before he could do that. But that wouldn't be earlier than the following day as he needed to see Silvestre before returning to Sierra Leone. He would also like to spend the night with his parents at the village. Silvestre had made it easy for him to travel across the borders without any problem. He had made available a military vehicle and escorts each time he had to travel. He was a friend indeed! And now he deserved to have first-hand information of the success eventually attained regarding their friend's immigration imbroglio. Richard arrived at his base around 9 a.m. British time and made a call immediately to his highly elated friend.

'Richard, I can never thank you enough for saving me a huge embarrassment,' he said.

'No, Donaldson. All thanks go to the Lord Jesus Christ,' Richard had responded.

'There we go again! Even when they visited the loo all thanks must go to Jesus! I hope he doesn't seize this opportunity to begin a sermon,' Donaldson said to himself. He later rang up his wife, who was at work, and the latter rang Amanda to share the good news.

A copy of the letter from Monrovia and a covering memo were forwarded to the Home Office by the embassy of Liberia about a week later. And within four days of its receipt, Donaldson received a letter from the Home Office, requesting him to come for his visa – the right to reside – which qualified him to be gainfully employed.

It was a great celebration in his family. At every opportunity, that evening, Samantha kept on congratulating her husband, hugging and kissing him. The children too were excited. Both of them sat on their father's laps for a long time until Samantha jokingly sent them to their bedroom. 'Hey, you girls!' she exclaimed. 'I hope you are not trying to snatch my husband from me. C'mon, go into your bedroom while I enjoy my husband!' she added. The kids laughed as they made for their room, casting furtive glances at their parents as they went. But as they closed the door behind them Samantha yelled, 'Hey girls! Come have these chocolates before you sleep.' Her excitement was uncontrollable. The kids came back, collected the chocolates and galloped towards their room. But their father stopped them, saying, 'Hey, Natasha and Celine, what do you say to your mum? What did I teach you about gratefulness?' And the children chorused, 'Thank you, Mum.'

Samantha woke early the following morning. As her daily practice, after observing her private prayer time, she made for the children's room to wake them up for family prayer. They had to sing songs of gratitude and thank the Lord for what He did for the family yesterday. They had to thank Him for answering their prayer. She had taught the children that each time they thanked God for what He had done for them it opened the door for more blessings. Their thanksgivings should be more than requests. So that morning, with everyone still in ecstatic mood, they sang praises unto the Lord. Donaldson, as usual, didn't join them but took out the Home Office letter and read it over as he lay in bed. As he held the letter in his hand he heard his wife dictating prayer points in the living room, 'Let's first thank the Lord for His intervention in your father's immigration matter.' He smiled. He wondered how 'the Lord' intervened in his immigration matter. Was he the one who discovered the error at the Liberian registry? Or, was he the one who wrote the Home Office letter? He then humorously checked the letter to see if it was signed by

Mr Jesus Christ or Mr Jesus Joseph, as his father was claimed to be Joseph. Or, it could be Mr Jesus Christ Joseph. And he laughed out loud.

Samantha left for work that morning, leaving behind her husband and the children who were still on school holiday. As soon as she left, Donaldson began to prepare for his journey to the Home Office via his solicitors. He was still dressing up in the bedroom when Natasha, his elder daughter, knocked at the door.

'Who is it?'

'It's me, Dad.'

'What can I do for you Natasha?' Natasha came in looking sad.

'What's the matter, Natasha?' asked her father.

'Dad, what's the word for a man who teaches others to do what himself doesn't do?' asked Natasha.

'Hypocrite, 'replied Donaldson, thinking that the question was part of her school homework.

'Does that mean you are a hypocrite, Dad?'

Donaldson was astounded. Dropping the necktie he was trying to knot, he asked:

'How do you mean?'

'You see, Dad, you always teach us not to be ungrateful. Last night when we forgot to thank Mum over the chocolates, you promptly corrected us. But I never heard you thank Jesus for anything. And this morning, as we were thanking Him on your behalf, we could all hear you laughing at us. You always mock us when we pray!' And she sobbed.

Donaldson was speechless. He could only draw her closer and wipe her tears. And after some moments he was able to say, 'You see, Natasha, I'm not being ungrateful to anyone. There are certain things you assume to be real or true at your age. But when you grow up and your sense of reasoning becomes clearer you will realise that they are all make believe.'

'Does that include Jesus, Dad?' asked Natasha disagreeably.

'Well, Natasha, you know I have to go out as soon as your sister's minder arrives. Why don't we postpone this discussion till another time?'

Donaldson's evasive reply was a ploy to escape a barrage of knotty questions from his highly intelligent, twelve-year-old high school daughter. As she turned around to leave the room there was a knock at the main door. She hurried out to check who it was. It was Auntie Michelle, Celine's minder. As Natasha opened the door Auntie Michelle could observe her countenance. She was the one who always let Auntie in and as soon as she came in Natasha would grab her hand and began to chat. But she only opened the door that morning, greeted her briefly and then turned back with her head bowed. But Auntie walked closer, and asked, 'Natasha, what have I done wrong? You don't want to talk to me this morning?' The girl didn't respond; she only stared away.

Auntie Michelle, a Filipino, was a childminder whose nursery was situated down the street. In her late forties, she was a Christian widow who had great penchant for kids. Apart from making living out of it, she liked to be in their company teaching them numbers or Christian songs. She taught the older ones reading and biblical stories. The children, especially those who belonged to her nursery, loved her. Natasha and her sister only stayed with her during the holiday, as she looked after the pre-nursery children.

'You don't want to talk to me? Okay, where is your Dad?' asked Auntie Michelle inquisitively. Just then Donaldson emerged from his bedroom.

'Good morning sir. Did you scold Natasha this morning?'

'Nobody scolded her, Auntie Michelle. We only had a discussion that she didn't like.'

'What discussion? Was it about her academics?'

'No. It was something trivial.'

But Natasha broke down in tears.

'Daddy, there you go again! Jesus Christ isn't trivial. He is God!' And turning to Auntie Michelle, she said, 'Auntie, Daddy hates Jesus. He always mocks us when Mummy prays with us. I heard him laughing at us this morning as we prayed, and he called Jesus Christ make believe.'

'What?' exclaimed Auntie Michelle.

Until then, the woman had not known Donaldson's position about God, and it genuinely surprised her. She was also somewhat gobsmacked by the little girl's exceptional passion for God. After some moments of silence, Auntie Michelle looked at Donaldson and said, 'Sir, I thank God for your child. You can never have a more convincing sermon about God. This is God Himself appealing to you. And any further means of appealing to you by Him may be appalling. Good day sir.'

Putting her hands across Natasha's shoulders, she said, 'C'mon Natasha. Stop crying. You have delivered God's message to your Dad. Leave the rest to Jesus to accomplish. Take your sister and your stuff and let's go.'

Donaldson could only watch bewilderedly as the trio left the flat. But there was something that refused to leave. It was the statement, 'And any further means of appealing to you by Him may be appalling!'

CHAPTER 16: PRIDE GOES BEFORE A FALL

Donaldson never imagined that it would take so long for him to secure a job. At first, he had applied for high profile banking jobs with banks like Halifax, Barclays and HSBC. With his intimidating CV, he had always believed that getting a good job would not be a problem. He thought he would have his choice of offers. The first job he applied for was as a Chief Financial Officer with HSBC. The job attracted an annual salary of £235K+. And he wasn't surprised to receive a letter of inviting him to interview within two weeks of submitting his CV. Now he eagerly looked forward to the interview, hoping to dominate his would-be interviewers. He hoped to lecture them with a few things that neither their university professors nor professional experience had taught them. In fact, he saw the interview as a mere formality.

About fifteen people had applied for the job with only three of them shortlisted for interview. Of the three, it was obvious that his CV was most outstanding. And having interviewed the other two applicants earlier, the interview panel had unanimously scored him highest. He had been warmly received at the interview with huge respect accorded him. And when it was time to address certain banking issues, his articulacy, knowledge and exactitude were applauded by his interviewers. He, indeed, sent them back to school! At the end of the interview, the chair of the panel and his colleagues shook his hand in admiration.

A week after the interview, Donaldson and Samantha were at a grocery shop. As he pushed the shopping cart along the aisle a woman suddenly approached him.

'Excuse me sir, are you Dr Weah?' she asked.

Donaldson stopped the cart. And, looking at her, he immediately recognised her.

'Yes, I am,' replied Donaldson. 'And you are Mrs Pierce. Right?' he asked.

'Yes, you're right,' replied the woman, smiling. 'As you pushed the cart past me I looked at you but wasn't so sure it was you. Pleased to meet you sir,' she added.

'Oh, so pleased to meet you too. Please meet my wife – Samantha.'

Turning to Samantha, who had purposely stopped checking her shopping list and was staring at the duo, he said, 'Darling, meet Mrs Melissa Pierce, member of the HSBC's interview panel.

'Good morning, Mrs Pearce.' said Samantha as she offered her hand.

After exchanging pleasantries, Donaldson and the woman discussed some issues relating to banking industry and then the last interview. The woman turned to Samantha and smilingly said, 'Madam, you have a very brilliant husband. Everyone was impressed by his performance, especially, the presentation. I personally believe he has better chances than the rest of the applicants.'

On getting home that morning, Samantha told her husband of her optimism about the job. All she needed to do now was to begin to thank God for answering her prayer. She then knelt down and began to thank God for the anticipated offer. But Donaldson held her both hands and helped her on her feet, saying, 'C'mon, darling, stand up. And don't be naive. Who else are they going to employ if not me? This is not an achievement. You know I'm worth more than this offer. And you don't have to bring Jesus into this.' Samantha could only look at her husband bewilderedly.

Donaldson received a letter from the bank about two weeks later. There was no doubt that it was the offer letter he had been expecting. He was on his way to toilet when it was dropped in the mail box. He wasn't so anxious about it since he apparently knew the contents. So, he had to visit the toilet first and then come back to pick it up. While in the toilet he visualised himself behind a broad executive table in a posh HSBC office. He was back again at the top. Although he was conquered in his home country, he was sure to conquer in Britain. And his conquest had just begun. The job, according to him, was to be a springboard needed to launch him to fulfilling his ambition of directing a British bank. Who knew? He could become Governor of Bank of England someday! He picked up the letter after leaving the toilet and tore it open on his way to bedroom. Holding it in his hand until he sat comfortably on a sofa, he then began to read:

Dr Donaldson Jerome Weah,
94 Lesley Street,
Bermondsey.
SE1 3AT

19th December 2001

Re: *Application for the post of a Chief Finance Officer*

Dear Dr Weah,

Our Selection Committee was left with an extremely difficult decision after interviewing all the applicants. This was due to everyone's impressive CV and their awesome presentation. But, based on some specific criteria, the committee was able to reach a unanimous decision. We regret to inform you that your application is not successful. Meanwhile, we shall keep your CV and contact information should we have another executive opening in future.

Thanks for your interest in working with us.

Yours sincerely,

Melissa Pierce (Mrs)

Director of Human Resources

Donaldson was dumbfounded. He felt a slight headache, with sweat oozing out of his forehead and bridge of his nose. It was a complete bombshell! He looked around the room, beginning from the sofa on which he was sitting. He then looked at himself down to his feet. Not satisfied, he pinched himself hard above the brow to ascertain he wasn't dreaming! After that he began to have a feeling he hadn't read the letter correctly. He spread it closer to his face and read it again. He then jumped on his bed to try to get some sleep. But sleep eluded him. He rose again and reached for the landline in the living room. He felt like calling the bank. What for? He replaced the receiver and went back to the bedroom. He let out a very long sigh as he sat thoughtfully at the edge of the bed. He rose again, walked to the sofa and picked up the letter again. He then remembered Auntie Michelle's warning, 'And any further means of appealing to you by God may be appalling!'

Was this a consequence of not believing in Jesus? He asked himself. It was very stupid of him to think that way. How could a dead-and-buried Jesus influence his success or failure? Besides, unsuccessful job applications couldn't be said to be appalling since there were a thousand and one other job opportunities out there. He brought out his Oxford

English dictionary and checked out the meaning of appalling. 'Yeah, failing to land a good job is only disappointing and not appalling,' he said to himself. 'But wait a minute,' he said to himself. 'Are you sure you haven't gone insane?' he asked. He then went back to the living room, opened the fridge and brought out four cans of Stella Artois which he gulped down in quick succession and returned to his bed. And within a couple of minutes, with the letter flung on the floor, he began to snore heavily.

It was Samantha who picked up the letter as she returned from work. Although she was highly disappointed, she knew she had to console him and encourage him to be strong. But she never needed to do all that. He was the first to rise very early the following morning. He then woke her and asked if she had read the letter. After she had nodded he quickly added, 'Darling, it's one of those things. Don't worry. I'm still expecting some more letters of interview. I strongly believe that one of them will click. Cheer up, honey and let's put that behind us.' Twitching her lips, she stared at him thoughtfully in a manner suggesting, 'Is that fake confidence?'

But that was the closest Donaldson ever got to landing a top job in England, as he was never invited for any banking interview again. After two years of unemployment, however, he decided to explore some other industries. But that didn't work either. Day in, day out, his hope of getting a job – any job – was turning to despair. And before long, his jobless situation and the attendant financial dependence were taking unprecedented toll on his demeanour. Although his wife had given him her bank card and freedom to take from her account, he never felt happy to be a financial 'parasite.' As he was daily beleaguered by the thought of his affluent past, coupled with the notion that a man ought to look after his wife and not vice versa, he became persistently moody. And within a very short period depression set in. He no longer played with his children and seldom chatted with his wife. The situation became so bad for him that he found every of his wife's encouraging words insulting. He had suddenly changed from a loving head of the family to a grumpy generalissimo.

For the first time, after many years, his wife decided to have a down-to-heart discussion with him regarding his predicament. She had to let him know the source. She had been advised by her pastor to go ahead, prayerfully. The pastor had said that sinners were easily preached to when their strength and ability had failed them. And helplessness, according to him, often played sinners into the waiting hands of Christ. So, one

Saturday afternoon, after a delicious lunch, Samantha sought an audience with her husband. Much as she would like them to start off with a prayer she didn't want to give him a premonition. So, she quickly muttered some few words of prayer and began by extolling his virtues.

'Darling, I can never thank you enough for your love right from the days of our courtship. It makes me feel on top of the world anytime I remember that my husband is a loving and loveable genius. Yes, you are still a genius despite what you are currently passing through. For I always know that tough times never last but tough men do. Talking about toughness, I never doubt your strength and ability to confront unpleasant situations such as the one you are facing. However, to ride upon a tough time one must be tougher than time. But the fact remains that you can't be tougher than time except that the owner of time enables you. He is the one that subdues the time. And like a horse, He bridles it, saddles it and then sets you on it for a joyous ride. Darling, I know you are a master of rhetoric!' Donaldson managed to subdue a smile of approval at this juncture.

Samantha continued, 'And I'm not so good at speeches. But darling, allow me to tread on a forbidden terrain for your sake; my sake and for the sake of our children. I'm convinced that you know the terrain that I'm talking about. It's a terrain which you have forbidden me from treading for so long. It's high time you gave your life to Jesus Christ. There is no assurance of success elsewhere. His words say, 'By strength shall no man prevail.' Honey, please let's invite God to stop the storms in our life and put us on a better path again!' And she began to sob.

Donaldson rose from his chair and walked over to her. Holding her both hands, he helped her rise from the sofa and positioned her head on his chest. Without saying a word, he continued to stroke her shoulders until she stopped crying. He then went to the bedside cupboard, pulled out the last of its four drawers and brought out a file jacket. And from the file jacket, he brought out four sheets of different newspapers. He then walked back to her and gestured to her to sit down. And after she had sat down he began, 'Darling, I have been anxiously waiting for a day like this. I knew that you would speak to me about Jesus in reference to my prevailing circumstances. I knew it. And I have prepared myself for it. If my circumstances are attributable to my sin or stance about Jesus, to what shall we attribute the following?' he asked as he handed her one of the sheets. It was a newspaper report of a popular American pastor who was involved in an air crash that killed all passengers onboard.

According to the report, the pastor was coming from a meeting where he was a guest preacher.

After she had finished reading, he handed her another one with the caption, 'Evangelist Craig loses wife to cancer.' And after that was the one captioned, 'Church building collapses: seventy killed, several injured.' The last one was about a pastor's son who was arraigned among armed robbers in Lagos, Nigeria. According to the report, the boy had claimed that he got involved in the robbery in order to pay for his father's overdue surgery. According to him, the hospital had refused to proceed on the operation unless a deposit was paid. After Samantha had read all the reports, he asked again, 'To what shall we attribute those circumstances if mine were attributed to godlessness?' Samantha was stupefied.

And after he had waited in vain for her response, he continued, 'You see, darling, I always say to you that all this 'Jesus, salvation, heavenly mansion and hellfire' are nonsense. Let's forget about those so-called children or servants of God who couldn't be saved from their gruesome and untimely deaths; let's consider the pastor whose son joined an armed robbery gang in order to pay for his father's surgery. It is obvious that the boy must have joined the gang after all legitimate avenues of getting the needed cash had been explored without a positive result. We can then infer that it wasn't only his pastor father that was financially incapacitated – all the members of his congregation were, although we don't know the size of the congregation. If there is a God, why didn't he provide for his servant? Where were the miracles to heal the pastor and Pastor Craig's wife? My conclusion: God is a myth! As for my present situation, you just watch me. Life is made up of crests and troughs. I have once been on the crest and now on the trough. But watch out, I'm approaching the crest again.'

When he had finished speaking he reached for his trainers and put them on. And after he had carefully laced them up he wore his winter jacket and made for the door. Looking back, he said to his wife, 'I'm off to Peckham. Don't bother to make dinner for me as I might come back very late.' She could only stare at him with mouth agape as he exited the bedroom.

Donaldson had mingled with certain men of his own race. He had been able to locate meeting points for African big boys at Peckham in South East London and Finchley Road, West End. He believed that there was no way he could get on his feet as a lone ranger, so he needed to move with people that really mattered. While the meeting point at Peckham was an African-owned beer joint, that at Finchley Road was a

149

private flat secretly or illegally converted to a recreation centre for ostentatious middle-aged Africans. Armed with his wife's bank card, he was able to buy these people drinks and make friends. He was particularly close to a Nigerian called Raymond, and a Ghanaian called Kofi. The two men were very close. It didn't take Donaldson long to discover that they were business partners and co-owners of the property at Finchley Road. But he was yet to find out what they dealt in. The two men were very rich – much richer than the rest of the group. They cruised about the city in the latest brands of expensive wonder cars. Apart from the one at Finchley Road, each of them had properties elsewhere. And often, under the influence of alcohol, they bragged about their fleet of cars and palatial edifices in their respective home countries. The two men always reminded Donaldson of his flamboyant past.

Ever since he began his adventure with these people he never came home earlier than midnight. Samantha had noticed that he was always dropped off in various expensive cars which were fully occupied by men of his race. Another thing she noticed was that he never ate his dinner nor made another one when he returned. As soon as he came back home he took off his clothing, put on his pyjamas and then went to bathroom. After that he would sit on the sofa for a long time, speaking to some people in Pidgin English on his phone before coming to join her in bed.

One night, as he finished speaking on phone, Samantha asked, 'Darling, who are those people you always speak to at night? Don't they go to work in the morning?'

'They are my friends,' he retorted. And, looking at her indignantly, he asked, 'Does everyone in this country have to do morning shift like you?'

'But you go out to meet them every evening. What shift do they do and what days of the week do they work?' asked Samantha angrily.

'Hey, madam,' began Donaldson, 'since when did you become a member of the Gestapo?' he asked.

'Darling, mind your language,' appealed Samantha. 'And don't call me a Nazi,' she added.

'Then stop behaving like one. And if I must let you know, not everyone in this country is an employee like you. My friends are successful business tycoons.'

'What do they deal in?' asked Samantha further.

'But you just told me you were not a member of the Gestapo. What sort of questions are you asking me?'

'I'm your wife and I have a responsibility to ensure you are not courting the devil,' she replied.

'Alright, alright,' said Donaldson, 'shall I start courting your dead-and-buried Jesus?' he asked. And, laughing hysterically, he buried himself under the duvet.

But Samantha wasn't provoked. She realised that it wasn't her husband's natural behaviour. So, she had to intensify her intercession for him.

The following evening, as he was about to go out, he called his wife and said, 'I knew the reason you were asking me those stinking questions last night. Have your card and, henceforth, I stop being your gigolo.'

'I'm so sorry, darling. I never meant it that way. I was only concerned....'

But he threw the card at her and left the flat, banging the door behind him. Peeping through the window, Samantha and her children could see him climb into an expensive Lexus jeep to join four men who were already seated in the car. It was the first time they came to pick him up. Their destination was the pub at Peckham.

But something remarkable happened that evening as they alighted from their vehicle. An elderly Caribbean man in his eighties approached Donaldson and beckoned to him. At first, he ignored him, but the elderly man followed him and tapped his shoulder from behind. Looking back, Donaldson asked, 'What can I do for you sir?'

'Can you spare me a few minutes of your time? I have something very important to discuss with you,' said the man.

One of Donaldson's friends, who thought the old man had come to beg for money, opened his wallet and offered him a ten-pound note. But the elderly man politely refused the money, insisting on speaking to Donaldson privately.

'Would you like to come in, so we may talk over some bottles of beer?' asked Donaldson.

'No,' replied the man, 'I prefer we have a seat over there,' pointing at one of the benches in front of Peckham library.

Donaldson told his friends to excuse him for a minute.

'Young man, I want you to listen attentively to this story,' the man said as they sat next to each other on a bench. 'Once upon a time, a farmer saw a lonely lion cub in his farm and brought it home to be raised among his flock of sheep. And as the cub grew up it shared similar characteristics with the sheep, including bleating. Amazingly, anytime the sheep saw a wild animal and bolted the lion cub also ran. One day, the sheep and the cub saw a grown-up lion approach them and they all began to run. But the old lion recognised the cub as his long missing child. He then ran after it, grabbed it and brought it back home. As it continued to bleat, the old lion brought a mirror and asked the cub to look at its own image. The cub was surprised to discover that it looked exactly like its captor and entirely differed from its playmates. The father lion then revealed himself to his child and taught him attributes of a lion, including roaring. He made his son understand that he was born to rule over all other animals and didn't belong to group of sheep. The young lion thus had his identity returned. And within a very short time he began to exhibit all the attributes of the king of beasts again.'

Pausing for a while, the old man asked, 'Did you understand the story?'

'Well,' said Donaldson, 'the story is interesting, but I really don't understand what you are trying to achieve with it.'

'Young man,' said the man, 'as you alighted from the car the other time, I immediately realised that you didn't belong to the group I saw you with. Like the lion cub, you are destined to rule over them, but you have lost your identity. You certainly know what to do to have your identity returned. May the Lord help you as you do it!'

Without allowing Donaldson further queries, the man rose and left.

Donaldson sat there for some moments, meditating on the message. He quite understood the story now and he knew that it was true. Had it not been for the war in his country he wouldn't have migrated to Britain in the first place. Maybe by now he would have become the central bank governor or a minister with a significant portfolio. Or maybe his application to the World Bank would have been granted long ago. The man was quite right – he didn't belong with the group. But how would he recover the so-called identity? Another thing was that the group had promised to help him on his feet again. Wouldn't it be stupid of him to quit a group that had given him a ray of hope? What about quitting after achieving his objective? But the man said he knew what to do to recover his identity. What exactly was it? Oh yes, he knew! The man was preaching Jesus!

'What a clever way to preach Jesus!' he said to himself as he rose to leave.

He apologised to his friends as he returned to their midst. They asked him what was discussed. And when he told them that the man had been preaching, they all laughed. Donaldson laughed too.

'The man had a clever way of preaching, mates. It took me moments after he had left before realising that he had been preaching,' said Donaldson. And they all laughed again.

'Donaldson, you shouldn't have given him an audience in the first place,' said Kofi.

'They are all hypocrites,' added Raymond. Continuing, he said, 'There was a Christian nincompoop who stalked me for several weeks requesting my audience. The idiot never relented even when I told him point-blank that I wasn't interested. You know what? Everywhere I parked my car his tracts were stuck to my windscreen until I couldn't bear it any longer. I called the police and had charges pressed against him. The son-of-a-bitch was slammed with three months suspended sentence for stalking and harassment. And ever since then I haven't seen his ugly face nor had any of his stinking tracts stuck to my windscreen.'

'There was this couple who wanted to preach Jesus to me too,' beginning another member of the group. 'But I made a request that set them back on their heels. Looking at the woman seductively, I told her husband that I would be ready to give my life to Jesus if he allowed me a quick one with his beautiful wife.'

They all laughed hysterically.

CHAPTER 17: WITHOUT CHRIST THERE ARE CRISES!

Samantha was on the route 188 bus on her way home. Although she had obtained a small Ford car by hire purchase, she seldom used it. It was for Donaldson. As she returned from work that Friday evening the bus was filled up with all sorts of noisy 'thank-God-it's-Friday' passengers, mostly antisocial teenage girls who spoke, sang and screamed at the top of their voices. Due to the noise, her mobile phone, which was kept in her handbag, rang several times without her knowing. She got home later to discover that she had missed seven calls from the same caller. It was a strange landline number. She then reached for the home landline to call the caller back.

'Hello, this is London Metropolitan Police. What can I do for you?' replied a male voice. Samantha missed a heartbeat. 'London Metropolitan Police?' she asked herself.

'I am Mrs Samantha Weah. I missed your calls. That's why I'm calling back,' she replied.

'Oh, so you are Mr Donaldson Weah's wife?'

'Yes, officer,' she nervously replied. 'Please, what exactly is the matter?' she managed to ask.

'Your husband has been arrested and is being detained here.'

'What for? I mean what has he done?'

'Sorry madam. That cannot be disclosed on phone. If you need further information you need to come to the station at Finchley Road. Good night.'

Samantha was confused. Ever since her husband joined the Peckham group he no longer stayed with the children at home. They were kept at Auntie Michelle's nursery until she returned from work around 6 p.m. But as the nursery had closed for the day she was confused over what to do. She didn't want to leave the children alone at home and she wouldn't like to take them along. Besides, her husband had taken the car out that evening. In the end, she took a cab and travelled with her children.

Raymond and Kofi were internet scammers who defrauded people in a number of countries, notably the United States of America. For quite some time they had been hunted by the FBI, working in collaboration with the London Metropolitan Police. The fraudsters and their accomplices were eventually nabbed by the Bureau in London. Three men, including Donaldson, had been arrested along with the kingpins and the investigation promptly commenced. First, the Metropolitan Police had to promptly seek a court injunction to keep the suspects beyond the constitutional twenty-four hours. And next would be legal proceedings to extradite them to the States for trial. Samantha, who was in tears, had requested to speak to her husband.

'Darling, are you really part of them?' she asked.

'Darling, trust me. I didn't even know that they were fraudsters. They told me they were importers and exporters.'

The next thing for Samantha was to get a good lawyer for her husband. Through Amanda and her husband, the same lawyers who argued his immigration case were contacted again. Among the five suspects only Donaldson was granted bail. And when the case began he was the only one excluded; the rest were duly extradited to the United States to stand trial for fraud and money laundering, among several other charges. The concealment of facts charge that was earlier pressed against him was thrown out by the court. The lawyers had once again demonstrated great legal skills. More importantly, they had demonstrated Christ's love by responding at the time of trouble. Before they departed the court premises one of the lawyers called Donaldson aside and said, 'Mr Weah, your immigration document is not irrevocable. So, stay out of trouble.'

Shame could be seen boldly written in Donaldson's face as he arrived home with his wife. Apart from some fruit which he ate immediately he returned that afternoon, he neither ate his lunch nor dinner. With eyes widely opened he just lay in bed all day sighing intermittently. His mind was engrossed by his sad situation as he ruminated on his status back home in Liberia, compared to his shame and reproach in Britain. He kept on remembering the lawyer's advice: He should stay out of trouble! So, his prevailing circumstances had now turned him into a delinquent? He could also imagine what his wife would be thinking now, 'I warned him not to court the devil.' He gave a deep sigh once again, carving a picture of a footballer who scored a decisive own-goal at a cup final. He thought of his friends back home in Liberia, especially Richard, Silvestre and Gabriel who still maintained their respective statuses despite the war. 'Life is truly a wave of troughs and crests,' he opined. But it seemed to him that his own troughs were larger than crests. Although the troughs may be as large as anything, the crests would emerge again. After all, there was always light at the end of a tunnel.

'Not every tunnel has light at its end,' interrupted Samantha.

'How do you mean?' Donaldson asked, surprised. 'And how did you know my thoughts?' he added.

'But you weren't thinking; you were soliloquising, darling,' replied Samantha.

'Really?' he asked.

'Like I was saying, there will be light at the end of the tunnel if and only if Jesus Christ is invited into the tunnel. You see, darling, when Jesus accompanied three Hebrew guys in the fiery furnace they came out smiling. And when He accompanied his disciples during a raging storm they weren't consumed. Darling, stop hanging on your deceptive philosophy; let's invite Jesus Christ today to have your destiny restored. Philosophies give way, but Jesus is the rock of ages; He never gives way but makes a way.'

When Samantha thought her husband would be upset by her preaching he just gave a half smile and asked, 'Darling, aren't you fed up of me?'

'Never!' she replied. And she added, 'Darling, you are the most loving husband on earth. You have demonstrated unconditional love for me right from the days of our courtship. God has used you to erase my anguish and my tear-soaked memories. And, talking about being presentable, you are very handsome, articulate and brilliant. When we were still courting I always prayed that you rubbed off those qualities of yours on our children. And God answered my prayers. Both of them are very beautiful and exceptionally brilliant....'

'Excuse me,' interrupted Donaldson. 'Talking about brilliance, it's very difficult to say which one of us the children have taken after. But, talking about beauty, everyone knows that it's you!' he added smilingly.

'Thank you darling but I know what I'm talking about,' said Samantha.

'And so do I,' replied Donaldson.

And both of them laughed. After that, Donaldson apologised for not heeding her warning about his swindler friends. He also apologised for being slack towards his family. But, regarding Jesus, he promised to think very deeply about the issue. He still needed some more time.

The monthly premium on Samantha's car was really affecting the family's finances. There were still other bills to be paid, such as energy, television licence, telephone, etc. Had she known that her husband would not get a job quickly she would not have acquired it. Donaldson knew that the car was a source of worry to his wife, even though she didn't show it. And after three years of joblessness he made up his mind to do any job, even cleaning, to support his wife. Without informing her he started looking for menial jobs. As soon as he dropped her off at work and children at school he would park the car at home and set out on the public bus.

One morning, as he sat on the upper deck of a packed bus, a man in a three-piece suit took a seat beside him. Donaldson liked the way he was dressed. It was obvious that the man was a private security officer as he had a badge on his jacket. After exchanging greetings, Donaldson made inquiry about his company. Beaming, the man told him that the security outfit was new, and that recruitment of new staff was still on. Donaldson followed him to Tottenham Court Road, where the company – Hawk Security – was situated. He was given two forms to complete – one for him and the other for someone, not a member of his family, who could attest to his good behaviour.

How to get the attestation form completed without his wife's knowledge or assistance was the only problem. He really didn't want her to know about his search for any kind of job until he was able to secure one. As soon as he came back home he quickly completed the applicant's form and attached copies of his passport. Turning the TV and stereo off, he began to think of what to do about the other form. Yes, he had an idea! He took the car key, walked briskly out of the flat and locked the entrance door. He jumped into the car and started the engine. It was around 11 a.m. The traffic wasn't much on London roads at this time. And within half an hour he was at his lawyers' chamber at Finsbury Park.

'Sir, she will object my taking up the job. And I really must do something to support her financially,' he had told the lawyers in response to one of their questions. The form was duly completed, signed and stamped. Donaldson was more than happy. He headed straight to the office of Hawk Security as soon as he left the lawyers. Luckily for him, there was an opening at a nightclub along Piccadilly Circus. He would work ten hours – 8 p.m. to 6 a.m. – for five days, from Wednesday to Sunday. He loved the schedule as it would allow him to drop his family off in the morning. He didn't tell his wife about the job until the evening he was going to start. He had perfectly concealed his uniform somewhere in the room. And when it was about time to leave for work he just told her that he had something very important to tell her.

'Darling,' he began, 'for three years now all the financial responsibilities of this family are shouldered by you without complaints

157

or regrets. But I want to tell you that any reasonable husband will stop at nothing in assisting a dutiful wife like you. The monthly bills we incur in this family are too much for only you to bear. For that reason, I have got myself a job you might not like.'

'What job?' she asked.

'Security guard,' he replied.

Samantha was shocked.

'Security guard?' she asked repeatedly.

No, she would not allow him to do it. It was unheard of. A leading banker turning a security guard! No! 'Darling, you can't take that job. No, you can't. We must wait a little more until God provides a job of your qualifications. After all, I'm not complaining,' she added.

But Donaldson rose and opened the wardrobe where he kept his uniform. He brought it out and showed it to her, saying, 'You see, darling, my mind is made up. All arrangements have been concluded regarding this job. Here's my uniform and I'm starting tonight. I can do this job while I look for a better one. It is ten hours for five days which will greatly enhance our finances. Darling, please allow me to do it.'

It was emotional departure as he left for work that evening. As soon as he left, Samantha withdrew to the bedroom. She arched herself up in bed and ruminated on her husband's life before the civil war. She visualised him as he gave a scintillating speech at the Trade Department's party. She also visualised him posing for photographs with the Liberian president and other people that mattered in the society. She still had in her memory, the picture of his expansive office at the Central Bank of Liberia. She could still remember the first day she visited his office. Like a perfect gentleman that he was, he rose immediately and offered her his hand, saying, 'Darling, welcome to my pint-sized office,' an expression that generated laughter between them. She also recollected the first time she visited his home – the introduction and the luscious delicacies in her honour. 'Oh Lord, please have mercy on my husband. Please, touch his stony heart and make it yield to you. After all, you said that the heart of a king is in your hand,' she said as she began to sob.

The nightclub where Donaldson worked was one of the biggest in London. There were only two guards on duty from Sunday to Thursday. But, due to a larger turnout of clubbers, four guards worked on Friday and Saturday. Donaldson's colleague on Wednesday, Thursday and Sunday nights was a fifty-year old Greek whose name was Christos.

Christos worked from Sunday through Thursday and was relieved on Friday and Saturday by three men, two of them Africans and the other a Brazilian. Of all his colleagues at the club, the only person Donaldson enjoyed working with was Christos. He was very charismatic and hardworking. It was Christos who put him through the rudiments of the job, keeping an eye on him as he got accustomed to it.

Donaldson never enjoyed working with the two Africans. They talked a lot about their secret dates and criticised every female reveller.

'Look, this one looks like a demon,' one of them would say.

'Ha, that one has overdone her makeup. She makes me sick. She looks exactly like a Jezebel,' the other would remark.

They also liked to talk about their greedy relatives in Africa who frequently solicited financial assistance from them. One of them had told a story of his uncle who swindled him of a very large sum. He had sent the money to him to help build a house. But he arrived in Africa to discover that the uncle never built any house and that the photograph he sent to him was that of someone else's property.

It didn't take long before the owners and staff of the nightclub began to love Donaldson. Apart from his towering height which was a deterrent to troublemakers he was very punctual and hardworking. Out of sheer generosity, the club allowed every security guard two free cans of beer after midnight. But Donaldson never went for it. When the manager asked if he didn't take alcohol, he replied, 'I do drink beer, but I don't believe in drinking while on duty.' The amazed manager then instructed his staff to allow him to take his beer home if he so wished.

Meanwhile, Donaldson's attitude towards the job he initially considered as transitory had gradually changed. He never liked a job that involved standing or walking about for ten hours. After all, there were other security jobs which didn't involve standing for so long. Anytime there was an opening for such, he believed that his experience at Hawk would be an advantage. And he would also be able to quote them as his reference. But, with his tremendously growing popularity at Hawk and the nightclub, he began to enjoy the job. As for his wife, she had stopped asking him to quit. One thing had further endeared him to her. As he arrived from work on the first payday, he brought out his pay packet and handed it to her, saying, 'Darling, I received my first wages last night. Take it. Everything is for your wardrobe. Ever since our arrival in London you have never bought more than one dress in a year. Please, don't refuse it because I want you to dress better than all your colleagues at work. Buy beautiful shoes, bags and jewellery as well. If the money is not enough I promise you my next wages as well.' Samantha was dumbfounded. She could only stare at him with mouth agape.

'But ... but ....'

'Sh-hhh,' interrupted Donaldson as she tried to utter some words. Putting his forefinger across her lips, he whispered, 'Darling, no buts and no ifs. It's all yours!'

But she eventually managed to say, 'Honey, you need new clothing and shoes too.'

'Yes, darling,' he replied. Surveying his uniform from the collar of his coat to his boots, he added, 'Here's a new beautiful three-piece suit and a pair of fine shoes. I still have two more sets of these in the wardrobe. I don't need more than these for now.'

Samantha didn't say anything afterwards but kept staring at him as he drove that morning. 'Oh my God,' she thought. 'What a caring husband, loving father and selfless individual Donny is! Lord, please crown these amazing qualities with the salvation of his soul,' she added with tears rolling down her cheeks. But Donaldson was stupefied as he saw her through the driving mirror.

'Honey, why are you crying?' he asked.

'Me? Crying?' Samantha was startled. 'No, I'm not crying. The joy of the Lord is my strength,' she concluded.

'C'mon, darling, and wipe your tears. I know what you are thinking and why you are crying,' said Donaldson as he drove on.

It was Donaldson's fourth month at the job. The family's finances had improved, and he had decided to live joyfully in the present. He would stop thinking about his past and accept whatever fate had brought his way. Although his was an ignominious story of falling from grace, he would try to forget the past. He would try not to be psychologically affected by his transformation from a banker, who had the whole world at his feet, to a security guard who was subjected to insults from miscreants. But as much as he would love to forget his past there were some people who derived pleasure in teasing him about the political situation of his country. He always regretted the stupid mistake he made which played into their hands. One of the regular revellers, who looked gentlemanly, had asked him the country he came from. But a few nights later, when the man and his friends were drunk, they began to tease him. Some called him Samuel Doe's brother while some called him a coward for running away from war. The revellers eventually nicknamed him Sergeant Doe. And it didn't take long before he was being called this by everyone at the club.

Despite being reminded of where he came from he would try not to let his past affect his present. After all, the greatest gift of nature was life. If he lived, he might have a better future. Who knew? He remembered his colleagues at the Central Bank of Liberia who were murdered by their abductors. What if he had been killed too? He sighed and thanked his stars. He then realised that if he was serious about forgetting the past he had to forget everything that had to do with it.

Those were the thoughts on Donaldson's mind as he sat on the bus going home from work one Sunday morning. And he was so engrossed that he was oblivious of a man that took a seat beside him until he was interrupted by the man.

'Good morning my son,' said the man.

Donaldson was greatly surprised to discover that the passenger sitting next to him was the same old Caribbean man who had spoken to him in Peckham some seven months ago! He could only stammer a reply. After that, the duo stared at each other in silence for some moments. The silence was eventually broken by the old man:

'Congratulations on your new job,' he said.

It was another shock for Donaldson.

'How did you know it's my new job?' he asked.

'But I know that Hawk is a new security outfit in this city and there's their badge on your uniform.' replied the man as Donaldson managed a smile.

'Okay, but where are you going this early in the morning?' asked Donaldson.

'I've come to see you.'

'Me? What convinced you that I was on this bus?' asked Donaldson who could no longer hide his amazement.

'Son, I see you go to work every evening and return early in the morning,' the man said. 'But let's skip all those trivialities and address my purpose of visit,' he added.

'The purpose of visit?' Donaldson asked, surprised.

'Yes,' replied the man. Continuing, he said, 'I have come to ask if you have found your identity.'

'Old man, please stop speaking to me in parables. I don't understand them. What is this identity you've been talking about?' asked Donaldson almost angrily.

'Don't be naive, young man. Your identity has to do with your celestial ancestry, reason for your existence here on earth and your destination when you cease to exist here. Which of these have you found out?'

'Why is it important I find out?' asked Donaldson with a pinched face.

'Because they hold the key to your living a fulfilled life, which entails earthly prosperity and more importantly, prosperity beyond,' replied the old man. But, changing the course of their discussion, he suddenly asked, 'Where are your friends? I mean the ones I saw you with at Peckham some months ago.'

Turning his face away, Donaldson replied, 'They're fine.'

'Fine?' the old man asked inquisitively. 'Are you sure they're fine? Where are they now?'

That was yet another bombshell. It seemed the man knew everything. But Donaldson decided not to answer any of the questions. And while the old man waited for his response there went the automatic announcement, 'Bermondsey Station!' That was Donaldson's destination. But as he rose to leave, the man said, 'Son, you are still a lion cub in the midst of sheep. And it's your last chance to recover your identity, I'm afraid.'

Without saying a word, Donaldson descended the stairs to the lower deck of the bus and exited. But he was visibly agitated. Who was the old man and how did he know everything about him? He knew about his job, his commute and the fate of his friends. He asked him to find out his identity! He had not time for any 'celestial origin' but he was particularly troubled by the statement, 'it's your last chance to recover your identity, I'm afraid.' 'This man is scaremongering,' he concluded.

CHAPTER 18: FIRST LONDON MIRACLE CRUSADE

The rate at which atheism was gaining ground everywhere was a major concern for Evangelist David Clooney. There were old and new atheistic theories out there which were aimed at disproving the existence of God. These theories were impediments to soul winning, while they acted as clogs in the wheel of spiritual growth of believers. As a matter of fact, many new converts had backslid due to these theories. What about stories of the so-called new discoveries often captioned on the front pages of popular newspapers and magazines which tended to discredit the biblical account of creation? Such captions included, 'GOD IS A MYTH'; ORIGIN OF SPOKEN LANGUAGES TRACED TO ORANGUTAN!' etc. The evangelist was always shattered any time he saw such captions. His feelings were similar to what he had when there was news about a stabbing among the youth. Something urgent must be done to break evangelical ground, especially in notable cites of Europe and America where atheist beliefs thrived. There were only two scriptural ways of confronting the problem. And these were prayer and increased evangelism. It was high time the children of God woke up from their dangerous slumber and confronted the spiritual menace. Evangelism must be prioritised. After all, the great commission was for all Christians and not just for a few True, the evangelists were just people whose hearts were specially burdened and equipped by God for soul winning. That didn't mean that they were the only ones who were charged with evangelical responsibilities. The responsibility of evangelists, among others, was to encourage and mobilise other children of God in the area of soul winning. Evangelist Clooney couldn't understand why the church suddenly switched off from its massive responsibility. From the beginning of the year the Lord had been speaking to him about holding crusades in three notable cities. These were London, New York and Brisbane.

The London crusade was to come up first. The venue would be the main bowl of Wembley stadium. It would be a huge effort trying to carry other churches along. To stage a citywide crusade, he had learnt that local churches must be directly involved. Although his ministry was still young, he manifested, by the mercy of God, several gifts of the Holy Spirit needed for the work. Such gifts included healing and deliverance, word of wisdom, word of knowledge and prophecy. And, talking about physical blessings, the Lord had raised lots of financial supporters for his ministry in many countries. There were lots of churches who paid donations to his ministry. The story of his ministry was that of obedience and zeal. He was practising as a medical doctor when God called him to full-time evangelism. He never hesitated. He immediately dropped his stethoscope for a Bible and microphone. That was only a year after he had given his life to Christ. He still remembered his first mission with a heart full of praises for the Lord. It was that mission that highlighted how the Lord wanted to use him in the work of the ministry. It was during the annual convention of his church in London. The pastor of the church was the first to receive the revelation about his evangelistic ministry. When told about it, David Clooney only said, 'If that's the will of the Lord I'm ready.' The pastor was surprised. He was surprised because Christian professionals rarely heed a full-time calling immediately. The pastor remembered how long it took him to be converted from top civil engineer to a full-time pastor. But here was a young medical professional who was ready to forsake all for Christ – just like Simon Peter had done!

David Clooney had his first chance of mounting the pulpit on the final day of the three-day convention. It was believed that the invited guests needed to be witnessed to as many still didn't know the difference between church-going and giving one's life to Christ. And so, David Clooney was given a rare opportunity of exhibiting his God-given evangelistic gift. After a brief opening prayer, he went on to read a Bible passage which he had prayerfully selected from Romans 5:12–21. But as he was still reading the scripture something remarkable took place. A mentally disabled preteen boy, who suddenly broke loose from his accompanying grandmother, ran towards the pulpit. And before the ushers could overtake him he was already standing before David Clooney, yelling, 'You lie. Grace didn't come through anybody. Nobody has grace!' But as the ushers tried to take him away David commanded them to leave him alone. Turning to the boy, he said, 'You evil spirit, I command you to come out of him in the name of Jesus Christ!' There was a piercing scream from the boy after which he dropped on the floor and began to roll over. The boy then lay flat and convulsed rigorously for some moments. There was a loud scream. A few moments later he was sitting up looking at David, perfectly well. He rose and looked about the auditorium. He then began to sob. His grandmother broke from the congregation and ran to embrace him, weeping profusely as she did.

'Joshua!' she called out to the boy.

'Yes, grandma,' replied the boy.

The old woman told how the boy's father, who was her only child, had developed a strange sickness and died. And precisely a year after his father's death, the boy too suddenly had a protracted headache which was diagnosed as a migraine. Later he began to exhibit mental disabilities which gradually developed into full-blown insanity. When there seemed to be no medical solution she had taken him to several Christian meetings of which the convention was one. There was a tumultuous thanksgivings and praises unto the Lord at the convention, the kind that the assembly had never witnessed before. When the altar call was made at the end of David's sermon, more than sixty guests came out to give their lives to Jesus Christ with most of them signifying their intention to become members of the church.

That event was all it took David for his ministry to take off. After the convention he began to receive invitations to minister at both church events and open-air crusades. His first invitational mission was held at a Pentecostal church in Reading while the next one was at the Celtic Park in Glasgow, where more signs and wonders took place. He had also been invited to Canada, Australia and the Republic of Ireland. Ever since his mission at the Celtic Park he had a packed schedule and he became a household name among Christians in Europe and America. His first Christian book, titled 'He's Ready When You Are' was a bestseller too.

The planned London crusade was to coincide with his ministry's fifteenth anniversary. And lots of churches, both orthodox and non-orthodox, had been co-opted into its planning. A circular, which stated the objectives of the crusade as well as its modus operandi, had gone around these churches as a starting point. A meeting was then held with representatives of the assemblies at a location in London. It was after the meeting that banners and fliers were printed. There were also advertisement slots on printed and electronic media. The crusade was scheduled to be held in the evenings with workers seminars taking place in the mornings. Several experienced Christian preachers were invited from various countries to teach at the seminars. For about forty days which preceded the events a powerful prayer chain was in existence among the participating churches. One of the invited preachers had emphasised at the seminar that whenever children of God came together harmoniously in prayer the kingdom of darkness must surely bow. Indeed, the kingdom of Satan bowed right from the first day of the crusade. A notable atheist, a Professor at Oxford University, gave his life to Christ!

The three-day crusade was televised live on Christian television. The first day was primarily for praise and worship. The publicity given to the event was so huge that all the available seats were filled up before the commencement of the programme. The programme commenced at 6 p.m. prompt with an opening prayer after which the whole stadium became lively with God's praises.

At around 7 p.m., without being introduced, Evangelist Clooney mounted the pulpit wearing a white suit with a white shirt and a white tie with black stripes. That was his style – he never liked to be introduced. He disliked being applauded. He believed all applause, glory, honour and praises should be given to God, and God only. And as he mounted the pulpit, many who hadn't seen him before didn't know that it was the evangelist they had been waiting for until the whole stadium erupted in clapping, jumping and whistling. But the evangelist had a way of diverting attention from himself. 'Yes! Keep on clapping for Jesus, the King of kings and Lord of lords! He is the Rose of Sharon and the fourth Man in the fiery furnace! He is the Lion of the tribe of Judah and He is the unchangeable Changer! C'mon, you can do better than that!' he said. After that he burst into a very popular worship song with a specially organised choir taking over from him.

After the first stanza of the song he gestured to the choir to pause and said, 'We had designed this night to be a preamble. That is, we intended to bring the throne of God down to this arena through praises and worship with a few interludes of prayers and a brief sermon. But God won't make it a preamble. He's into action right away! He just told me now that healings have commenced in the body of some people in this place. Oh, thank you Jesus!'

Indeed, God really moved through the opening day's activities. Lots of people received healing and lots came out to give their lives to Christ. But the most astonishing was the miracle that took place in the home of another university professor, a renowned atheist whose eighteen-year old son was a terminal cancer patient. The boy had just been discharged from hospital so he might die at home with his family. But the son urged his parents to tune to Christian TV. Not willing to deny him any of his last wishes, the parents reluctantly obliged. Coincidentally or miraculously, it was at that point that the evangelist asked everyone watching the crusade via TV to lay their hands on their TV set for prayer. The boy obeyed. And as the prayer was still on, he fell into a deep slumber and began to dream. He was in a very large surgery room awaiting a surgical operation. And the only surgeon, who was dressed in all white, looked at him with a smile as he lay in surgical bed and said, 'You'll be fine, son. Without being anesthetised, the surgeon placed a surgical knife upon his cancerous part and removed a big lump of flesh. He then began to apply the sutures. But, amazingly, the boy didn't feel any pain whatsoever throughout the operation. He didn't even feel the touch of the knife or needle! After the operation the surgeon gestured to him to rise. Putting his right hand across his shoulders, he said, 'Son, it is done. You may go back home to your parents now and tell them that I love them.' Falling before the surgeon, the boy repeatedly thanked him until he woke up.

Still thanking the surgeon as he woke, the boy gently opened his eyes, surveyed the room for some moments and then jumped to his feet. His parents were greatly amazed.

'What's the matter?' they both asked.

'I've seen the Lord,' the boy replied. 'He has healed me and given me a new lease of life,' he added.

'How do you mean?' asked his bewildered parents.

After explaining his encounter with the miraculous doctor, the boy was taken immediately to the hospital where stupefied oncologists confirmed that his cancer had disappeared! The news soon hit everywhere, including the media.

The professor and his wife were at the crusade the following evening to testify to the Lord's miracle and to surrender their lives to the Lord.

The three-day crusade was a meeting point for children of God in London and beyond. There were various activity groups to belong. These included Choir, Ushering, Security, Counselling, Follow-up, Technical, Cleaning etc. While Amanda was a leader of the Counselling group, Samantha had registered with the Ushering group.

Despite Samantha's increased enthusiasm as the crusade drew nearer, she wasn't able to attend the event. Disaster had struck on the first day of the crusade. As part of her morning routine, she had prepared breakfast for her family and was expecting her husband who always returned from work around seven o' clock. The first thing he normally did on his return from work was to brush his teeth and then eat his breakfast. He would then warm the car engine in preparation for dropping his family members off at school or work. But it was an odd morning as Samantha and the children waited endlessly for him. Her start time at work was nine o' clock and so was the children's school time. But a few minutes before nine o' clock Donaldson was nowhere to be found. All efforts to reach him on his mobile were abortive as the phone kept ringing without being picked up. She suddenly began to feel that something unpleasant must have happened. She then went into the bedroom and searched his folders for his employers' number. But her phone suddenly rang. It was her husband's employers. And she nearly passed out when she was told that her husband was at the intensive care unit of the St Thomas hospital.

The incident which led to his hospitalisation took place around 3 a.m. A group of four trouble-making, heavily drunk yobs had been ordered out of the club. As Donaldson led them out, one of them grabbed his collar from behind and said, 'Mr Samuel Doe, go back to your own country.' Donaldson turned around, grabbed the yob's hand and tried to tear it from his collar. Just then, there was a great thump! Another yob had smashed his head with an empty beer bottle. And, as he fell on the floor facedown, another one stabbed him at the back and left the knife hanging there while they all fled. It was a great commotion at the club. Everyone, including the clubbers and passers-by, fled the scene at once. Within a few minutes, a team of police-accompanied paramedics arrived at the scene. But the knife couldn't be removed without surgery. It sank deep into his back. He was rushed to hospital.

He was still in a coma when Samantha arrived at the hospital. She had earlier on called her boss and explained what happened. She had also contacted her children's schools. With the situation of her husband, however, she was granted a two-week compassionate leave by her employers. But when he didn't come around within the two weeks, she had to take her annual leave entitlements. The medical experts in charge had told her that her husband had a fractured skull and had had his spinal column pierced. With tears rolling down her cheeks, she had asked about his chances of surviving. But the doctors only said, 'We shall surely try our best. For now, we've not been able to assess the extent of damage to the skull, but we are aware that the knife penetrated his lamina and entered the spinal cord at the T11 level, sustaining fatal bony injury in the process. The neurologists cannot establish yet if there is intramedullary of the cord.' But Samantha didn't seem to understand the explanation.

Donaldson remained in a coma more than three weeks after the surgery, with his dutiful wife always waiting upon him with prayers. Her church pastor, together with some members also paid regular visits. Amanda too was as supportive as ever. She always joined her friend at the hospital as soon as she finished work. And, while she was around, Samantha had an opportunity of rushing home to see her children. Auntie Michelle was sleeping in to look after them. The children were very agitated, eagerly looking forward to their father's return. Each time they heard the clicking of the main door locks, they both rushed towards the door to discover that it was only their mother! And there went the usual questions, 'Mum, where is Dad? When is he coming back?' But she always tried to hide her emotion as she replied, 'Just pray for your Dad. He will soon be back.' She, however, had a great fear about her husband's situation. This fear was borne out of his glaring enmity against the Lord. Should he die in that position his destination was obvious. She missed a heartbeat anytime she thought of it. The Bible had made it clear that if anyone's name was not found written in the book of life, he was thrown into the lake of fire. That was the main reason she wept at night and seldom ate. Encouraging her was, therefore, a herculean task for Amanda, her only bosom friend.

Samantha seemed to have lost all sense of Christian reasoning. There was an occasion when Amanda asked, 'Don't you believe that the Lord is at work?' But she asked almost disagreeably, 'Over a sinner and one of His worst enemies?'

'Yes, Samantha,' replied Amanda after a smile. 'He is at work ... for your sake. Did you read the story of Noah? The Bible didn't say that God found all his family members righteous. He was the only one that was recorded in the Bible as being righteous. But God also saved his family members from the earthly catastrophe, for his sake. That is why we say that His mercy endures forever. Look at all these years that we have been praying for salvation of your husband. Do you think God will not grant our request? Sure, He will. The Bible says that the effectual fervent prayer of the righteous avails much. C'mon, Samantha! Where is your faith?'

That was the first time Samantha heartily smiled since her husband's hospitalisation.

CHAPTER 19: HOLINESS UNTO THE LORD

Weeks after the powerful crusade, Evangelist Clooney still had lots to do. He had to supervise the follow-up of the new converts. There were several responsibilities he never delegated. And supervision of follow-up was chief among them. There was a large diagram of four concentric circles pasted on one of the walls of his moderately decorated office. The diagram was used to illustrate four stages of the work of his ministry. The smallest of the circle was labelled 'Evangelism.' This was followed by one labelled 'Conversion,' which referred to the moment sinners came forward to accept Jesus Christ. The next circle represented 'Distribution.' That is, distribution of converts among participating churches, while 'Follow-up' was the fourth and largest. In the speech he delivered at the pre-crusade seminar, he explained the reason for the size of each circle:

'Although the task of winning souls is enormously large, but that of keeping them is much larger. It is evident that the life of a backslid convert is much more horrible than it was before his conversion. That explains why Jesus didn't ask us to 'make converts of all nations' but 'make disciples of all nations.' Conversion is the beginning of the Christian journey while discipleship is the period when the Christian grows and learns to be a soldier for his Lord.

'As there is no point recruiting a soldier that would be taken out easily by the weakest of opponents, there is no point for evangelism if there is no adequate provision for the converts afterwards. Between Conversion and Follow-up lies Distribution, which is depicted by a circle almost the same size as that of Follow-up. They must join churches where holiness is the watchword. Some would say that righteousness, like salvation, is a gift to every believer and the Lord has bestowed same upon the church. While that is true, the Lord still expects holiness from us. Holiness is not work done to attain salvation. By the way, salvation is not attained by any work on the part of man. On the contrary, holiness is the work generated by righteousness of Christ or salvation. In other words, holiness is the fruit of righteousness. And holy living by Christians is what Apostle Paul refers to as work, in the book of Second Timothy. 'Faith without work is a dead faith,' therefore, implies, 'Christianity without holy living is not Christianity.' That phenomenon which makes the neighbours of a new convert realise that he has become a Christian without seeing him carrying the Bible or going to church, is the work generated in him by salvation or the righteousness of Christ. So we can infer that righteousness is an internal spiritual endowment of a Christian due to salvation, while holiness is his external physical attribute due to righteousness. Hence, when a thief stopped stealing, or a smoker stopped smoking, or a fornicator stopped fornicating, or a liar stopped lying, or a slanderer stopped slandering, etc, as a result of giving their lives to Christ, the work is said to be done by their salvation.

The task of spiritually uprooting juvenile crimes also remained uppermost in Clooney's mind. The next youth rally as well as hospital and prison evangelisms were being planned. Letters had been forwarded to the management of selected hospitals and prisons to that effect. Top among patients to be visited were victims of knife or gun crime and the aged. It was during Donaldson's fourth week in a coma that Evangelist Clooney and his team visited his hospital. They were at the hospital for more than four hours going from one ward to another, praying for patients and taking their contact addresses. At the end of his visit the evangelist decided to see the Chief Medical Officer of the hospital in his office before leaving. He had to walk a distance along the corridor, to the South East ward, towards the Intensive care unit, before taking the lift to the office. Meanwhile, Amanda, who wasn't aware of the evangelist's presence at the hospital, had gone to see one of the doctors in charge of Donaldson's case on the upper floor and was returning in the same lift. As she alighted from the lift the first person she met was the evangelist. She greeted him ecstatically. Although he missed the lift so as to return her warm greetings, he didn't seem to recognise her. But before she could introduce herself, one of the evangelist's entourage, who knew her very well, turned to the evangelist and said, 'Sir, this is Sister Amanda Ashley, one of our counselling leaders at the last crusade. She is wife of Pastor Paul Ashley of the Divine Light Evangelical Church, and daughter of Reverend Wilberforce.'

'Oh, my goodness!' exclaimed the evangelist. 'Please, pardon my short memory,' he added. Beaming, Amanda replied, 'That's alright sir. I can understand the enormity of your responsibilities. We are all proud of you sir.'

From there, a long dialogue ensued between them. First, they talked about the success of the last crusade, and then about the just-concluded hospital evangelism. He later asked what she had come to do at the hospital. Amanda told him about Donaldson. She said, 'His wife is a very close friend and a colleague at work. She is also a prominent member of our church.'

'What about the husband?' the evangelist asked.

Staring away morosely, she replied, 'He doesn't believe in God. We've done everything humanly possible about his salvation, and now we have resorted to only prayer.'

'Well, Sister,' beginning the evangelist, 'nothing is humanly possible about the salvation of souls. Everything is done by Christ through his atoning blood. Can we see him at once?'

The evangelist was led to the intensive care unit where Donaldson was still lying in a coma. It was around 6 p.m. and Samantha had briefly gone home to see her children. Amanda would take her leave as soon as she returned. That was the daily routine. The evangelist asked a team of nursing staff nearby if he could come near the patient. And they obliged. But as he and Amanda walked towards Donaldson's bed, the evangelist suddenly fell on his knees and gave a terrifying shriek, saying, 'No, Lord! Remember your mercy and unfailing love. Remember your words, Lord. You said you don't delight in a sinner's death. Lord, remember your pain and the cross. Remember your covenant with me – You said anything that I ask in your name shall be done for me. Lord, you said 'anything' and not 'some of the things!' Lord, it will be an overwhelming victory for the enemy should you be adamant. Consider also the souls that will be won for You here today as a result of this forgiveness!'

Crowd of hospital staff and relatives of patients gathered round the evangelist and watched as he knelt down head bowed, resting his two hands on the floor. A senior nursing staff, who didn't want to be put in trouble by the action, thought the evangelist needed to be reminded that he was in a hospital ward – an intensive care unit for that matter. But she was cautioned by her colleagues as she tried to approach him. After some moments, the evangelist gave thanks and rose. With his eyeballs turned red and a small pool of water on the floor where he knelt, it was obvious that the evangelist had been shedding tears as he prayed. He summoned the unit staff and apologised to them. He then told them that the patient will come around from coma in less than an hour and that he will be back to see him in two weeks' time. Everyone in the unit was astounded by the evangelist's conviction as he spoke. But he still remained gloomy as Amanda saw him off at the corridor. Anxious to get some clues, Amanda asked, 'I hope everything is alright sir?'

'Yes, Sister,' he replied, 'The Lord has broken the covenant of death for now,' he added.

'The Lord has broken the covenant of death for now?' Amanda kept asking herself as she walked back to the unit. She didn't understand what that meant. Did it mean Donaldson would eventually die after coming around? But the evangelist said he would come back in two weeks to see him. Did that mean he intended to see him before he died? Amanda made up her mind not to tell her friend about the worrying statement.

No sooner did the evangelist leave than Samantha arrived. She was promptly told about his visit and the prophecy about her husband coming around. Although she was very happy about the prospect of speaking to her husband again, she rued the missed chance of meeting the evangelist for the first time. She had missed the last crusade, she didn't even have the chance of watching the live telecast. The major reason she wanted to attend the three-day crusade was to bring her husband's salvation before God. She had planned to speak to the evangelist if she had an opportunity during the pre-crusade seminar. But she missed the seminar too, and so was unable to ask the evangelist to pray for her husband.

Amanda wasn't in a hurry to leave that evening. She was anxious to see the evangelist's prophecy fulfilled. The nursing staff too couldn't hide their feelings. Everyone was apprehensive. The head of nursing staff kept checking on Donaldson at regular intervals. And exactly fifty minutes after the prophecy, the unfathomable took place. Suddenly, there was a loud sneeze from one of the patients. It was Donaldson! The room went wild with jubilation. Even the unbelievers joined the rest as they repeatedly chorused 'Thank You Jesus.' Donaldson slowly opened his eyes and looked about the room. He couldn't understand what all those people were doing in 'his bedroom.' Samantha, who was already standing next to his bed, held his hand with one hand and raised the other in God's praises. He then turned to his wife and stammered, 'What are these people doing in our room?' Samantha didn't know what to say. She only stroked his forehead and said, 'That's alright darling.'

The consultant was promptly informed. And within a few moments he and his team came down to see the patient who had been their focal point for almost four weeks. Samantha and her friend were politely asked to vacate the room while the curtains were drawn. Donaldson surveyed the members of the consulting team one after the other trying to figure out who they were and what they were doing in his home. And as the consultant placed his stethoscope on his chest, he asked, 'Please, who are you guys and who invited you here?' But the consultant didn't mince words.

'Mr Weah, this is not your home. You are in intensive care unit of the St Thomas's hospital. You had been in a coma for four weeks after sustaining serious head and back injuries at your place of work.'

'Injuries?' he asked. He then tried to stroke his shaved head with his right hand. But his head was totally covered with heavily padded bandages.

'How did you say I sustained the injuries?' he asked inquisitively.

But the consultant remained calm as he painstakingly replied, 'You see, Mr Weah, the most important thing is that you came around from coma with your mind intact. You were brought here four weeks ago by paramedics with those injuries. We may not be able to explain to you the incident that led to them. But first thing is to assess you and carry out our next responsibility now that you are back. If you would like to speak to your wife she will be allowed to speak to you when we are done.'

Looking in the consultant's eye, he shook his head miserably. Feeling uncomfortable lying on his side for so long, he tried to roll over. But that wasn't possible. He tried once again but couldn't. He then tried to sit up. But that wasn't possible either. He then rolled down the duvet to discover that his trunk was fully bandaged. He was greatly disturbed. With mouth agape, he then stared away trying to recollect the circumstances that led to his current predicament. How did he sustain the injuries? Was he run over by a drunken lorry driver? He needed Samantha to explain to him, he concluded.

The assessment was completed. The heart and circulatory system were in perfect condition. And the consulting team were happy at the rate the wounds were healing. But there was an issue that they needed to discuss with the patient or his next of kin. The consultant called his team aside and had a brief talk with them. It was decided that they speak to his wife first.

The consultant spoke to Sam in his office. Joined by Amanda, she followed the team as they walked through the corridor to the lift. After the consultant and his team had left the unit Donaldson was served a liquid meal. He was also provided with a bottle of water. He had to be placed on liquid meals for some time because of the situation of his throat. A team of nursing staff helped him sit up by raising the bed's headboard to an appropriate Fowler's position. And after their leader had congratulated him he unclipped his case file from the top bar of the bed and read through it. He told him some of the instructions that were newly included by the consulting team. A follow-up surgery was to be done the following week and he should only take liquid foods until further notice.

'And when am I going to be discharged?' he asked sombrely.

'I have no idea sir,' she replied, 'But not any time soon.'

'Why?' he asked.

'Because we need to ensure that everything is perfect before discharging you,' replied the nursing staff as she prepared his injection.

Samantha and Amanda sat next to each other in the consultant's office.

'Good evening ladies,' said the consultant. And turning to Samantha, he said, 'Mrs Weah, I would like to speak to you alone.' But as Amanda rose to vacate the office her friend gestured to her to sit down.

'Sir, you may go ahead. She is the only one I have, apart from my husband,' she said to the consultant.

'Alright,' said the consultant. He then began by congratulating her on her husband's coming around. After that he explained how complicated the back surgery was, as the knife severed his spine. And all their efforts to restore the spinal cord had been futile.

'And what does that imply sir?' asked Samantha as the expert paused to clear his throat.

'You see, a severed spinal cord is a break in the network of nerve cells in the spine. This cord can be severed due to a traumatic injury. If this happens, it can cause paralysis below the point of the damage, which can be total or partial, depending on the level of injury and degree of impairment of the cord.'

'I hope none of those applies to my husband,' Samantha cut in.

'That's where I'm going, Mrs Weah. Your husband has suffered total paralysis as a result.' But Samantha threw herself on the floor before the man could finish his statement. She burst into tears and cried bitterly. Amanda could do nothing to console her friend as she was also shedding tears. Some invited staff of the social welfare department came in and began to console the two of them.

The news of Donaldson's paralysis was not broken to him until two days later when he was moved to the Accident Ward. Although Samantha told him all he wanted to know about the circumstances that led to his hospitalisation, she answered evasively when he asked what the consultant discussed with her. Now he could recollect all the events of that night – the hustle and bustle characteristic of the nightclub, the menacing yobs and their subsequent teasing. Lastly, he recollected the sudden explosion in his head. Before he was told about his disability, Amanda had asked him if he had ever heard of an evangelist called David Clooney. But all he knew about him was the massively advertised crusade in which his wife was anxiously waiting to participate. She then told him about the evangelist's visit, intercession and prophecy which promptly came to pass. She also told him about his promise to return in two weeks' time.

Amanda said, 'Donny, I know that you don't believe in God but He's the One responsible for your coming around from the coma and being alive today. I was bringing the evangelist to the intensive care unit to pray with you when, suddenly as we entered the room, God revealed something to him about you. To the amazement of everyone in the room, he fell on his knees and prayed agonisingly for close to a quarter of an hour. When he rose, we could all see that he had been crying as he prayed. His eyeballs were red, and his tears were collected on the spot where he knelt. At the end of his prayer he thanked God and then told the nursing staff that you would come around in less than hour. Nobody, except me, believed him. As our daily routine since you arrived here, I was supposed to leave when your wife arrived from home. But I waited to see you come around according to the words of the prophecy of the evangelist. Indeed, exactly fifty minutes after the prophecy, there was a loud sneeze from you! And for the first time in four weeks, you opened your eyes and looked Samantha in the eye. The whole unit went into uncontrollable jubilations. However, there was one thing I noticed about the evangelist as he left that evening – he looked very disturbed. When I asked him if everything was alright the reply he gave me was so agitating I decided not to tell Samantha. He only said, "The Lord has broken the covenant of death for now."'

Also listening was a lady nurse who brought Donaldson's previous case file from intensive care unit. 'Yes,' interjected the lady, 'we all celebrated your coming around which was obviously a miracle. I gave my life to Christ that night. Before then I used to think that I was being pestered by a Christian friend when she preached Jesus to me. But I went straight to her house when I finished my shift that night and asked her to teach me to give my life to Christ. With the way the evangelist prayed and the miracle that promptly followed that evening, only a fool will still doubt the Lord,' she added as he clipped the file to the top bar of Donaldson's bed and left.

Amanda continued as soon as the lady left. She explained how disturbed she was by the last word of the evangelist's reply. 'What did he mean by the Lord breaking the covenant of death for now? I couldn't understand what that meant. I hoped it didn't mean that you would come around temporarily and then pass on. I regretted not asking the evangelist what he meant by the statement before we departed. Realising my mistake, I ran after him perhaps he was still waiting for the lift. But he was gone. I then began to pray and meditate upon the statement until this morning when the Lord gave me the meaning through the book of Leviticus chapter twenty-six and verses twenty-seven to twenty-eight, 'Yet if in spite of this you do not obey Me, but act with hostility against Me, then I will act with wrathful hostility against you, and I, even I, will punish you seven times for your sins.' The Lord must have told the evangelist what He revealed to me in that scripture. That is, if you disobey Him despite this miracle of bringing you to life….' Scared of pronouncing what the consequence of the disobedience might be, Amanda left it to be imagined by everyone, especially, Donaldson.

At that moment, a team of three social welfare officers came in. After exchanging pleasantries with Samantha and Amanda, they all shook hands with Donaldson in turn. Only Samantha and Amanda knew their mission. After cracking a few jokes with him their leader began, 'Mr Weah, as you are quite aware, being in a coma for four weeks and to be back is phenomenal. Many never return. And many who return don't return with their complete mind. Being in a long coma as a result of serious head or back injuries sometimes leaves an indelible mark in terms of certain disabilities.'

'Our team of experts, who rub shoulders with the best in the world, have really tried their best to ensure that the indelible mark that I talk about is minimal as far as your case is concerned. I don't know if you are already aware that the knife injuries really affected your spinal cord and the surgeons really tried their best to ensure that your mobility was retained. But, unfortunately, the havoc was so much that the said mobility will have to be restricted to a wheelchair.'

'Meaning?' asked Donaldson inquisitively while tears rolled down Samantha's face.

When it was explained to him in a clearer term he roared like a lion, hitting both sides of his head rigorously with clenched fists as he wept. 'I'm finished … I'm finished … I'm finished…,' he lamented. The officers then beckoned to a male nurse holding a white tray nearby. The nurse came instantly, took a syringe from his tray and injected Donaldson. It was a sedative.

CHAPTER 20: HIS MERCY ENDURES FOREVER

Evangelist Clooney returned to the St Thomas hospital four days ahead of his schedule. He had travelled to Australia the same week he first visited Donaldson. But he didn't forget to mark the next visit in his official diary. While in Australia, he kept praying for Donaldson's salvation and for words that would bring about a turning point to his life, when he met him again. Ever since he saw him he couldn't keep his mind away from him. The evangelist never felt alright whenever he encountered a soul that was gliding towards destruction. The Lord just had to show mercy.

It was Saturday morning. Evangelist Clooney and his wife had a prayer of agreement before setting out. They first bound all the demons that were assigned against Donaldson's salvation. They also bound all the stray demons within and around the hospital. After that, they committed his heart to the hand of God and then thanked God for their answered prayer. Only a few people recognised him as he arrived at the intensive care unit in a white T-shirt over blue jeans. He went straight to the head of the unit and introduced himself and his wife. It was through the introduction that other excited staff realised that it was the guest they had been expecting. The unit head ecstatically recounted how the evangelist's prophecy promptly came to pass and how the events of the evening had motivated her and some of her colleagues to give their lives to Christ. The evangelist was very happy. He and his wife were then led to Donaldson's new ward.

There was a change in aura as the evangelist entered the sprawling room. All the staff in the room stopped what they were doing and stared at the evangelist and his wife as they were led in by top staff. Although they didn't know who the guests were, they were quite sure that they were VIP's of some sort. The lady first took the evangelist to the head of the ward – an Asian man in his forties – and introduced him. After exchanging greetings with the evangelist and his wife, the purpose of the visit was revealed to the ward head. He, together with the lady and the evangelists, then headed towards Donaldson's bed space.

'Good morning, Mr Weah,' said the ward head. 'You have very important visitors this morning,' he added. Donaldson, who was reading a sport magazine, dropped it immediately and looked at the evangelist. His instinct told him that it was the evangelist Amanda spoke to him about.

'Evangelist Clooney?' he asked.

The evangelist nodded in the affirmative and then introduced his wife. There was only one visitor's chair allotted to each patient in the room. But the ward head hurriedly brought one more because of the couple. The evangelist promptly stood up and shook his hand. While doing that, he asked the ward head if he was born again. But he smilingly replied that he used to attend church in India, but his volume of hospital responsibilities and duty schedule didn't allow him to attend church regularly since he came to Britain. Promising to see him later, the evangelist opened his briefcase and brought out one of the books he authored. He took his pen and signed it, titled *Keeping the Fire Burning* to the lady.

When the couple were left alone with Donaldson, the evangelist said, 'Good morning Mr Weah. I hope you feel better now.'

'Yes,' replied Donaldson, 'Thank you very much.'

'I didn't meet your missus last time I was here. Is she around today?'

'No. She has to attend to the kids at home, but she might be here before you leave.'

The evangelist then began by telling him what the Spirit of God revealed to him during his first visit. God had revealed that, even though he was an orphan, he was divinely nurtured and specially catered for. He grew up with spectacular aura of authority built around him. And where others experienced demotions he had raked in promotions upon promotions. Every door he knocked had opened and every button he pressed sounded. At a tender age, God had made him sit in the position of authority where the buck stopped at his table and orders carried out at mere gesticulation. God had made him a cynosure of all eyes and envy of all his peers. Blessed with divine charisma, God had made him a warmer of every heart and pleaser of every soul. Bestowed with enormous wisdom, God had made him a versatile speaker who was applauded by kings and princes. He had caught attentions of ambassadors of nations and wined and dined with presidents. Shinning like a million stars in his chosen profession, he had effected business growth and brightened up economic atmospheres. And rather than look for wealth, it was wealth that looked for him. Despite his disdain for God he was blessed with a God-fearing wife and charming children. And despite his haughtiness God had sent various messengers to him and had even spoken to him through a lunatic.

'Excuse me, evangelist,' Donaldson cut in. 'Did you say God had sent a lunatic to preach to me?'

179

'Yes, Mr Weah, replied the evangelist. 'That was what the Spirit said to me.'

That was amazing! Donaldson had never told anybody about the incident which took place in Liberia long before he got married. But the evangelist dropped another bombshell when he said, 'But the Lord Himself had appeared to you in your dream and in person too.'

'How do you mean sir?' asked Donaldson.

'What about the dream you had shortly before leaving Liberia? Who did you think the man who delivered you from those creatures was?' the evangelist asked.

Donaldson's mouth was agape. He remembered the frightening dream which he had kept within himself since then. Everything now seemed to him like a dream. So, God knew all that he had kept within himself and He had revealed them to the evangelist! Oh, he also said God had appeared to him in person. No. That wasn't possible!

'Did you say God had also appeared to me physically?' he asked.

'Yes, Mr Weah,' replied the evangelist.

'No,' he said, 'If God had appeared to me physically I would have stopped doubting His existence,' he added. But the evangelist burst into laughter.

'Sure, He appeared to you physically. But the mistake you made was you expected Him to introduce Himself to you as God! Okay, has anyone ever asked about your missing identity?'

'My goodness!' screamed Donaldson as he remembered the old Caribbean man. 'Was that the Lord?' he asked inquisitively. He knew it! He knew that there was something about the old man that wasn't natural. How he came to know about his commute and his convicted friends remained a puzzle to him.

The evangelist smiled.

'Mr Weah, I want to confess that I have never seen a person who has enjoyed the grace and love of God more than you do. When I saw you for the first time two weeks ago, the Lord told me that you were already in the snare of the enemy and you would never come back from the coma. But looking at you, I was filled with compassion and began to cry to the Lord for you. In the end, the Lord said He would give you another chance for the sake of your wife in whom He greatly delights and who continually makes supplications for you. But I must warn you from Leviticus chapter twenty-six and verses twenty-seven and twenty-eight, *"Yet if in spite of this you do not obey Me, but act with hostility against Me, then I will act with wrathful hostility against you, and I, even I, will punish you seven times for your sins."'*

Donaldson marvelled at the Bible verses. They were the same verses quoted by Amanda, a proof that the same God had spoken to them! Jittery, he then asked, 'What shall I do now? Evangelist, are you sure the Lord has not started punishing me for my sins already? Look, it has been confirmed that I will spend the rest of my life in a wheelchair. My hope and aspirations have gone down the drain. My skill, talents and brilliance have all evaded me. But if truly the Lord can still accept me I count all those as nothing!' And he sobbed.

The evangelist and his wife couldn't control their emotion. The evangelist took two white handkerchiefs from his briefcase, wiped his tears and those of his wife with one of them and Donaldson's with the other. When he had stopped crying, the evangelist said, 'Mr Weah, God has not started punishing you. In fact, he had his massive umbrella over you. But it was you who gradually moved away from its cover, into the waiting arms of the enemy. And I can assure you that with your decision for Him today you are adequately covered again. And, as for all that you believe you have lost, including your mobility, listen to the word of God in the book of Job chapter fourteen and verse seven, *'For there is hope of a tree, if it be cut down, that it will sprout again, and that the tender branch thereof will not cease.'* Listen again to the Book of Isaiah chapter one and verses eighteen and nineteen, *'Come now, and let us reason together, saith the Lord: though your sins be as scarlet, they shall be as white as snow; though they be red like crimson, they shall be as wool. If ye be willing and obedient, ye shall eat the good of the land.'* The arms of the Lord are always stretched to receive. He never casts away those who come to Him. He will surely accept you. He's even waiting for you as we talk.'

'Ha, evangelist,' Donaldson cried out, 'I have been so stupid. I have wasted lots of time and allowed earthly circumstances and knowledge to pitch me against my Maker. I don't care if I never walk again. And I don't care if I die a pauper but please teach me to give my life to Jesus.'

'What?' exclaimed the evangelist and his wife. 'You mean you want to give your life to Christ?' asked the evangelist joyfully. He was greatly astonished by Donaldson's resolution. He had never seen a new convert so desperate. And after he had led him to Christ the trio prayed and sang solemnly unto the Lord. But as the evangelist encouraged him in the Word of God all the people who had earlier on preached to him flicked through his memory. These included Agnes, his former secretary; the lunatic; the wealthy couple in the Aston Martin; Amanda; Samantha; Pastor Isaac; his Liberian friends; the old Caribbean man; Natasha, his own daughter; and Auntie Michelle. He then remembered Aunty Michelle's words, 'And any further means of appealing to you by Him may be appalling.' How correct she was!

Donaldson gestured to the evangelist to come nearer. The evangelist moved closer to him. And, stretching his both arms forward, the duo was locked in a bear hug. They were in this position when Amanda and her husband, together with Samantha, arrived.

'Oh, Samantha, Evangelist Clooney is here already,' Amanda said ecstatically as they approached Donaldson's bed space. But as the evangelist turned around to greet them, Samantha couldn't believe what she saw.

'Dave!' she exclaimed.

'Samantha!' the evangelist responded.

Then there was a palpable silence. Samantha and Evangelist Clooney stared at each other bewilderedly while the rest of the people gazed at them in turn. As Samantha turned around to speak, her eyes caught the evangelist's wife, who had also risen from her seat.

'Bridget!' she exclaimed.

'Samantha!' Bridget exclaimed.

With both hands on cheeks, mouth agape and eyes wide open, Bridget stared at Samantha speechlessly. At that moment, Amanda walked closer to Samantha and asked:

'Samantha, what's the matter? What's going on?'

'This is Bridget and that's Dave,' replied Samantha solemnly. Turning to Donaldson, she repeated, 'Honey, this couple are Dave and Bridget!'

Pointing to the couple in utter disbelief, Donaldson asked, 'Did you mean that Evangelist Clooney and his wife are the treacherous Dave and Bridget?'

'Yes, darling,' Samantha replied. 'His real name is David Hales.'

'This is incredible!' said Donaldson.

Everyone was speechless as they stared thoughtfully at the evangelist. And after some moments of silence, the evangelist calmly began, 'Pastor, Brother Donaldson and Sister Amanda, I want to confess to you all that my wife and I were truly treacherous. We had been the instrument of the devil. We were heartbreakers, backstabbers and betrayers. Samantha is right – I used to be David Hales before I met the Lord.

Evangelist David Clooney was born to an Australian father who had come to work in London at that time. His father's full name was also David Clooney. His mother, Nicole, was brought up together with an elder brother by a single mother. But after their mother's death, her brother took to drugs, alcohols and various social vices and seldom came home to look after his sister. And not long after their mother's death he was convicted of rape and sentenced to seven years imprisonment. Before his incarceration, he had let out one of their three rooms to David Clooney (Senior) who worked at one of the retail shops as a sales assistant. With incarceration of her brother, who was the breadwinner of the family, life became miserable for Nicole. But she soon had their tenant David Clooney to thank. Apart from paying his rent as at when due, he also took care of her financial needs. It wasn't long, however, before they fell in love and started sleeping together. Trouble, however, ensued when Nicole became pregnant and turned down David's abortion suggestion. A month before her delivery, David disappeared with all his belongings and was nowhere to be found. Nicole later gave birth to a bouncing baby boy whom she named after her absconded lover.

Some years later, Nicole met a South African Christian who showed her real godly love. A wedding was arranged, and they became husband and wife.

The husband, Nathaniel Hales, proved to be God-sent. He really took care of her and her son. Not only that, he regularly visited her brother in jail and preached the gospel to him. After his release from a Manchester prison, the guy became a very strong Christian. He came back to his married sister in London and apologised to her and her husband. With their council flat already repossessed, he returned to his fellow-converts in Manchester where he later founded a church. However, a year before Evangelist Clooney graduated from the university, Nathaniel Hales decided to return to South Africa with his wife and three children, including the evangelist. But the evangelist decided to stay behind, partly because of his education and partly because of Samantha. His stepfather then transferred the ownership of his four-bed room apartment to him and left sufficient funds in his account to complete his university education. All this time Dave didn't reveal the truth about his paternity to Samantha. The reason for this was, ever before he met Samantha, he had vowed to consign his real father to the past. To him, he had been long buried in the sea of oblivion and nothing or nobody would compel him to bring him back to life. There was only one man he really wanted to know and present as his father. And that was the kind-hearted Mr Nathaniel Hales. He always rued the day he discovered that he wasn't his real father; he had wished he didn't know!

Evangelist Clooney became a Christian through his stepfather not long after he jilted Samantha and got married to Bridget. His stepfather, who had come to London with his wife to attend the wedding, was displeased when he later learned about the circumstances surrounding his marriage. He felt for Samantha. He then called the newly-married couple and had a talk with them. He told them that both of them, especially, Bridget had committed a grievous sin against God by humiliating a loving and caring individual. Although they were married in church, that wouldn't stop them from being penalised for their sins of fornication and betrayal. For them to escape the impending wrath of God, they needed to give their lives to Jesus Christ and ask for Samantha's forgiveness. Although Evangelist Clooney had always been preached to by his stepfather ever before the latter went back to South Africa, he never seemed to be interested. But the night-after-the-wedding preaching was so incisive the two of them gave their lives to Christ. Both of them started attending Mr Nathaniel Hales' old Pentecostal church at Lewisham and were personally introduced to the pastor by Mr Hales before returning to South Africa. The pastor took over immediately, regularly visiting the couple at home for counselling and Bible study until they became strong in faith and prominent members of the church. It was during one of the visits to their home that God revealed to the pastor that Evangelist Clooney was to be a vital instrument in His hand.

It was during his first year in high school that he was told the story of his father for the first time. Before then, he had always wondered why his surname was different to that of his siblings. Touched by the inhuman treatment meted out to his mother, he hated his father and abhorred his name. As everyone was used to calling him the abhorred name, he cleverly made a slight change in its spelling and pronunciation. He changed David to Davies and promptly adopted his stepfather's surname. He was hence called and referred to as Davies Hales or simply, Dave. A few years after he had changed his name, his absconded father came begging. Having discovered that Nicole was married with children, he begged that he might be reconciled to his son. But young Dave refused to forgive him. Mr Clooney then went back to Australia a dejected person.

Many years later, after Dave became a Christian, he realised that there were three things he had to do to have a perfect relationship with God. One, he had to forgive his father; two, he had to revert to his original names; and three, he had to look for Samantha and apologise heartily. None of them was difficult for him as he had grown in faith. So, he picked up his phone, called his father and spoke to him for the first time after many years. The following day, he went to court to officially change his name. As for meeting Samantha, he found out that she was in Liberia working at the British consulate.

The couple arrived in Monrovia in the heat of the civil war. As all flights to the country had been suspended, they had to take a flight to Sierra Leone where they passed the night. The following morning, they hired a chauffeur-driven car and headed to Monrovia. Crossing the Sierra Leone-Liberia border was one of the most dangerous things to do during the Liberian civil war. There were Sierra Leonean and Liberian troops at their respective sides of the border, while Charles Taylor's and Yormie Johnson's rebels were everywhere shooting sporadically. These rebels didn't really pose any threat to white travellers. The major threat was from the militias loyal to the assassinated president. Based on America's alleged complicity in the capture and eventual murder of President Doe, Americans and other white expatriates passing through villages or towns under the militias' control faced a great risk. As the couple travelled in their hired car, they could see corpses scattered everywhere. And so many times they had to come out of their car to convince some heavily-armed militias that they weren't Americans.

'Hey, Americans, you killed our president. Didn't you?' asked a group of armed men as the couple came out of their car at one roadblock.

'Gentlemen, we're not Americans. We're Britons,' replied the evangelist.

The leader of the militia then regarded them for some moments before saying:

'What have you got to prove your nationality?'

The evangelist opened his briefcase and brought out their passports. The man took them and walked a short distance away and showed the passports to some of his members. After about five minutes he returned to the couple and asked: 'Have you got firearms in the car?'

'No,' replied the evangelist.

'Are you sure?' he asked. 'If I search the car and find any, I will put this in your nostrils,' he added, pointing a pistol at the evangelist.

Two of his men walked over to the car. One got into it while the other opened the boot. After a thorough search of the car the couple and their chauffeur were released to continue their journey.

The journey from the border town of Bo to Monrovia, which was supposed to take two hours, took almost nine hours! They arrived in Monrovia late in the evening and lodged in a three-star hotel with their chauffeur. After committing Samantha's heart unto the hand of God and rehearsing their pleading, they set out on a journey to the embassy the following morning. But, alas, the whole building was locked! On inquiry, they discovered that the embassy was closed about three weeks earlier with all the staff members evacuated. They then returned to London and promptly contacted the Foreign Office for information about Samantha. But they were gobsmacked to learn that she wasn't among the evacuated staff; she had resigned her appointment shortly before evacuation took place. The office couldn't clarify whether she was still in Liberia.

The couple, however, went through hell returning to Sierra Leone from Monrovia. A few kilometres before Bo, they were stopped by a group of militiamen who ordered them out of their car. After they had been duly searched, their leader looked into Evangelist Clooney's eyes and said, 'Without any doubts, both of you are American spies.' He was a hefty man in military camouflage that didn't seem to have been washed for ages; it was dirty and had blood stains all over it. He wore a very rough dreadlock that flung over his shoulders down to his chest and back. His big eyeballs, together with his protruding upper front teeth, made him look very scary. As he spoke, he had a fat roll of marijuana dangling between his lips. He held a riffle in his left hand and a long dagger in the right. 'Now, move that way!' he commanded, pointing to a narrow bush path. Before Evangelist Clooney could say a word, a man grabbed his collar from behind and pushed him along. Another man put his rifle at the back of Bridget's head and pushed her along. 'Move, you American swine!' they yelled as they pushed the couple along.

The couple were taken to an empty, bullet-riddled bungalow a few yards away. Two iron chairs were given to them to sit on while the gang members, about fifteen of them, deliberated. A few moments later, another group of armed men, led by a man in sunglasses, entered the building. The man in sunglasses approached the evangelist and asked: 'White man, are you truly an American spy?' The evangelist looked into his eyes. Without saying a word, he opened his briefcase and brought out their passports and a Bible.

'Gentleman, we're not Americans. We are British. I'm an evangelist and here's my wife. We came to this country to look for a friend who used to work at the British embassy in Monrovia,' said the evangelist.

The man regarded the couple for some moments and then turned around. Walking over to the group who brought the couple, he said to their leader, 'Scorpion, let's release these people; they are not spies.' But the hefty man with protruding teeth, referred to as scorpion, became annoyed.

'Who are you to ask me to release them,' he asked.

'Who are you, too, to make a unilateral decision?' fumed the sunglass man. 'By the way, who made you our leader?' he added.

From there, a heated argument ensued between the two groups. The argument eventually resulted in a bloody confrontation. And as the melee continued there was suddenly an amplified announcement from outside the building: "This building is completely surrounded by the Liberian federal troops. Drop your guns and put your two hands over your head." But they didn't obey. And shootings were exchanged for a quarter of an hour before the federal troops could gain access into the building. The confrontation, which had several members of the militia dead, left Bridget left arm seriously wounded. It was the evangelists' chauffeur who had gone to report their abduction to the federal troops. The troops didn't normally wade into abduction matter, but what happened that day was indeed a miracle. Bridget was taken to a Sierra Leonean hospital where a number of bullets were removed from her arm. Considering the medical standards of the hospital, however, the couple opted for an urgent return to London.

'But much as the medical experts tried….'

Evangelist Clooney didn't bother to complete the statement. Rather he took Bridget's left arm and rolled up her sleeve to reveal a prosthetic arm!

'N-o-o-o-o!' exclaimed Samantha. Throwing herself on the floor, she began to weep.

No one could console her as everyone was either weeping or battling against their tears. Amanda wept until her handkerchief got soaked. Donaldson held his forehead in both hands. When he raised his face, his eyeballs were as red as heated iron. Amanda's husband held his right thumb against a tooth as he repeatedly said: 'Oh Lord Jesus!' The hospital staff, who didn't know what really happened, came around and asked questions to which no one responded. Bridget, whose head had been resting on Evangelist Clooney's shoulder as she wept, suddenly broke from her husband and knelt before Samantha, saying: 'Samantha, you have done for me more than anyone could do for their cousin. You actually played my mother by giving me happiness and my livelihood. You made me a star in a profession you actually introduced me to. But I repaid your kindness with evil and your love with hatred, causing you unimaginable pain. Please, stop weeping for me. I deserve what I got. Although the Lord has forgiven me, I need your forgiveness too. Please, tell me you have forgiven me!'

But Samantha wept all the more. After a few moments she rose, wiped her tears and helped Bridget up. Putting both her arms across her cousin's shoulders, she said, 'Bridget, although what you did to me was so painful, I never wished you this. What is there for me to forgive? We were once lost like sheep without a shepherd, but Christ's love found us all and brought us home. All those events took place during our period of Godlessness.' Turning to Evangelist Clooney, she said, 'Dave, I want to thank you for taking very good care of my sweet cousin. I still love her as much as I used to, and nothing can separate her love from my heart!' Everyone sighed.

It was Donaldson who spoke next.

'So, it's really true that if anyone is in Christ he is a new creature – old things are passed away and all things have become new,' he said. Samantha was startled.

'Darling, do you realise you have just quoted a very important Bible verse?' she asked.

'Yes,' replied Donaldson, smiling.

'And do you believe what you have just quoted?' asked Amanda.

'Why not?' replied Donaldson. 'Am I not a living proof? Before Evangelist Clooney arrived here less than two hours ago, I was a stinking sinner – Satan's stooge. But now I am God's friend – the apple of His eye.'

'Oh my God,' exclaimed Samantha gleefully. 'Evangelist, what exactly did you do to my husband?' she queried sarcastically.

'Nothing more than what the Lord instructed me to do,' replied Evangelist Clooney smilingly.

And the three couples joined hands as they solemnly worshipped the Lord.

CHAPTER 21: A POUND OF SATAN'S FLESH

Donaldson was discharged from hospital about three weeks after his encounter with God. A week before his discharge, some officials of the social support department came to show him some wheelchair catalogues to choose from. And, assisted by his wife, he had chosen an easily affordable one. The officials were to return the following day for the payment. But Amanda and her husband went behind Donaldson and Samantha's back to pay for it. Donaldson and his wife were astonished when the wheelchair arrived with an official receipt. And it took almost a year, after a further twist of events, before they found out who the Good Samaritans were.

After Donaldson's discharge, Evangelist Clooney and Bridget travelled to Brisbane, Australia to spend some weeks with the evangelist's ageing father. His father had appealed to him to relocate to Brisbane as he remained unmarried and with no other children. Besides, the old man had inherited a sprawling mansion from his deceased father, which he wanted the evangelist and his family of five – the couple and three children – to inhabit and inherit. But the evangelist had politely told him that he could only be paying him a regular visit for the meantime. While the couple was away, Bridget and Samantha maintained regular communication via phone and email.

The morning after Donaldson arrived from the hospital, after his family members had left for work or school, he went into his room to pray. After bolting the door and confirming that all window blinds were fully drawn, he bowed his head and prayed tearfully, 'Oh my merciful God, this is my very first time of conversing with you one-on-one. That's why today will be remembered for the rest of my life. What have I got to say, Lord? Not so much. First, I want to thank you once again for your love and mercy that saved me. Having realised that it was my soul that the enemy was really after and not just my finance or health, I want to thank you for frustrating his plans. Lord, I've also come to let you know that the great deal of my time wasted in the enemy's camp hurts me badly. Lord, I'm still hurting … really hurting. And each time I remember my period of enmity against you I loathe myself. Two things I, therefore, ask of you Lord: That You may help me to forgive myself as You have forgiven me, and, that You may help me to take my own pound of flesh from Satan. Empower me, O Lord, to set his captives free and preach good news to the poor. Dear Lord, where my physical ability has failed You let my physical disability compensate. I ask all these in the name of Your only begotten son Jesus Christ.' And he wept bitterly.

There was someone knocking at the main door. He quickly wiped his tears, lifted himself into his wheelchair and rushed out of the bedroom. Using a device on the main door, he first set the door ajar to see who it was. It was the old Caribbean man! Donaldson was elated as he let him in. There was always coffee left behind for him in a vacuum flask. So, Donaldson offered his guest a seat and quickly served him a coffee. The old man looked about the living room as his host served him.

'Thank you, my son,' he said after taking a sip. 'The coffee is just as hot as I wanted it,' he added.

'Yes,' replied Donaldson, 'It's very cold outside. We're having the coldest winter of the decade,' he added.

'My son, it's always cold outside – winter, spring, autumn or summer,' replied the old man. 'That's why I'm happy you found this warm embrace at last. Stay within and you will never experience the biting cold,' he added.

After a long pause, the man suddenly asked, 'Now my son, have you found your identity?'

'Yes, old man. Just a minute,' replied Donaldson as he elatedly wheeled towards the bedroom. He came back holding an identity card which was made of fine gold. The old man rose as Donaldson brought it. He took it from him ecstatically and admired it for some moments.

'Yeah,' he said, 'you got it, my son. You have truly got it. You got it at last!' Handing it back to Donaldson, he said, 'Now put it on and let's see how fitting it is.'

Donaldson collected it and suspended it by wearing its immaculate lanyard around his neck.

'Oh, smashing!' exclaimed the old man. 'Now listen to me: never remove it from your neck for whatever reason. It is neither transferrable nor lendable. Keep it there perpetually. It is your eternal inheritance.' And without bothering to finish his coffee, he gestured that he was ready to leave. But when Donaldson reminded him of the need to finish his hot coffee, he replied, 'Son, what warms me up is not hot coffee but recovered identities.' But as he was about to exit the flat a small envelope fell off his jacket. Donaldson picked it up and wheeled after him.

'Sir, you dropped this envelope,' he said.

But the old man looked back casually and replied, 'That's yours, son. Bye for now.'

Donaldson bolted the door after the old man had gone out and then opened the envelope. In it was a small piece of paper on which a Bible verse was written.

His neck now began to ache. He slowly opened his eyes and realised that he had slept off while praying. Oh, he had been dreaming! The old Caribbean man had paid him a visit and had had a coffee in his living room! Wow! It was true that in his dream he'd finally got the required identity! Wait a minute – the old man had given him a Bible verse. Oh, what was it? Trying to recollect the verse, he held an index finger against his forehead and closed his eyes. Everywhere was apparently silent, except for the rhythmic ticking of wall clocks in the bedroom and living room. One second, … two seconds, … three seconds, … thirty seconds – he recollected! He quickly reached for his Bible. It was a very beautiful KJV preacher's Bible presented to him by Amanda's husband. Donaldson liked the pastor's perfectly coined compliments written in cursives on the first blank page, *'Presented to Brother Donaldson Jerome Weah, a prolific labourer in the Vineyard of our God. Go on, brother – hammer the devil!'* He opened the given verse and read. It was the ninth verse of Haggai chapter two, *'The glory of this latter house shall be greater than of the former, saith the LORD of hosts: and in this place will I give peace, saith the LORD of hosts.'* He was very happy. Now oblivious of his aching neck, he continued to praise the Lord.

Still wanting to assist his wife financially, he registered for weekly disability benefits. Although the stipend was meagre, he believed it would take care of some of their various bills. And, as he did when he received his first security wages, he invited his wife into their bedroom and handed the cash to her. Samantha was greatly surprised. She couldn't imagine him queuing up for benefits. And when she asked him how he felt queuing up for benefits, he simply replied that his pride only lay in Christ and His service. She could only stare at him thoughtfully. His next payment was spent on the printing of handbills which he used to summarise his life as a God hater and then God lover. He also acquired a battery-driven megaphone. He intended to distribute the handbills as he witnessed publicly. And after he had obtained all he needed for the solo-evangelism, he embarked on a seven-day fasting and prayer to dedicate the materials and to seek God's direction over how and where to start. After the seven-day programme he came up with the idea of Trafalgar Square as the venue, while witnessing would take place 5 p.m. Monday to Friday. He was very excited about it. He had told his wife that witnessing for Christ was the greatest of all jobs.

The only thing that he was waiting for was his water baptism which would come up next Sunday after the church service. Although he could start witnessing before water baptism, like Jesus, he wanted to fulfil all righteousness. Once that was out of the way he could launch out immediately. He was so excited that, on Saturday morning, he positioned his wheelchair before the standing mirror in his bedroom. Looking at his own image as he sat in the wheelchair clutching his Bible and megaphone, he said, 'Satan, the battle line is drawn. I know you are mocking my physical disability, but I don't need physical ability to defeat you. I'm only going out there to stage a repeat of what my Lord has done already. You and I know who is going to win this battle.' And he laughed scornfully, not knowing that his wife had been eavesdropping.

'Darling, you challenge me,' she said as she came in.

'How do you mean?' he asked.

'Your faith and determination make me look like a beginner in Christ,' she declared.

'You can't talk like that, darling,' said Donaldson, realising that his wife had overheard him. 'After all, you are my spiritual mother,' he added. And they both laughed.

The couple's protracted laughter attracted their inquisitive children who were doing their school homework in the living room. Natasha was surprised to see her father holding the Bible and megaphone as they came into their parents' bedroom. When her mother explained that the megaphone was an equipment of her father's proposed solo-evangelism, the girl was very happy. And when she was further told that the evangelism would daily take place, she said, 'Daddy, I've got an idea. You see, most people don't like to listen to things that have to do with God. So, one needs something to arrest their attention. If you allow me, I can always come with you and play my violin as a starter. There's no doubt that lots of people, including the tourists, will like to watch a young girl playing the violin. And as they gather to watch we can then have interludes of preaching.'

It wasn't only in academics that Natasha was the best student in her school; she was also the best in some of the school's extracurricular activities. She had represented her school at that year's edition of an interschool violin competition and came first. Among the prizes received by her was a very beautiful violin which she often played to entertain her parents and their guests.

Her parents looked at each other without saying a word. Once again, their daughter had proved that she was not just a child, but one sent to them for a specific purpose. Her father beckoned to her. And as she came up he placed his hand round her shoulders and asked, 'Natasha, where do you get all these ideas of yours from?' But his wife swiftly cut in.

'Stop pretending, darling,' she said. 'The answer is too obvious. A tiger cub is always a tiger!' Pretending he didn't understand what she meant, he smilingly asked, 'And what does that mean?'

'Sure, you know what I mean. You know that all your qualities were rubbed off on your children!' They both laughed again.

Trafalgar Square in London was a tourist centre built in 1840 in commemoration of the British naval Battle of Trafalgar. Everyday people gathered there for tourist or recreational purposes, especially during the summer to see Nelson's Column.

Although it was winter, there were lots of people at the square on the day Donaldson and his daughter first witnessed there. As previously rehearsed, Natasha started by playing her violin to the admiration of a very small number of people which gradually became a large crowd. A brief notice was, however, displayed to prevent the people from dropping coins at the feet of the girl. It read, *'Please, drop no coins. Just enjoy.'* After she had played a few secular songs, Natasha changed to Christian ones. As it was December, she started with *'Amazing Grace'* and then some very popular Christmas carols, such as *'Silent Night'* and *'While Shepherds Watch Their Flocks.'*

Amid a vociferous ovation, Donaldson gestured to his daughter to stop playing. He then turned on his megaphone and addressed the people, saying, 'Ladies and gentlemen, I want to thank you for appreciating the musical gift exhibited by this young girl. Don't you worry – you will still have some more. But there's a basic truth we need to share before she continues. It is a truth many of you will turn your back against and leave the moment I unveil it. And I cannot blame anyone for leaving because I had also turned my back against this truth all my life until recently. During my period of ignorance everyone who believed in this truth was a numskull. That was the period I stupidly championed its negation. But I wasn't doing that without a reason. In fact, if anyone here thinks he's got a reason to be obstinate I had scores of them.'

There was total silence as his audience tried to fathom what he was driving at. Many of them believed he was one of those civil right activists who openly criticised certain policies of the government. Their belief was hinged on the fact that Trafalgar Square, at that time, was a place where individuals or group of individuals publicly expressed their disdain for some governmental policies. But the way this activist chose to pass his message across was entirely different. He had employed the power of music and suspense, holding his audience spellbound. But one thing that was quite observable was that he didn't sound anti-government. He must be one of those state-sponsored canvassers.

After waiting endlessly for him to make his point, one middle-aged listener raised his hand and yelled, 'Mister, what is this truth you keep on emphasising?'

Donaldson look at him smilingly and said, 'Thank you very much sir. The truth that I antagonised all these years, but which saved me from destruction is Jesus Christ. There is heaven and there is hell. But Jesus can save you from the power of hell and give you earthly peace.'

His reply was greeted with various reactions from the audience. Some hissed and began to walk away while some just walked away quietly. Some of them laughed scornfully as they walked away. A bald, elderly man among them quipped, 'What a clever bigot!' Within a few moments only a handful of listeners were left standing before Donaldson. Not discouraged by the exodus, he continued to preach. He talked about how man fell in the Garden of Eden and how Jesus came and offered redemption through a blood sacrifice. He then spoke about himself – his professional status and former atheistic posture. He told of how he met Jesus in a peculiar way. Although the people listened with rapt attention and responded to the closing prayer, no one came forward to give their life to Jesus. After the closing prayer, he distributed two leaflets – a Christian tract and the one containing his personal testimony. Natasha then played 'Amazing Grace' to close the meeting.

Amanda and her pastor husband came visiting later that evening. They were both surprised when they learned about the evangelical adventure of Donaldson and his daughter. They particularly marvelled at the sudden and glorious transformation of a recalcitrant. But when the pastor congratulated him and his daughter on their exploits, Donaldson smilingly replied that the outreach wasn't all that successful as no one came out to give their life to Christ.

'That is where you are wrong,' replied the pastor. 'No evangelical effort is a failure. Soul winning begins from the spirit and then manifests physically. And the process is divided into four: cultivation, planting, tending, and harvesting. Sometimes a soul passes through all four before being saved. The stage when a sinner turns down frequent appeals to be preached to is the cultivation stage. There are lots of obstacles when you cultivate a land for farming. There are stubborn roots to be uprooted and unwanted trees to be felled. All these can constitute discouragement. Cultivation stage is the stage where your labour of prayer is directed to transforming the stony heart of a sinner to that of flesh.

'The stage when he now listens, whether intentionally or by accident, is planting or sowing. That is, you are sowing the seed of salvation in that soul. Tending is the stage when he listens wilfully but hasn't made up his mind to accept the Lord. At this stage, as you bombard his soul with the Word of God, you are helping to protect and water the seed already sown by you or someone else. The last stage is when the seed finally germinates, and the person gives their life to Christ. This is the harvesting stage. That is, the soul is harvested for Christ. Before a soul is finally saved it sometimes takes witnessing from various Christians who, through their preaching, move the soul from one stage to the next until it finally gets to harvesting stage. However, every labourer involved in this salvation chain has put in equal contributions, regardless who finally harvested the soul. In fact, all of them are harvesters.

'You see, when you spoke to a sinner and he promptly decided for Jesus you may be harvesting the soul on which some people had earlier on laboured through cultivation, planting or tending. That is what the apostle Paul means in the book of the First Corinthians chapter three and verse six, '*I have planted, Apollos watered; but God gave the increase.*' What am I saying? An evangelist does not only harvest but ably contributes to the chain of cultivation, planting, tending and harvesting.' Looking Donaldson in the eye, he added, 'By witnessing today, you have done at least three things – cultivation, planting and tending. And who knows, next time it may be harvesting.'

Donaldson was very happy. He meditated on the pastor's encouraging speech with elation boldly written in his eyes. 'Christians are the happiest and most knowledgeable people on earth,' he said to himself as he collected his cup of coffee from his wife. But as he lifted the cup to his mouth, his mobile phone suddenly rang. It was a strange number.

'Hello,' he said as he picked up the call.

'Is that Pastor Donaldson Weah?' asked the caller.

'Yes, this is Dr Donaldson Weah. Please, who's on the line?'

'My name is Arthur Lucas. I was at Trafalgar Square this evening and will like to speak to you privately. How can I see you tomorrow morning sir?'

'Sure, you can see me. But I must call you back to fix the venue and time. Is this your number?'

'Yes sir. Thank you very much sir.'

'You're welcome.'

Donaldson dropped the phone and stared at the ceiling ecstatically, to the bewilderment of everyone. After some moments of silence his wife asked, 'Who was that, honey?' But he turned to the pastor and said, 'Pastor, it seems our outreach really went beyond cultivation, planting and tending; I can perceive a harvest.'

After sharing his joy with his wife and guests he called Arthur back and scheduled a meeting for 10 a.m. at the Divine Light Evangelical Church. His pastor – Amanda's husband – had advised that they meet at the church in case his assistance was needed.

Luckily for Arthur, the church wasn't far from Loughborough Estate where he lived. Samantha would drop her husband off at the church on her way to work while the pastor would drop him off at home when he finished with his potential convert. It wasn't easy for Samantha to help Donaldson into the car or out of it; it was a very big task. But she never complained.

Donaldson arrived at the church office about ten minutes ahead of schedule and was surprised to see Arthur already waiting for him. He had been waiting for almost a quarter of an hour reading a newspaper at the bus stop adjacent to the church building. It was a very large building that used to house a supermarket. It was initially obtained by the church on a five-year lease, but before the lease ran out, arrangements were concluded to buy the building. The funds for its purchase were raised by the three richest members of the congregation, although every member contributed towards its renovation and decoration. At the dedication of the auditorium, the General Overseer of the church, Reverend Stuart Wilberforce, had compared the members' hearts of giving to those of the children of Israel when they gave their riches to build a house for God.

Immediately Arthur saw Donaldson's struggle to come out of the car he walked to him and shook his hand in greeting. He also greeted Samantha and joined her in helping Donaldson come out. And after Donaldson had been helped into his wheelchair he introduced himself.

The duo entered the church office, accompanied by Samantha. The trio was received by the pastor who had arrived in his office much earlier. After exchanging pleasantries, Samantha kissed her husband and bade everyone farewell as she left for work. As soon as she left, Donaldson and Arthur went into the ushers' room while the pastor retired to his office.

As the duo sat at a table facing each other in the ushers' room Arthur thrust his hand into the side pocket of his trousers and brought out a small dark bottle. Placing it on the table, he asked if Donaldson knew what the content was. Donaldson regarded the bottle for a while, took it and then read the inscription on it. What! It was arsenic, one of the deadliest poisons of that time.

'What are you doing with this?' he asked.

'Well,' said Arthur, 'I need to let you know that yesterday evening was to be my last on earth. I only came to Trafalgar Square for my last walk before departing. Then I saw you addressing a crowd nearby. But when I listened to your sermon and read your story I became confused. Something then told me that I needed to speak to you.'

Arthur Lucas was a Brazilian in his twenties. A half-orphan who had lost his father in infancy, he came to Britain for a bachelor's degree in Computer Engineering. He remained his mother's only child as she never remarried. However, two years before he completed his programme, his academics suffered an unprecedented setback. His uncle, who was responsible for his sponsorship, suddenly died. Although he had a part-time job, the proceeds could only pay his monthly rent and food. And to compound his misery, his pensioner mother was diagnosed with cancer back home in Brazil and needed a very large deposit for surgery.

Confused over what to do, one day he made up his mind and contacted one of the university's so-called 'big guys' for help. The 'big guys' were those students who lived ostentatious life and cruised about the city in expensive state-of-the-art cars. The one he contacted was Desmond Ashworth, an American and a final year Bachelor of Arts student in European History. Desmond's response had been a surprise, 'My guy, I ain't gonna give you fish but teach how to fish,' he had said. 'Sure, I'm gonna lend you some bucks but you're gonna work for it. And if you work hard, oh boy, I swear you're gonna get more than enough bucks to save your mama,' he added as he puffed stylishly at a fat cigar. He invited Arthur to his posh, three-bed room off-campus apartment that evening and handed to him a medium-size envelope. 'That's two thousand pounds,' he said. Arthur was gobsmacked. He didn't need that much. Even a thousand pounds was enough to take care of the whole bill. But Desmond was upset when he told him this.

'C'mon, stop behaving like a kid,' he said. 'You've just told me that you lost your sponsor. Where are you gonna get your fees from? I told you that you're gonna earn more than this when you start working for yourself.'

'What kind of job is it? I hope it is not criminal?' stammered Arthur.

'Come off it, mate,' Desmond furiously responded. 'Do I look like a criminal?' he asked. And continuing, he said, 'Look, my old man is rich. He's a top property guru. He's got megabuck shares in almost every big business in the New York. I tell you, me-e-n, he's a megabucks fella.'

Indeed, Desmond's father was very rich, but his son had chosen a path of crime. He belonged to a gang who impersonated plain clothes police and seized drugs from dealers within and without England. The drugs, which were sold through their underground networks within and without the country, yielded much more money for them since no capitals were involved. Desmond only revealed the truth about the business to Arthur after arriving in Glasgow for their clandestine operation but assured him of a passive role. That night, he was only asked to sit in the car and keep the engine running while the rest of them – four of them – went into a property. As frightened as he was, he knew that he could be ruthlessly dealt with should he decide to back off at that moment. So he planned to withdraw after that operation. But, having got wind of the impostors' activities, the drug barons had laid an ambush for them. This resulted in a fiery exchange between the two criminal groups. And by the time the police arrived at the scene three men were already dead, two from Desmond's group. All the men, including Arthur, were arrested and charged for various offences which included illegal possession or use of firearms, drug dealing, murder, public disorder, impersonation and aiding and abetting. Arthur, who received the least sentence, was given two years imprisonment.

During his period of incarceration news spread fast to England and Brazil. There were, however, various versions of the news. Some said the gang had tried to rob a bank at gunpoint while some said they had gone for vengeance killing. The former was received by Arthur's recuperating mother about three months into his sentence. And within a few months of its receipt she bade the world farewell. Believing that Arthur would come back home someday, she left a note for him before she died.

After a year of his imprisonment Arthur was paroled, but he was to be deported back to Brazil. But, having discovered that his student visa was still valid, a humanitarian organisation swiftly swung into action, fighting against his deportation. The organisation first spoke to his university and received confirmation that he could continue with his studies. After obtaining a court injunction stopping the immigration department from deporting him, the organisation then prayed the court to allow him to complete his studies. As his visa validity didn't cover the rest of his programme, its renewal was subject to obtaining a sponsor from Brazil, UK or anywhere.

Arthur contacted Brazil as soon as he was released from the immigration camp and discovered that his mother had died the same week he was released from prison. What a tragedy! He had lost his idol – the one who had shown him immeasurable love and affection right from babyhood; the one for whom he had strived to be successful in life. He remembered all his sweet promises for her – that he would buy her a mansion and great cars; that he would only marry a wife of her choice and have her tell his children – her grandchildren – ancient stories; that he would tell his children that she was the best mother the earth had ever produced. But now the course of the story had tragically changed! It was now a story of a well-loved child who repaid her mother's love with sorrow and death; a story that began with a mother's shower of love and ended with cruelty from her stupid ex-con son. And he cried aloud roaring like a starving lion. The reality that he was the cause of the death of the same mother whose love he had daily strived to repay, coupled with the thought of his wasted time and the lifelong 'ex-con' prefix that he had acquired, had taken an unprecedented toll on his psychology. He lost interest in everything; not even a renewed student visa or completing his studies. He needed to meet his mother to apologise to her. He cried every hour and everyday

Donaldson was barely able to hide his emotion after the story. Before responding, he held both Arthur's hands and prayed that the Spirit of God would take control and calm the storm in his life. He then began by saying that he could see the hand of God in all the stages of his story. He could see His hand working for his parole; the hand was there at the point of deportation; the hand was there working to make him complete his studies as evident by the university's readiness to reabsorb him and the authority's readiness to renew his student visa; and the hand was there to stop him taking his life and going to eternal damnation. What a loving God! No mother's love can compare to His agape love. No. Not here or anywhere else!

Weeping profusely, Arthur was led to Christ by Donaldson. The pastor was invited to pray for him. For the first time since he was in elementary school in Brazil, Arthur attended the church service the next Sunday where he met the surprise of his life. As he was waiting to exchange pleasantries with Donaldson and his family after the service, a Brazilian man in his early sixties walked to him from behind and said to him in Portuguese, 'Good morning, Arthur. How was the service?'

'Good morning sir,' Arthur replied as he turned around in utter disbelief. 'The service was great sir,' he added.

'The pastor discussed you with me during the week and when I saw you as you were being introduced to the church this morning, you resembled someone I knew back home in Brazil.'

'Who is that sir?' asked Arthur.

'How are you related to one Rafael Hugo Lucas of Itabuna city of Bahia state?' Arthur was thrown off balance.

'That was my father sir,' he replied.

'A former high school teacher?' the man probed further.

'Yes sir. But he died about twenty-four years ago, when I was still an infant.'

'My goodness!' exclaimed the man. 'So you're Rafael's son! And the pastor told me that Alicia, his wife, is also dead?'

'Yes sir. That was my mother. She died about three months ago,' replied Arthur with an emotion-laden voice.

The man took Arthur to his wife who was waiting in the car. He introduced him to her and then took him to his home. The man was one of the three wealthiest members who bankrolled the acquisition of the church building. At his home he revealed that Arthur's father was his best friend when he was in Itabuna. They attended the same high school and university but only lost contact after he got a scholarship to study aeronautic engineering in Britain, where he married a British wife and became a citizen.

Arthur moved into the mansion of his new benefactors – Mr and Mrs Ricardo Giovanni. And, without wasting time, all the necessary documentation for the renewal of his visa was provided by the engineer. Donaldson was very happy to have been used to save a soul from the claws of the devil. One day, as he sat in his wheel chair clutching his Bible, he grinned at his image in the full-size mirror in front of him and said,

'Satan, what did I tell you? Didn't I say that I needed no physical ability to defeat you? Take note of the scores: Donaldson 1 – Satan 0, and the game continues.'

On Mr Giovanni's suggestion and sponsorship, Arthur travelled to Brazil to organise a headstone for his mother. He was accompanied by the generous couple and their eldest son who was about four years younger than Arthur. As he arrived in his family home that night a neighbour brought the letter left for him by his mother. He tore it open and read:

Arthur my loving son,

When I received the news of your incarceration in the UK I didn't have to think twice about what could have compelled you to join the criminal gang. I knew that anything you did was because of me. But I knew that you couldn't hurt a fly; you have the same heart as your father's – caring and tender. He always believed in hard work and that's the path you have also chosen. I know that you sincerely love me, and you will never do anything that will cause me any pain. So, stop feeling guilty! But there is one request I want to make of you. You see, I'm going home with pride and joy. Why? Because I gave my life to Jesus Christ a few months before I wrote this letter. I'm going home as a beloved of Christ. But my joy will not be complete if you don't give your life to Him too. Arthur, do you wish to meet your loving mother again? I bet you do! My dear son, the only way we can joyfully meet again is by giving your life to Jesus Christ. And as soon as I drop my pen I will begin to pray for salvation of your soul until I breathe my last.

Good bye.

Your loving mother,

Alicia Lucas

'Hallelujah! Thank you, Jesus!' Arthur exclaimed. Staring at the large portrait of his mother, he muttered tearfully, 'Mum, sure we're going to meet again in that glorious city where we shall part no more.'

CHAPTER 22: THE IDENTITY

Donaldson continued the work of evangelism with amazing zeal. He became so obsessed with this task that he seemed oblivious to his physical disability. He no longer thought of his past achievements except when he had to mention them when sharing testimonies of God's merciful forbearance towards him. And, except for evangelistic purposes, he never wanted to remember those so-called achievements again. The only thing he wanted to remember was the day he gave his life to Jesus Christ. And, indeed, the way he celebrated the first anniversary of his becoming a Christian amazed every member of his church. A few weeks before, he had appealed to the pastor to spare him a considerable length of time during the service to share his testimony. In his speech during the celebration, he had said that the only birthday he loved to remember and celebrate was the day he became born again. And at the end of the speech he and members of his family rendered a well-rehearsed 'Amazing Grace' in front of the congregation while Natasha played her violin to their admiration. Eulogising his zeal for God's work and commitment to church activities, the pastor had prompted laughter among the congregation when he joked, 'As a result of the bashing he daily receives from Brother Donaldson, Satan has started praying to God for mercy!'

Also speaking at the occasion, Arthur Lucas recounted how God had used Donaldson's ministry to save him from the grip of Satan and death. About five more members, two of them with their family members, also came out to thank God who had used Donaldson for their conversion. And after the service that day, Donaldson and his family treated every member to soft drinks with assorted cakes and biscuits. Four days later, after the midweek service, the pastor invited him to his office and told him what God said about him. 'Brother, last night when I was praying, God spoke about returning all that the enemy has stolen from you. I believe that includes your professional status and job. Did you apply for a job lately?' But when he replied that he hadn't, the pastor added, 'But I saw you receiving an offer letter. It could be a spiritual letter, anyway. Well, I will pray for more light on this.'

About three weeks later, as Donaldson lay in bed after his family members had gone out he heard mail dropped in the mailbox. There were two of them – one for him and the other for his wife. He tore his own open. My goodness! It was an executive offer from HSBC – the same post of a Chief Financial Officer! The candidate previously employed didn't stay very long. Donaldson picked up his mobile and called his wife. Samantha couldn't wait to see the letter. She took permission from her boss, jumped into the car and came back home. After his wife had arrived, Donaldson called the pastor to inform him. But the pastor dropped a bombshell, 'Brother Donaldson, I congratulate you on the offer but that isn't the letter God spoke to me about. The Lord said the letter will come with a conspicuous sign. We have to wait further for the actual letter.'

Highly displeased, Samantha took the phone from her husband and replied:

'Pastor, I think the sign the Lord is talking about is the letter itself.'

'No,' the pastor replied, 'The letter is not a sign but a miracle. But not every miracle comes from God. That's why God sometimes accompanies His miracles with a sign – a sign to know that the miracle is truly from Him.'

'But, Pastor, the sign might follow later,' said Samantha, frowning.

'Yes, I agree with you. But we must be very careful not to jump for a penny at expense of a pound. You see, sometimes there are petty miracles intended by the enemy to rob us of the major ones.'

'So, what's your advice sir? I shouldn't accept the offer?' cut in Donaldson.

'That is it, brother. Don't accept it yet.' replied the pastor, to Samantha's chagrin. But after he had thanked the pastor and hung up, Donaldson turned to his sad wife and said, 'Darling, perhaps you should listen to the pastor. You are experienced enough to know Ephesians chapter three and verse twenty says, *'Now to Him who is able to do immeasurably more than all we ask or imagine, according to His power that is at work within us.'* Besides, we weren't even looking forward to any offer. Were we? Don't let us be distracted by the enemy but keep on serving the Lord who will surely reward us here on earth and then in heaven.'

'Alright, Senior Evangelist Donaldson Jerome Weah,' said Samantha, smiling. And they both laughed.

Two months after that, Donaldson received a parcel sent through DHL. It was from the embassy of Republic of Liberia in London. He couldn't imagine what the message was all about as he hadn't got anything to do with the embassy since his immigration imbroglio some years back. He curiously tore it open and reached for a white, sealed envelope. He carefully opened the envelope and brought out a letter written on the Liberian Ministry of Finance's letterhead.

From: The Honourable Minister of Finance
Through: The Embassy of Federal Republic of Liberia
To: Dr Donaldson Jerome Weah

REBUILDING OUR NATION

Date: 4th May 2005

Dear Dr Weah,

I'm writing to inform you that, as the clouds over our dear nation have finally settled, there is need for our collective rebuilding of the nation. We've got lots to do to put it on the right footing again and then propel its machinery. This is the reason why every strategic position must be manned by the best brains of the nation. The era of political appeasement in the sharing of official responsibilities is over. In appreciation of your colossal prowess in the areas of finance and administration, I have received an instruction from her Excellency, the executive president, to invite you to man the post of the governor of the Central Bank of Liberia with immediate effect.

Kindly liaise with the Ambassador for further briefing.

Please, accept my congratulations.

Long live Federal Republic of Liberia!

Sincerely yours,

Jacob Belleh

Honourable Minister of Finance

Donaldson couldn't believe his eyes. He wiped his face with the back of his hand twice and read the letter over again. He was being invited by the president to assume the post of the Central Bank governor! But he was in a big dilemma. Much as he loved to serve his country, he wouldn't dare to relocate his family who were very happy in United Kingdom. He was experienced enough to realise that the correct sequence of happiness was, 'yourself, family and nation.' That is, happiness flows from the individual to family and from family to nation. You can only make your family happy if you are happy yourself. And for a nation to be happy the constituent families must be happy. Regarding the appointment, he knew he didn't have any say. His line of action would be decided by his family. But he would not call his wife at that moment as he didn't want her distracted. He would tell her when she returned from work. He then picked up his mobile and called the pastor. But the pastor asked, 'And what sign did you notice as you received the parcel?'

'Sign?' asked Donaldson. 'I didn't see any sign,' he added.

'Then that is not the offer,' said the pastor.

Samantha was very happy it wasn't the offer God spoke about. As much as she would not like to stand in the way of her husband she didn't like to go back to Liberia. A few days later, Donaldson sent a polite reply to the minister explaining why he wouldn't be able to take up the appointment at that moment.

Donaldson concentrated on his evangelical activities until about two months later when he received yet another parcel. It was from the Central Bank of Liberia. As it was Saturday, his wife and children were at home that morning. It was Natasha who opened the door and signed for the parcel. And as her father opened the parcel the rest of the family cast inquisitive glances. The first thing he observed as he brought out a glossy letter paper from a white envelope content of the parcel was the United Nations logo on its right corner. With Samantha also reading over his shoulder, he then rushed through the lines.

From: Personal Assistant to the President, World Bank
Through: The Governor, Central Bank of Liberia
To Dr Donaldson Jerome Weah

APPOINTMENT TO THE POST OF VICE PRESIDENT

Date: 23rd September 2005

Dear Dr Weah,

I, first and foremost, wish to tender my unreserved apologies for sending this letter late. It was due to the just-concluded scheduling and rescheduling of certain official responsibilities here. Having realised that your CV, which had been in our archive over the years, qualifies you for the above-mentioned post, we have shortlisted you among two other applicants. The date of interview is 17th October 2005 at 10.00 a.m. prompt. If you are interested in the post and will be able to attend the interview kindly give me a call on the number on top of this letter as soon as possible. For visa formality, kindly present this letter at the nearest US consulate.

Thank you.

Yours sincerely,

Phil K. Schmidt

Personal Assistant to the President

The couple finished reading the letter at the same time and stared at each other with mouth agape. 'Mum, what is it? Dad, what is it?' asked their curious children. Samantha took the letter from her husband without saying a word and read through again. 'Thank you, Jesus! Thank you, Jesus!' she suddenly exclaimed. Holding the letter aloft, she began to run to and fro the living room speaking in tongues as her husband stared away. No longer able to bear the suspense, Natasha grabbed her mother by her pyjamas and begged, 'Mum, please tell us what the good news is.' Ignoring her daughter, she walked briskly to her husband and said, 'Darling, I know you are thinking about the accompanying sign.' Bringing the letter to his view, she said, 'Look. The sign is in this phrase, 'CV … qualifies you for the job.' And I strongly believe that the interview is going to be a mere formality. The Lord has given you the job!

Donaldson collected the letter and regarded the highlighted words. The woman was right. That was the sign the pastor was talking about. Otherwise, how could they still reckon with his CV which was submitted almost twenty years ago! Yes, it was a sign that God had opened His book of remembrance concerning him just as He did concerning Mordecai. Turning to his wife, he said, 'Darling, you're quite right. It is, indeed, the sign the pastor said would accompany the letter.' Happy at being proved right, Samantha turned to her children and said, 'Hurrah, your father is going to become Vice President of the World Bank!' The children were elated. Like children who were meeting their father for the first time after several years of separation, they ran towards him and gave him a bear-like hug. But the children's combined momentum threw the wheelchair off balance with Donaldson tumbling and falling flat on the floor. His wife ran to him and grabbed him from the armpits as she tried to lift him onto the sofa. But he felt an agonising wave pass through the whole of his back and screamed very loudly. Next, he felt some sensation along his vertebrae that seemed to make it as heavy and stiff as iron. Neither able to sit on the sofa nor return to his position on the floor, his instinct told him to stand up by leaning the back of his thighs against the armrest of the sofa. He did that successfully without feeling any pain! Something then told him he could stand without continuing to lean against the sofa. Like a movie full of film-tricks, he slowly took a step away from the chair.

Then the second, third, fourth ... and then continued to walk! His wife was stupefied. She sprawled on the floor and continued to roll over, weeping and shouting 'hallelujah' as she did. The children jumped into their father's hands as he repeated, 'Lord, if this is a dream, please, I don't want it to end!'

'Pastor, are you and Amanda at home? Please, come over quickly. It's happening here.' That was Samantha calling the pastor after the reality of the miracle was dawning on the family. And, in response to the pastor's probing, she said, 'No. I won't tell you. I want both of you to come here and see for yourselves.'

Donaldson was the one who rose and opened the door as the pastor and his wife arrived. And as the couple looked at him bewilderedly, he gave the letter to the pastor and said, 'Pastor, welcome to our new dawn. My miraculous healing is the accompanying sign that the Lord meant. But I'm not really sure which of the two miracles I have received in quick succession this morning is actually a sign to the other – each of them is too big to be an accompanying sign!' Still dumbfounded, the pastor read through the letter and passed it to his wife. And, not knowing what to do still, he looked upward and said, 'God of Abraham, Isaac and Jacob, You have rendered me perplexed again this morning with your astonishing deeds. Lord, You always know how to daze Your children. You are God who does a new thing every new day.' Apparently short of further words, he fell on his knees and just remained silent. Everyone in the house, including the children followed suit. Suddenly, as they remained in this posture, tears began to roll down everyone's face; an indication of worshipping hearts with a powerful move of the Holy Spirit. Later the pastor burst into a popular song, 'Who's like unto thee, O Lord?' and was chorused by all.

It was total commotion at church the next day as Donaldson was mobbed by members who competed to hug him. Songs and beats which ignited rhapsodies of praise were started at once by the choir. Everyone sang at the top of their voice and clapped their hands vociferously. Some members, who were drunk of the Holy Spirit, displayed fascinating dance steps to the high tempo praise songs, running to and fro through the auditorium as they rigorously danced. Sensing the movement of the Holy Spirit, the pastor allowed the scenario to continue for as long as the Spirit allowed. It didn't really matter if all they did that day was praise the Lord; that was how the Father wanted it.

After a lengthy session of praise, the pastor eventually mounted the pulpit to give the sermon which he had specifically prepared the previous day. It was titled 'The Identity.' The pastor began by emphasising that the reason Jesus came here was to identify with us. This He did by forsaking his heavenly splendour and came through a woman's womb, passing through the stages of infancy, preteen and teen just like us. And if the game of football was in existence during His time He would have participated in five-a-side with other children at the community ground. The pastor, however, prompted laughter when he added that the Lord might have even been a top striker or agile goalkeeper! Continuing, he said that the Lord, like anyone of us when we were children, ran errands for His parents and other elders who were His creatures. The Bible made it clear that He rejoiced with those who rejoiced and wept with those who wept. He even conversed with condemned robbers at the tail end of His life, giving one of them a first-class ticket to paradise!

Now, as he identified with us to the point of death He beseeched us to identify with His Father in heaven as well. And as He gave up the ghost on the cross He returned to us the identity that was confiscated from our first parents. But, unfortunately, only a few people accepted this identity. Most people were still going about the world without the identity even though it was free, though it cost the Lord His blood. What was the significance of the identity? It qualified its holder for righteous living, because it was made of the righteous blood of Christ. That was the reason why only Christianity, among other religions, was synonymous to holiness. And that was the reason it was only Christianity that was always subject to the world's scrutiny. That also explained why it didn't really matter when other leaders of religion did anything wrong. But when a renowned Christian did the same it became a big scandal and front-page news. The identity does not only qualify us for righteousness, it ensures prosperity both on earth and in heaven. However, the meaning of prosperity, from the world's point of view, was earthly riches or affluence. From the heaven's point of view, the pastor said that it was combination of righteousness, peace and joy in the Holy Spirit. Therefore, to an identity-carrying Christian, wealth or affluence is an offspring of righteousness. That explained why the Bible said, 'Seek ye the kingdom of God and its righteousness and all these things (all your godly aspirations) shall be added unto you.'

Donaldson was surprised that the pastor spoke about identity exactly like the old Caribbean man. The old man must be speaking through him, he had concluded.

Speaking further, the pastor said, 'If you use your identity accordingly, no power of darkness can sit on your inheritance and no demon can ever block your way to your destiny. Brethren, our God can amaze his children with both open and hidden miracles. As soon as Brother Donaldson arrived here this morning you could all see the miracle that has taken place in his life. This is an example of open miracle. But there is another miracle that is currently unknown to you. And I want to announce to you that we have in our midst this morning the new Vice President of the World Bank!' Everyone then began to look about the auditorium trying to fish out a visitor whose appearance matched the designation. The pastor paused for some moments to enjoy the game of suspense. Smiling, he said, 'You are all trying to find out who the person is among us. Well, I have the honour of introducing to you this morning the new Vice President of the World Bank, in the person of Dr Donaldson Jerome Weah. May Dr Weah rise please?' The pandemonium that greeted the introduction was simply indescribable, as Donaldson rose from a seat next to his wife's.

In conclusion, the pastor said there were five categories of people in the world: those who hadn't got the heavenly identity, those who hid their own, those whose identity had become blurred, those who had lost theirs and, lastly, those who had their identity intact and put it on perpetually for the kingdom purpose. According to him, the first four categories in that order, referred to those who were not Christians, those who were Christians but not manifesting traits or discharging the responsibilities expected of Christians, those who committed secret sins, and those who had completely wandered away from faith. As the presence of God was always in the auditorium, he beseeched those who knew that their identity was hidden, blurred or lost to begin to pray. Lots of members responded vociferously. And after he had allowed enough time for personal prayers he prayed for the people, category by category.

Lastly, while all eyes remained closed he asked all members who were not born again yet to raise their hands. Lots of people, especially new members, responded. And after confessional prayers, he prayed for them, saying, 'Lord Jesus, these ones have hearkened unto you by coming to identify with your Father. They have come to you for heavenly identity, so they may fulfil your plan and purpose for their lives on earth and in heaven. Lord, as you present them their identity today, I ask that it will never be hidden, stolen nor go blurred. Lord, let this new identity chart a heavenly course to their destiny. These I ask in the name of our Lord Jesus Christ. Amen.'

CHAPTER 23: THE GLORY OF THE LATTER HOUSE

Donaldson had a successful interview and assumed office at the Washington DC headquarters of the World Bank about four weeks later. It took only two weeks to obtain his diplomatic passport. Luckily, his children were on vacation while his wife hurriedly applied for a four-week annual holiday, so the family might spend his first four weeks together in the US. He had really wanted his wife to resign her appointment at the Foreign Office and join him immediately, saying that his income was more than enough for them. Indeed, his income was much higher than what he would earn as an executive of HSBC or governor of the Central Bank of Liberia. But Samantha didn't want to leave the Foreign Office unceremoniously. She still remembered how her bosses had rallied around her when seeking re-absorption to the Foreign Office and felt she should give them enough notice. Besides, the cordiality between her and her colleagues demanded that.

Donaldson was temporarily accommodated in a luxury hotel for the first three weeks before being allocated an official residence. The residence was an expansive ultra-modern property which used to house the Australian Ambassador. Among the facilities in the properties were a very large garden, swimming pool and a garage large enough to hold up to a dozen cars. The family's first night at the property was spent dedicating it to God through prayer, praise and worship. It was a very exciting time before the Lord as the family sang and prayed from 12 midnight till 4 a.m. Donaldson didn't forget to dedicate his luxurious office to God also. On his first day at work, after being conducted around the facilities, he retired to his office to pray. Without bothering to bolt the door from within, he knelt and worshipped the Lord. All the top officials of the bank, who came to say hello and found him praying, were greatly amazed and turned back one after the other. Among them was the president of the bank. They also noticed that he had replaced a large painting of a semi-nude woman in a conspicuous position of the office with one of a great hand holding the earth, with the caption, '*He holds the whole world in His hand.*' The president stared thoughtfully at the new painting as he waited for his vice to round off his prayer. Realising that his boss was still waiting, Donaldson rounded off quickly and rose. Smiling, he said, 'I'm sorry sir, but I needed to invite my mentor to take charge.'

'Your mentor?' asked the president.

'Yes sir,' replied Donaldson, 'He is Jesus Christ!'

'Oh, Jesus Christ!' said the president. 'So, you believe in Jesus?' he asked smilingly.

'I am not only a believer sir; I am His servant.'

'Really?' said the president, unable to hide his surprise. 'You are a pastor then.'

'No. I'm an evangelist.'

'What is the difference between an evangelist and a pastor?' asked the president.

With that question Donaldson immediately realised that his boss had created an opportunity to be witnessed to. He then began, 'While the responsibilities of the pastor are basically directed towards making church members grow in the knowledge of God, those of the evangelist are directed towards winning new members to the kingdom of God. So, when someone reminds you that no matter how long you live on earth you will surely die and then give account of how you spent your life, that person is an evangelist. Or, he may ask you to forsake your sinful life and accept Jesus Christ as your personal Lord and Saviour, so you may live peacefully and joyfully here, and later reign with the Lord instead of being eternally damned. You see, many people believe that their exalted position and affluence are the greatest things that can ever happen to a man. But the Bible says, 'What shall it profit a man if he gains the whole world and loses his soul?' Why would anyone allow the luxuries of a temporary place of abode to prevent them from enjoying the luxuries of a permanent place of abode? There are two permanent places of abode – heaven and hell. While we still live we have an opportunity of choosing where we are going to spend our eternity. Sir, if anyone exposes you to these realities, that person is an evangelist.'

There was a long silence after which the president said, 'Thank you, Dr Weah. I've only come to say hello and personally welcome you to the world's greatest financial institution. I will be speaking to you about several official issues this week.' But, according to his pastor, Donaldson had covered at least one of the stages of soul winning, namely, cultivation, planting, and tending. And if God provided more opportunities he would follow that up, maybe to the stage of harvesting.

As the vice president, Donaldson's responsibilities included liaising with national governments through their respective central banks, over economic matters. He organised international conferences under the auspices of the United Nations Economic Council and gave speeches at national conferences. He was also the head of the advisory committee of the World Bank on economic matters, whose responsibilities included suggesting and monitoring World Bank projects in developing nations. Because of his glaring positive influences on development projects in these nations, he was idolised by their governments and people. He was accorded great respect by the heads of state and government wherever he went. And, because of the presence of God with him, he was loved and respected at work and beyond.

Two months after arriving in the US, his wife and children joined him permanently. After high school, Natasha secured admission to Harvard University to study Law while Samantha worked with the Washington Post as a Business Manager. Much as her husband wanted her to be a full-time housewife she really wanted to work. Not just because of earnings but, according to her, she wanted to continue to make use of her professional experience to effect business growth. Like he always did when he received his first wages, Donaldson invited his wife to their bedroom and handed his bank card to her, saying, 'Darling, I want to thank God for giving me an opportunity to play my role as your husband and father of my charming children. I want to thank you too for being there for me at all times. With you as my wife, I never felt any vacuum left behind by my mother. You are more than a wife to me. Here is my first salary minus my tithe. Spend it any way you like.' Samantha looked at the bank card and laughed hysterically.

'Darling, what am I going to do with this lot of money?' asked Samantha.

'Well, you may like to buy the whole of Washington DC,' replied Donaldson jokingly.

After much persuasion, Samantha collected the bank card with a thankful kiss. But the following Saturday, she took her two children out shopping. She bought beautiful dresses, shoes, bags and jewels for herself and children. She then bought five beautiful three-piece suits, shirts, four pairs of shoes and two expensive wristwatches for her husband. She also bought some beautiful household utensils. Donaldson was flabbergasted when she presented the stuff to him as she returned his bank card. And, on checking his bank accounts, he was more amazed to discover that all that was spent wasn't up to a tenth. The family continued to live happily together serving the Lord.

Although the couple attended a new church in Washington DC, they still maintained a very strong link with their London church. There wasn't a week that they didn't communicate with the pastor and his wife. As a matter of fact, Samantha and Amanda communicated almost every day. Donaldson paid a total of twenty percent of his monthly earnings as a tithe – a tenth to his local assembly and the other tenth to his London church. Six months after their arrival in their palatial mansion, they hosted three couples who were very important in their lives – his London pastor and Amanda; his local pastor and his wife; and Evangelist Clooney and Bridget. The get-together was simply glorious. The couples were given the royal treatment by their hosts. Apart from their local pastor and his wife, the invited couples spent the weekend with them in their mansion. Samantha and Bridget were very happy as they conversed throughout the night. The men also spoke extensively about the deplorable situation of the world in reference to God's end-time calendar. They also talked about the backsliding rate of Christians as prophesised by the Lord. On Sunday, the guests worshipped with their hosts at their church. The local pastor was used to have great servants of God and their spouses worshipping with them. And on Sunday evening, when their guests were about to leave, Samantha lavished Amanda and Bridget with expensive gifts, promising to repay their visit together with her husband.

Within his first two years in office Donaldson had visited lots of developing nations, either to give a speech or to make suggestions towards revamping their ailing economy. He also wrote and launched two books, titled, *'Evolving a Viable Economy'* and *'Catching up With the Rest – Effective Use of Available Resources.'* The books, which were basically meant to provide practical aids to experts and teachers in the fields of Finance, Business and Economics, found their ways into world top universities' libraries. Two years later, he followed them up with another two titles, *'Capital Projects as a Tool for Economic Development: The World Bank Perspective'* and *'A Banking System That Propels the Economy.'* Apart from his position at the centre stage of world banking, the books further exposed his academic prowess that he was later conferred with honorary professorship by the school of Financial Economics of the Oxford University.

The Triumphant Entry

It was three years after his World Bank appointment that Donaldson was able to visit his home country. It was the first time since he left for Britain during the civil war. There were several development projects being executed in Liberia by the World Bank, with some of them due for commissioning. And his boss had given him a rare privilege of leading a World Bank delegation to the country. Posters had been printed and announcements made on all Liberian media, with government and people eagerly looking forward to the epoch-making event. The projects to be commissioned included a five hundred-kilometre dual carriageway and a thousand low-cost two-bedroom apartments for those who lost their homes during the war. Realising that he would need to meet a few old pals and relatives, Donaldson and his wife had fixed part of their respective annual leave coinciding with the visit. It was a glorious home-coming. The venue of the event – the Monrovia terminal of the newly constructed road – was agog with dignitaries from all walks of life in attendance and all sorts of traditional dancers taking to the floor. Lots of beautiful canopies were erected with a red carpet rolled out from a lavishly decorated rostrum. Those seated on the canopied rostrum included the executive president and vice president of the country; members of the three arms of the government; traditional rulers and top business executives. Others included the military and police bigwigs. Among the invited VIP's were Donaldson's old friends. Donaldson and his entourage, which included his wife, children and four top officials of the World Bank, had arrived in Liberia the previous night and were lodged at the prestigious Hotel Africa. Many school pupils were invited to line up either side of the road, from the visitors' hotel to the event venue. These children were a beauty to watch as they appeared in their various school uniforms, waving Liberian flags. About five minutes before the commencement of the programme a convoy of four police-driven black Mercedes jeeps arrived, escorted by police vans and motorcyclists. The backseat of each of the first two Mercedes cars was occupied by two World Bank officials who waved to the cheering crowd. Donaldson and his family were in the third car while the fourth contained the Honourable Minister of Works and Housing and the Secretary to the federal government, who had earlier on gone to the hotel to fetch their august visitors. As the visitors stepped on the red carpet everyone, including the president, rose. And as they arrived at their front row seats the national anthem was played by the military band, to the applause of mammoth crowd of elated spectators.

After the national anthem, a lady MC held the microphone and began, 'The president of the Federal Republic of Liberia, the vice president, the royal fathers, members of the federal and regional governments, invited guests, distinguished ladies and gentlemen, I have the privilege of introducing to you the following officials of the World Bank: From my right we have Mr Leonard Miller, the project director. Could Mr Miller rise for recognition, please? Thank you. Next to him is Mrs Anfisa Vyacheslav … and next is Miss Anita Da Silva … and next is Mr Gandulf Waldebert.' There was a round of applause as each of the officials rose. The pre-emptive cheers as Donaldson was about to be introduced, however, compelled the lady MC to pause for some moments before saying, 'Can members of the audience lend me their ears, please?' And as the noise slightly subsided she continued, 'Seated next to the executive president of the Federal Republic of Liberia is the person we all know very well. He was born and bred among us, and I've once had the privilege of being his personal secretary. He is an illustrious son of this land; an epitome of banking and business. He is the vice president of the World Bank. Ladies and gentlemen, please welcome Professor Donaldson Jerome Weah and his wife! The resultant cheers were so vociferous that the highest volume of the highly-efficient public address system in use was completely neutralised.

Donaldson stared thoughtfully at the MC as he stood up for recognition. He was astonished by what she said. She was once his personal secretary? Where and when was that? The pictures of all the secretaries he had worked with ran through his mind. But she didn't resemble any of them. As he and his wife sat down he whispered in her ear, asking if she recognised the lady. She didn't. But she had an idea. She took her copy of the event programme and opened the page which had the list of officiating staff. Last on the list was, 'MC –Mrs Agnes George (Director of Protocol, the presidency).' She showed it to her husband. 'My goodness!' he exclaimed. 'Is this Agnes?' he asked unconsciously. But the Liberian president, who thought that the question was directed at her, replied, 'Yes, Professor Weah. That's Mrs Agnes George. I needed honest and dedicated people around me when I assumed this office. And I found her a Christian with distinction, so I snatched her from her previous employers.' Donaldson had found it extremely difficult to believe that it was Agnes. Not only because she looked too young, but it was the first time he saw her in native attires. She wore a multicoloured long boubou with flamboyant head-tie to match. She wore a beautiful chain of beads round her neck and the same type for earrings. And, unlike most of the people that he left behind in Liberia, she didn't seem to be affected by the diabolical cloud that enveloped the nation for so long. Her girlish smile and smart walk were still noticeable as she bounced up and down the podium. The only thing that looked old about her was the pair of prescription glasses she wore. Donaldson wondered how happy she would be when she found out that he had become a child of God too. He couldn't wait to let her know. He then scribbled a note and sent it to her through a member of the ushering team. The latter quickly read through the note and suppressed a smile. *'Agnes, I would like to see you. I'll be around for a week. If you provide me with your number, I'll give you a call.'*

It was Donaldson's turn to give a speech after the Liberian president. The president had begun by thanking the World Bank for the economic and development projects embarked upon in Liberia. She had thanked the hierarchy of the bank for their timely contributions towards rebuilding the nation. Turning to Donaldson and his wife, she said that she joined the people of Liberia in welcoming them back home. In her conclusion, she urged the people of Liberia to forget the past and work together to put the country on the ladder of development again.

Donaldson adjusted his necktie as he mounted the podium. It was the brightest opportunity for his old friends to catch a full view of him. Prior to that time, only General Silvestre Abrahams, who was a service chief, was seated a few chairs away from him. Others were seated next to each other, far opposite, among the invited dignitaries. And as Donaldson rose, Gabriel told his friends that he had never seen any recalcitrant so blessed by God. Richard replied that he could see that nothing had changed about God's love for their friend. But they all had the shock of their lives when Donaldson cleared his throat and said, 'Let us pray.' After the prayer, he said, 'I apologise if I have broken the protocol. But I must let you know that it's not only the World Bank that I represent at this occasion; I represent the almighty God anywhere I am.' His friends had never been so dazed. Agnes mouth was agape. General Abrahams regarded him in utter disbelief. The Christians at the venue chanted 'Hallelujah!' But they were in for more surprises. Continuing, he said, 'The devastating effects of war are not only immediate; they linger on. And the havocs, though hugely physical, are more psychological. Hence casualties are not just the dead and maimed but the able-bodied survivors as well. The beginning of a war is easily determined. But no one can accurately determine when it ends. Some wars never end – they recur. And some metamorphose into mistrusts and suspicions. Wars are Satan's vital tool for altering or truncating destinies.' At the end of his speech he said, 'Finally, the Bible says that righteousness exalts a nation, but sin is a reproach to all people. For a nation to experience prosperity, joy and peace, it must imbibe righteousness and allow God to rule. And for its people to be happy, they must eschew all evils. The World Bank can only build roads and erect structures, but it is only God who rebuilds crumbled lives and families. He is the only One who can rebuild individual lives, homes and our nation beyond expectation. It was He who rebuilt mine.

And it is not too late for anyone here to give their life to Him. Thank you. God bless our nation!

Samantha battled against joyful tears. Although she always trusted her husband when it came to speechmaking or rhetoric, that particular one was extraordinary. Agnes silently stared at her former boss as she took over the podium. His friends' heads remained bowed in awe of God. Interestingly, nobody could clap after the speech. It was a moment for sombre reflection. For half-an-hour or so, the people were spellbound by emotional rhetoric that was loaded with evangelical discharges.

Donaldson was mobbed by old pals and former colleagues at the end of the event. But he didn't have enough time for them because of his colleagues who must return to their hotel amid security. He would, however, be ready to receive them at his hotel anytime within that week. While his colleagues would leave for the US that night, he and his family would stay a week longer. Meanwhile, he had given his local number to his five closest friends and a few former colleagues. And his mobile had begun to ring as soon as his team started their journey back to the hotel.

Within an hour of their return to the hotel, lots of visitors were waiting for him at the reception. Among these were Agnes and her husband whom he first attended to. After exchanging pleasantries with them and introducing Samantha, he turned to Agnes with a false grimace and said, 'Agnes, I hope you're not here to preach your stinking sermon again.'

'No sir,' replied Agnes, 'On the contrary, I have come to listen to a sermon from an evangelist who turned a civic event into a Christian crusade this morning!'

The two couples laughed. After that they talked about the good old days at the Wuteve Bank, the civil war, its effects on their careers and the progress they had made so far after it. As they talked, Mrs Weah and Mr George listened with rapt attention with glasses of wine in their hands. And as Agnes and her husband prepared to leave, Donaldson brought out one of the Christian books he authored, titled, *Delivered From the Path of Doom,'* and said, 'Agnes, I know that there is a question on your mind that you aren't sure whether or not to ask. Have this book. It provides answers to that question and several others you might have.' Agnes received it with an affirmative smile.

'This man hasn't changed a bit; so humorous and intelligent,' she said to her husband as they climbed into their Range Rover. 'How did he know that I really desired to know how he became a Christian?' she asked as she read through the synopsis.

Much as he tried to be brief with Agnes, their conversation was punctuated by calls which he had to answer. Two of them were from the Liberian president and the Central Bank governor who wanted to personally express their gratitude. He really didn't have a problem with his old pals as they readily conceded to other visitors. Considering the saying, 'He who laughed last laughed the longest,' they wouldn't mind seeing him last. Besides, they really felt at home with Samantha already seated and chatting with them at the restaurant. Samantha hadn't lost a bit of her beauty. To these men, she was as charming as she was more than a decade ago.

After almost an hour, Donaldson eventually came to the restaurant to meet his friends. But as he tried to apologise for keeping them waiting, Richard joked, 'Mr Vice President, can you please keep your apology. We're not here to see you but our Queen Samantha!' Pretending to walk away, Donaldson replied, 'Alright then. I leave her with you while I go have my siesta.' But Samantha rose and ran after her husband, leaving their guests laughing and applauding. That was reminiscent of their boyish days!

'You guys haven't changed a bit!' said Donaldson laughingly. 'I really missed all of you!' he added.

'I'm not sure you did,' replied Lloyd.

'What do you mean, Lloyd?'

'If you truly missed us why did you change your number?' asked Gabriel.

'And why did you stop calling us even if you changed your number?' added Silvestre.

There were lots to talk about. But the restaurant wasn't an appropriate venue for such. He told his friends that his decision to stay a week longer was because of them. Donaldson and his friends once again flocked together for a week. He had earlier on narrated the pathetic circumstances that led to his becoming a Christian. Two aspects of his story that nearly drew tears from his friends' eyes were his security job and paralysis. But his becoming a child of God, miraculous healing and divine promotion remained the highlights of the story. It really broadened their faith in the God of love. Richard too had a surprise for him; Pastor Isaac's church had got a branch in Monrovia and he was the part-time pastor! The branch, which was attended by all his friends, had grown rapidly after the civil war with lots of miracles taking place. Their former clubhouse, which used to be a venue for all sorts of sinful practices, had been remodelled and converted to a church auditorium. Donaldson was delighted when he visited the place. On Sunday which preceded his departure date, Pastor Isaac was invited to Monrovia to lead a thanksgiving service. There, Donaldson announced his decision to start a Christian orphanage affiliated to the church. The objective of the orphanage was to ensure that no orphan grew up with his kind of belief. A church committee was promptly selected and a large part of the proceeds from his books was released for the project. His friends wouldn't like to be left out; they all supported financially. And within a very short time, a well-equipped orphanage with a nursery, elementary school and sports field was set up.

Nobel Prize

It was once again an emotional departure as the men saw their friend off at the airport. He had assured them of his regular visit and they had also promised him of a joint visit to the US at a date to be decided. But none of them knew that the date would be much sooner than they could imagine. A week after Donaldson returned to America he received a letter from the organisers of the Nobel awards. He had been selected for a Nobel award for Economic Sciences, with presentation gala taking place in a few weeks. Arriving with the letter were several invites which he distributed among his five friends: Evangelist and Mrs Clooney, Amanda and her husband, Pastor Isaac and his boss, the World Bank president.

In his acceptance speech at the award, Donaldson said, 'I owe this honour to the Almighty God through His Christ. I want to thank my boss, the World Bank president, for the freehand granted me to exhibit my professional and academic prowess. I also wish to thank my five childhood friends who came all the way from Liberia to celebrate with me. They are Richard, Silvestre, Lloyd, John and Gabriel. The following servants of God have always been an inspiration to me and I like to recognise their presence: Reverend and Mrs Henderson of my local church here in Washington, Pastor and Mrs Ashley from my church in London, Pastor Isaac from Liberia; and Evangelist and Mrs Clooney. Now could Mrs Amanda Ashley join me and my wife on the podium, please?'

As Amanda timidly walked down the long aisle to the podium, Donaldson continued, 'Ladies and gentlemen, there is a saying that behind every success of a man there must be a woman. But there are always two women in my own case. Mind you, I'm not polygamous! The one on my right is my ever-loving and devoted wife and mother. She is my jewel of inestimable value. The one on the left is my family angel.

She's an indefatigable instrument that God has used to knit my family together. She's a friend in need and a friend in deed. My success story will be shambolic without mentioning them both. And, in recognition of their immense contributions to my career and spiritual standard, I hereby dedicate the award to the two of them.' It was joyful noise all over the place. And the two women became emotional as they hugged each other.

The following morning, as Donaldson was having his quiet time, the old Caribbean man walked in quietly from behind and tapped his shoulder. He rose and greeted him. But the old man politely declined a seat when he was offered one by his host.

'What can I do for you sir,' asked Donaldson.

'You see,' began the old man, 'I have come to borrow something from you on behalf of someone else.'

'What is it sir?'

'You have to promise you'll lend me before I tell you what it is,' demanded the old man.

'That will be very stupid of me sir.'

'Stupid?' asked the man, 'Is there any possession you, as a child of God, cannot lend a fellow human being?'

'Yes, there is,' replied Donaldson.

'And what's that?' asked the old man.

Casting a quick look at his suspended identity card, Donaldson replied, 'Of course, my identity.' The old man looked into his eyes and smiled.

'You passed the test, son. You did brilliantly. Enjoy your eternal identity,' he said as he walked out of the room.

Donaldson gently opened his eyes. It was yet another dream.

www.ingramcontent.com/pod-product-compliance
Lightning Source LLC
Chambersburg PA
CBHW072354030726
47505CB00014B/1820

* 9 7 8 1 5 3 2 6 8 0 9 8 4 *